NeverSeen

THE FAELAND LEGENDS: BOOK ONE

BY
TAYLOR HUNTER

NEVERSEEN
Book One: The Faeland Legends

For inquiries, please contact:
Prepare For Rain Press
Boise, ID
prepareforrainpress.com

Edited by Kim Foster: kimfostereditor.com
Cover design by PFR Press graphic design team:
- medallion image by Prabath Wijayantha
- background image by Jifi Suchanek (CrazyMind314 on Pixabay)
Interior design by PFR Press Design Team

Print ISBN: 978-0-9889537-5-8

First printing, 2014
Revised cover, 2023

Published in the United States of America

DEDICATION

To my grandma's grandma,
who saw the unbelievable
with her own eyes.
To those who never stop believing
in what they can't see
and what they don't know for certain.
To all the dreamers in the world,
who stare contentedly into space
as they discover and recreate the universe
as the rest of the world
could have NeverSeen.

CONTENTS

Acknowledgments

Thanks first to my parents for supporting me and cheering me on. You've been my biggest fans through this whole process.

My gratitude to my friends, teachers, and fellow writers for their encouragement throughout my journey to becoming a published author – and, in a few cases, for being character inspiration sources.

I am grateful to everyone who collaborated with me to make this story possible, but especially Dad, who has given day and night, week after week to make this happen. I couldn't have done this without him, since he inspired me to write this to begin with.

And above all, thanks to God, The Master Storyteller, who brought me here in the first place.

FORWARD

Never let somebody tell you to get your head out of the clouds. When somebody tells you that, it usually means they're jealous of your creativity. Unless, of course, you're being irresponsible and not doing your chores. All I'm trying to say is, if you have a dream to write a book, make a movie, become the next Steve Jobs, or have the bestselling album on iTunes for five weeks in a row, don't let *anyone* tell you that you can't do it. *Because you can.* You can do anything if you really, truly want it. There's always that one thing that gives your soul the thrill nothing else can give you: the feeling that you can accomplish something that nobody else can accomplish, the sensation that there is a niche nobody but *you* can fill. Everyone is here for a reason. You just need to figure out *what that reason is.*

What are **YOU** here for?

Taylor Hunter

Boise, Idaho

January 2014

PROLOGUE

My eyes flew open as I choked on thick, black smoke pouring in through my open window. I thrashed in my bed, desperately tangled in my sheets, finally crashing to the floor, my legs released from their sheeted prison. Adrenalized from both a gasp of fresh air and the ultimate peril, I sprang from the hard ground and cast myself at the door, fumbling for the latch keeping me from escape. My head caught up with me.

Click. Out the door and running. *Crack!* Flat on the floor, a broken board above me. Head pounding. Hot blood racing down my cheek. *Have to race now. For my life. Can't stop. Not now. Not now.*

Thick, stinging smoke. Couldn't see, eyes burning. *Crawl to the front door. Reach, reach for it.* The handle. *Pull it back.*

Flames lick greedily up the stair from below. People running, falling, screaming. Everywhere. Toxic smoke cloaks them. Me. Everything. Cloaked in death. Parents, children, old, young, strong, weak—all cloaked. *All going. All gone.* My heart shrieked with horror. *Where are mine?*

Mom was gone, I already knew. Dad? Probably, he would've been one of the first there. The hummers would've felt it coming and fled, maybe dead. *Ash? Ash! Ashlee was with me!* I turned from the blinding horror and clambered across the floor, choking and coughing. Stood up, flew at her door. Head pounding, fist pounding on the door. As if hearing myself from far away, I screamed "Ashlee! Ash!

Open up! Now!" I didn't wait for an answer. My right heel would have a bruise for weeks if I lived.

The floor liked my face tonight. I cursed at the pain, "Troll-snot-owl-pellet-fingernail!" I struggled to stand. Was it me or the ground? One kept moving. I clawed at the wall for balance. Everything was too slow. I fought to keep consciousness as Ashlee's small frame slid out from under the bed and grabbed my waist. We started down the hall. There was only one window large enough to get us out of the master bedroom.

Nobody home. I knew that. The flames called our names as they slunk closer, trying to tempt us away from our shattered lives. Ashlee countered my weight as I grabbed the stool by the desk and hurled it with what strength I had at the window. Glass shards showered like the rain outside, and we followed them, the massive Temple tree groaning the sound of smoky death as it fell away from us. The flames howled at our escape, left without their final prize. We fell.

The tree gave itself to the river, its life source and only companion in death. We fell as the smoke tried to claim us. We fell. I couldn't breathe. Even the fresh air was naught more than poison. We fell as the air tried to wrap us in a cocoon of un-life, being the breath we had to have without giving us the ability to take it. We fell. I was drowning in smoky sleep, too exhausted to try to live. We fell. I heard voices calling. Hands were catching. Catching us.

The freezing, wet ground met my burning back. I gasped in pain and shock and then coughed and choked and gasped all over again uncontrollably. The hissing of a horrid, evil serpent filled my ears, then I felt it rumble through every fiber of my being as the tree collapsed into the river, spent of life save that of the fire viciously devouring it like a ravenous wild beast.

There was nothing but smoke. All was smoke. The ground. The sky. The people. All was smoke...all was smoke...allwassmokeall-wassmoke.

All.

Was.

Smoke.

Ashlee was smoke. Everyone was smoke. I was smoke. I was ash. Ash was falling. Everywhere. Falling like a demon's snowstorm. Everybody was there and nobody was there. All was smoke and ash. All was silent. Silent death. I wasn't dead yet. I didn't know how. I didn't know why. I didn't know.

I strained to open my eyes to see what was left.

From the starless, dead sky, stared two evil, blood red eyes, cursing at my tiny, choking soul, watching me die, wishing I was dead already. I thought I saw my rescuer, my mother, coming for us, to save us from the evil above, guarding us with her angelically beautiful silhouette, as the darkness closed about me, like a cool, wet cloth on a sweaty summer night. I passed out of knowledge and time.

CHAPTER ONE

GOOD MORNING

I awoke with a start, panting into my wet pillow. My sheets were in the worst shape I'd seen in ages, and that was saying something. I was drenched in sweat and very cold, despite the gentle touch of just-cool-enough, fresh, spring air coming in through my bedroom window. It wasn't yet dawn. Threads of cool, pale moonlight drifted through my curtain, unconcerned with my current mental state. I sat on the edge of my bed, shivering uncontrollably and hyperventilating. Well practiced in the art of breath control, I forced myself to slow down, altering my short, shallow gasps into elongated, enriching sighs. I stared at my sorry reflection in the portrait mirror on my dresser, which was as frustrated and disturbed as I was. Yet another night with an hour short on sleep. I had to get this out of my head.

My secret notebook emerged for the fourth night in a row from my dresser and was opened up embarrassingly on my desk in front of the window. My window was the perfect size for me. It had space enough to see the skyline but was small enough that you could go quite unnoticed behind the curtains as you contemplated the deep mysteries of the ages. But not tonight or for many past nights for me. I brushed last night's drawings of leaves and birds and creatures of lore and magic to the side and poured my horrifying nightmare onto the rapidly decreasing supply of blank sheets in my notebook. Every detail, every sensation was stripped to the bone and laid bare on those precious pages of my uppermost privacy and secrecy.

This notebook cradled my sanity. It was my dreamlog. It contained every strange dream I could recall; as such, it was volume twelve of my dreamlog series. Yeah, I had weird dreams a lot. But they weren't just weird. They were much more than that. And that was why this dream in particular was that much more terrifying to my sensitive little heart.

I didn't tell anyone about my secret notebook of dreams, with the exception of my best friend, Sameela O'Klurn. We looked out for each other and kept each other's secrets. She was the only person who knew I had a history of night terrors, but even then, I told her as little as I could. Sometimes the less you know, the safer you'll be if someone starts snooping.

Besides her, I had never told anyone else why I looked so tired and acted so jumpy sometimes, but I knew Ashleeka had figured me out a long time ago. Ashleeka is my seven-year-old sister, but she has wisdom beyond her years. She has an uncanny ability of perception and philosophy that blows my mind every day. But hardly anyone knows about it because she rarely speaks. To anyone—even her parents. She mostly talks to me and that's it. My name is Emmaline O'Meern.

By the time I shut my dreamlog an hour later, the sun was poking its sharp little nose into my window. Time's up. Gotta get ready for a new day. The dreamlog was tucked away into its place of secret misery and fear to eat away at my subconscious, again, all day.

Ah, just another day in the life.

I prepared my mind for the coming semi-chaos as I washed my sweaty face, combed my long, gnarly hair into a thick, gorgeous ponytail, and dressed up in my favorite indigo jumpsuit and turquoise-magenta-flowered sundress. After I packed my school things in my woven-leaf sack, I opened my door and headed for the kitchen down the hall to make breakfast for Mom and Ashleeka. Mom was due to have a baby any day, so we pitched in with everything from meals to laundry.

I was steadily chopping up various fruits for Mom when Ashleeka came in, guiding Mom's enormous, rotund form to a comfortable chair in the living room. Mom hobbled like an elder, clutching a cane for support. I knew I had been big and so had Ashlee, but never that big. Some people were thinking twins. Ashlee didn't think so. I trusted her more than the nurses. That may seem stupid, but if you knew what I knew, you wouldn't second-guess Ash for half a minute.

Ashlee skipped her way into the kitchen as I finished cutting the fruits and loaded them up on Mom's favorite plate: a smooth, pink stone she and Dad had found on their honeymoon by the river. Ashleeka took it to Mom for me as I started in on our lunches. I glanced at Mom to see how she was doing. She looked pale and tired as she quietly chewed on the fresh fruit. I couldn't remember the last time she could go someplace without help. All of us were hoping the baby would arrive soon to give Mom a break.

"Bats!" I swore as I ran my finger under the faucet. My attention had strayed too far, and my finger had a close encounter with a sharp blade. I struggled to stay cool and collected while I bandaged my hand by focusing on the birds and bees flying around outside the kitchen window. *Buzz-buzz*, said a bee, looking at me. Sometimes I liked them, sometimes they scared me. Ashleeka finished packing our lunches before I even realized what she was doing. I was distracted by what she was saying.

"Hey Eme," she stated in an authoritative whisper. "Mom needs to be taken to Skyglass before school. She'll need all the restful treatment she can get before her labor starts at seven tonight." Ashlee stopped in front of me and gave me a look like I wasn't paying attention. "Wait...what?" I sputtered.

"Hello? Didn't you hear anything I said? We need to get Mom ready to go to Skyglass. Go and pack some clothes and blankets for her, will you? Relax!" She shushed me before I could express my distress. "We don't have to get her there—that's taken care of. Just get some of her favorite things, okay?"

No, not okay, I thought as my heart threatened to pound itself out of my chest. Ashleeka sighed, took my hand, and led me to Mom's room. She stopped and stared at me squarely as a mother to a disobedient child. Her dark-blue eyes were laser focused on my deep hazel eyes. "Look, I'll do the packing. You just get her coat and act surprised when someone knocks on the front door," she instructed me. Before I could ask who would come knocking, somebody did. I ran to the door.

A messenger was waiting on the other side, holding a scroll. "Is Mrs. Sonyamay O'Meern present?" he inquired with the utmost politeness. Flustered, I found myself opening my mouth with nothing coming out. I merely pointed over to where Mom sat, barely awake on the comforter chair. He tipped his hat politely, saying, "I've been sent from Skyglass, ma'am. I have instructions to bring you back for prelabor care this morning. If you'd just get into the carriage, please."

I stood, shell-shocked, gaping like some dummy who had just heard he'd won a year's worth of free labor in his fields. "Uh...yeah. Sure. Um, just a minute," I mumbled as Ash came in with a small pack of clothes and helped Mom up from her chair. She hobbled slowly out the door, doing everything she could to not lose her balance. Honestly, it was torture to watch my mother go through that and be helpless to her needs. I remembered her coat and got it for her. It was dandelion yellow, her favorite color.

"Bye, Mom. I love you," I called as the messenger shut the carriage door and hopped into the driver's seat. She gave me something wonderful: a small smile, the likes of which I hadn't seen for far too long. The carriage flew off into openness beyond the tree. I stood for a minute, praying for her. Something started humming erratically by my head.

"Hey there, buddy, you ready for school?" I asked Frankle, one of my hummers. Studbum, my other one, zipped around my head and hovered in front of me to say, "Well, yeah, only since yesterday!" Ashlee pulled out our coats and sacks and locked the front door as I harnessed my hummingbirds. I helped Ash get her coat on as she harnessed Doolee and Buzzle, her hummers. We mounted and harnessed onto our leaf-sleds as we swung our packs on and gave a whistle.

Off we went!

Despite the fun I had being flown to and fro by hummers, I still couldn't wait for the final flying test. It was just two days from now, and I was nervous and excited all at once. Until you were fifteen, you had to travel by carriage or hummer, until your wings were large and strong enough to carry your weight. To finally fly anywhere, that was every teen faery's goal. Freedom can't always be bought or sold, nor should it. Bondage is one thing that the faery kingdom cannot stand. It is better to die trying to be free than to remain in captivity for all time.

Racing along the inside of the tree, we barreled toward the large knot-hole entrance. Sliding and bumping down the branch, I prepared for the Plunge. No more branch. Down we went. Very fast. But I feared not. The air supported me as it always did, and the hummers guided my course. Upward. We soared up and up and up through the fresh air, as we saw life stirring in the small stores and faeries emerging from their sleepy, blanketed world. Then we surged up through the branches of the massive habit-trees towards the wide, clouded sleepiness of the sky ...and then all turned as smooth as ice on a winter-land pond.

It was later than it appeared, I knew. The many clouds snuggling on the horizon were snuffing the sunlight, teasing us to turn back and crawl into our nice warm beds. The breeze, crisp and cool, drifted through the trees below us, playing the music of gentle waterfalls on the instruments of the new green leaves almost finished budding. The true water lay trickling far below, splashing and rolling like a majestic chaos of faeries in a dancing ring. The thrumming of our hummers' wings, the seeming chorus of a quiet, contented world surrounded me like a cozy blanket. I didn't want to, but I closed my eyes, just for a moment. Just a moment.

No, no, no, I pleaded as the ghostly images threatened to emerge from the cage of my subconscious, those horrid phantoms that were cursed to torment my mind. *No, please, not now! Not when I've just started to forget! Wake up! Wake up, Emmaline, dang it! Don't let this get out of control. WAKE UP!*

Someone else did it for me.

"Hey-ey, Emmaline! You're really cruising!" screeched a voice that, unfortunately, was very familiar to me. My eyelids retracted as my blood started boiling. Shadela Glump, my arch enemy for, well, as long as I can remember, darted wildly above me, like a hawk waiting to dive for its prey. Her harsh red-and-brown-speckled wings beat with the pride of a month's head start as she sneered at me, taunting, "Hey-ey, Emmaline! You dreamin' again? Huh? Dreamin' like a little bay-bee!"

It took everything I had to focus my energy forward as I recontemplated for the umpteenth time what the consequences would be if I played out my fantasies of revenge. Breathe in, breathe out. Breathe in, breathe out.

"Hey-ey, little Emmaline! Baby Emma! You still dreamin'? You dreamin' about when you'll be all gwowed up enough to use those pathetic little baby wings of yours? Huh? When's the baby's special day?" she hissed. I could feel those black, raven eyes of hers boring into my skull, waiting to scavenge off my anger and despair.

"Little baby! You know what I think? I think it's time for you to WAKE UP!"

She snapped her wings together and dove at me with the speed of a falcon. I waited and at the perfect millisecond, I vanished.

Shadela fluttered where I should have been. Far from being the smartest at school, she looked around below her as if I'd also dived, instead of rolling away in a sideways barrel, and then up above her as a trade of places. Which is exactly what I'd done.

She must have heard my sarcastic condolences for her intelligence: she snapped her head up at me and snarled like a wolf. "Ooh, you're a bad little baby! Time for a time-out!" she growled. Shadela shot up like a burst of fire, hitting my leaf-sled and knocking me off balance and off the sled. She cackled hysterically as I careened off course, helplessly unprepared, and sped out of control towards the Willow-Tree Market.

My heart pounded in my throat from the adrenaline rush. I couldn't get back up. Time was running out as I flew sideways towards the massive tree. My wings weren't ready for this. I tried to shift my weight. Almost...there...

It happened. I got upright a second before I burst into a chaos of foods and goods and astonished faeries. Faeries. Baskets. Branches. Leaves. Everything. Over. Under. Right. Left. Over over under left over right under roll. Basket faery branch basket basket faeries branch. On and on. Here and there and everywhere. Confusion. Alarm. Anger. Surrounding me. For a few seconds, I saw the sky calling. The drooping branches flew back as I exploded from the accidental chaos behind me. It was over. I was through. I was safe.

I spread my wings out, gliding, and slowed my heart rate. *Breathe.* In and out. In and out. *Slow down.* I found my sled and reharnessed. I let my hummers take control again. Peace came to me. Peace I could find in very few places and certainly not at night when I slept. My eyelids closed, but I knew I wouldn't sleep. I lay out on my leaf and slipped into a state of semiconsciousness, where I could dream of the beauty in the sky I saw without the intrusion of my demons. Knowledge let me by. I drifted on the current of nothingness. Nothing at all.

The little baby dreamt.

CHAPTER TWO

SKYGLASS

I was aware of many things surrounding me before I saw them. I was lying on a soft, cushy blanket of lamb's ear petals, wafting their light, milky scent as their soft hairs caressed my face. Strands of golden sunlight weaved across me, gently warming my tired form. Water trickled nearby in a small fountain for washing and drinking in peace. A kind breeze played with my auburn hair and greeted me with the faint smell of...well, everything lovely. I finally forced my eyes open.

I sat up dreamily on my bed. The nonchalant waving of tree branches far above came and went in my window. My pack was perched precariously on the edge of my chair at my desk. Except it wasn't my desk, or my chair, or my bed, or even my room. It wasn't my house or my habit-tree, either. I was on one of the highest levels of Skyglass, our sacred healing place in the largest tree known to our kind. It was an elder tree planted in NeverSeen by the First Ones, after they were made by the Great One.

I could feel the life of that ancient tree pulsing through every fiber of wood inside of it, the life of everyone who was and ever would be there: children, elders, fathers, mothers. And Mom, finally resting and waiting with love for the baby to come. Love. It wrapped itself around me in the fair breeze pouring in, the branches stretching their way to the High Sky, and the fountain of water waiting to quench the thirst of the poor, tired faery that stayed there. It was the perfect environment for rest and recovery. It had been a long day.

I attempted to recall what had occurred in my day by sweeping away the fog covering the harbor of my memory. It faded in the sort of way that you don't quite realize, until everything is crystal clear, and the water is smooth as glass as the little boat of the memory you desire to reexplore drifts closer to shore, and you peer inside to find the thing you seek.

I'd been semiconscious for about ten minutes before I heard the familiar rumble of sounds that told me I was nearing school. I pulled myself up and stretched and saw Ashleeka tailing me from some distance. Guess she wanted to see, from a safe distance, how I handled Shadela today. We waved good-bye as we split off for our different levels: younger faeries have class in the lower levels and work their way up to the top as they progress each year. She circled down to level two, far ahead of other kids her age at Sunray Elementary, as I circled up to level ten of Moonbeam Academy. It was my final year of schooling before I chose whom I would be apprenticed to. A lot of pressure was on us final-years to figure out what our goal in life was to be, and sometimes it kept us up at night. But, hey, I was already used to that, so what difference did that make?

I came in for a landing, and being well practiced, I was off my sled and walking before we stopped moving. I unhitched Frankle and Studbum to go off and replenish their sugar supply and hung up my leaf-sled on one of the hooks on the wall. After taking a deep breath, I walked out into the great hall and started my school day.

It had started well enough, with Ancient Runes being more fascinating—as always—than I could imagine. Scientific Studies were exciting, as we learned about the revolutionary breakthroughs of our ancestors, and Inventions Workshop thrilled me as I assembled the ideas of my own creation. My trouble started, however, in Advanced

Mathematics, as we were taking detailed notes on the subject of Number Sequence Study and the significance of certain sequential connections.

I'd just been massaging my sore hand after completing the extensive theorems from the board on what becomes of an invisible quantity of possibilities, when our instructor, Mrs. Plumbottle, asked us if anyone knew what an extensional was. "Anything at all?" she asked again as her cat-like gaze swept back and forth over our stupefied faces. Even I hadn't heard of an extensional.

"Well, *duh*," blurted somebody towards the back, "it's a cross of exceptional and extension! *Everyone* knows that!" I didn't have to turn around to know it was Waximitt St'ail, the biggest, most pompous, loud-mouthed clown I had ever known. I had the unfortunate schedule of having him in several classes. All the glitzy, short-skirted, caterpillar-eyelashed, popular girls practically worshiped him as they complimented him on his "vastly stupendous intelligence." The other troublemaker guys were snickering at Mrs. Plumbottle as she stared, extremely unimpressed, at the mess of kids hanging around together defiantly in the back of the room. She stared at the space above their heads for a minute.

"You know what I was just thinking?" she mused out loud. I knew something great was coming. "I think it would be so much easier to teach if all you kids couldn't talk," she continued. Mrs. Plumbottle looked around at all of us. "Wouldn't that be nice?" she inquired to the roomful of confused faces. "Don't you think that would be nice, Miss Emmaline?" she asked me. I couldn't help but smile as I nodded. She smiled as I laughed quietly to myself. I got her humor. The other kids just sat there, glaring.

Mrs. Plumbottle continued with the lesson. "An extensional," she began, "is anything that is perceived by our senses that can be translated to another. But more specifically," she added, "a mathematical extensional is one which can be represented by a mathematical formula or number sequence. Can anyone think of the most common one we know?" Mrs. Plumbottle asked the class.

"Is it the number pi?" I asked her.

"Right you are, Miss Emmaline!" she congratulated, as the rest of the class either groaned or snickered behind me. Someone behind me whispered, "Yeah, Emmaline, *you* tell us what it is! We're too dumb to figure it out!" "You sure know everything! I wish *I* were as smart as you!" someone else taunted. I did my best to ignore them and stay focused on Mrs. Plumbottle's review of what pi stood for, being the ratio of a circle's circumference to its diameter.

For the next half hour, Mrs. Plumbottle trained us how to solve simple extensionals. Most of us struggled for a while, but after she walked me through a more difficult problem, something clicked in my head. It finally made sense to me. Through that single complex formula, a reasonable answer could be established by means of quantiguminalistid configuration! I was nearly floating from excitement.

I was in the process of trying an extensional of my own making when Mrs. Plumbottle stopped us for a minute. She said we were going to do an experiment with an object of hers. I was deeply curious about it.

Mrs. Plumbottle pulled out a bizarre nut-like thing and showed it to the class. "This is a great little example of an extensional translation. I'll tell you how it works," she began as she set it on the table in front of her. "I'm going to try to smash this nut, and I want any of you to tell me if you think you know how it is internally structured in extensional form. Can you do that for me?" she asked of us. Most people sat back in their chairs, already accepting defeat, but I sat forward to get a closer look at it. We braced ourselves as Mrs. Plumbottle pulled a large mallet out of a drawer and brought it above her head.

I saw a wave of light explode out of the nut towards me. A roaring wind engulfed me as I tried to block out the extreme brightness that was trying to...I didn't know what. Every cell in my body felt like it was being separated from me, like I was being dissolved. I pushed as hard as I could away from the intensity drowning my senses. I started coming back, but everything was so blurry. My vision wouldn't focus. The grinding of wheels surrounded my ears. Then everything shifted into something comprehensible: a math and science room, filled with gaping students, blown away at the unbelievable event they had just witnessed.

"Ow," I moaned as I pulled myself off of the floor and back into my chair. Suddenly I realized nearly everyone was laughing and joking. About me. Apparently I was the only one to see anything and definitely the only one to fly backwards out of her chair and onto the hard floor. My cheeks turned red as the usually sneaky torments transformed into full-on catcalls and owl screeches. They pierced my soul, making me feel ashamed, despite having done no wrong. My tears, which I couldn't say if they were from embarrassment or the pain in my elbows, wings, and head, were just about to spill over.

"All right, that's *enough!*" yelled Mrs. Plumbottle, overcoming the jeering crowd of my class-"mates" by a level of volume exponentially higher than theirs combined. She gave them The Stare of the Accused. They fell silent, but their triumph was still very evident on their not-so-concealed, smirking faces.

"Are you alright, Miss Emmaline?"

I nodded. She could tell I lied.

"Any last questions before class is over?" She searched our faces for "a question mark on our foreheads," as she says. Nobody said zip.

Those few seconds felt like eternity before the bell rang. I packed my books into my bag as quickly as I could. People kept bumping purposely into the back of my chair on their way out, muttering their final stinging comments before they went. I tried to stand up to leave, but Waximitt flapped his wings in my face, snarling, "Sid down, ya smarty-pants, and git yer head on straight." I had no choice until they were all gone, heading to fill their growling bellies with all manner of poor foods and sweets optional at lunch time.

I pushed my chair back to the table a bit harder than I intended to. I mumbled an apology as I headed for the door. "Miss Emmaline," spoke Mrs. Plumbottle. I halted in my tracks.

"Yes?"

"Would you do me a favor, please?"

"Um...what is it?"

"Could you draw what you saw on the board, please? It would mean a great deal to me," she explained as she sat down at her desk in the back corner. "I'm doing some research," she continued, "about the number of people who can translate extensionals naturally in their head. Don't worry, it's not a test," she replied to the nervous expression on my face. "I just want to see what you can do. Alright? Good!" she concluded cheerfully, as she ruffled through some test papers from yesterday.

I went to the front and drew everything I could remember, starting with a giant swirling figure on the left. *That's strange*, I thought as I wrote the rest on the board. *I don't actually remember seeing any of this in the wave of light. Maybe that's part of the translation process*, I wondered as I finished my masterpiece. I put down the pen and stepped back.

Guinolia Nut = 8's approximate quantical configimagine, factoring quirbal plunification

I picked my bag up off the floor and turned to see Mrs. Plumbottle gaping at what I had covered her board with. Looking back and forth between her and the board, I grew concerned.

"Is everything alright, Mrs. Plumbottle?"

She had a strange look in her eyes, like she couldn't—or didn't—want to comprehend what she was seeing. "What?" she asked me, perplexed. "Oh, no, everything's fine...you did very well, I must say. You're excused now, Miss Emmaline," she answered, acting like nothing had happened at all.

I left the room with far graver concerns than being worried about people laughing in my face for the next week. *First that dream, and then Mom and Ashlee, and now this?* I interrogated myself as I headed for the lunchroom. *What in God's name is going on around here?*

I sat in virtual silence for the lunch hour as my lunch buddies joked around about whatever new funny thing they heard through the grapevine. Completely engrossed in my neural complexities, I beat my memory to death as I recapped what had happened in the past couple of hours. The dream of the burning tree. Ashlee predicting Mom's delivery being today. And now this incident in Advanced Math. Why hadn't anyone else seen anything? I mean, I knew it was unlikely, but seriously, was it just me? And why did Mrs. Plumbottle react so strongly to my translation? I knew at that moment she was hiding something from me, but I didn't know then how unbelievably bigger the scale was of that something and how greatly it would affect the rest of my life.

And then the day got even better.

Stupid me, I cursed at myself as I sprinted down the hall. In my extreme self-absorption, I'd somehow managed to completely miss the first bell and in about ten seconds would have my first "late" to one of my favorite classes, Astronomical Phenomena. If there was one thing I hated about school more than the kids out to make my life a living furnace, it was being late.

Come on, move faster, you dumb, brainless toadfish! I slapped at myself as halfway down the hall, the tardy bell rang, vibrating my delicate soul. *Troll snot!* I swore. *Sorry, God,* I repented, as I gave it my all to reach the stairs before the bell finished echoing. I'd be late for sure. There was no way to get up those steep, winding stairs in a second, even if I flew, which I couldn't. Not before the test. If I tried now, I would never fly. Until I got angel wings, anyway.

I felt a sudden burst of power like no adrenaline I'd felt before as I leapt up the stairs in the terrible silence. The amber glow of the new spring sun flooded my vision as I entered the tall-windowed stair tower...

And then there was nothing.

What in Skyglass..., I thought as I looked around, startled out of my skin. I was surrounded by...outer space? *Geez,* I half joked, *this is like that weird show* The Midnight Realm *that the guys were making fun of.* But it wasn't. It was much weirder than that.

I was enveloped in darkness, the darkness of outer-world areas. And stars. There were stars everywhere! Blue stars, red stars, green stars, purple stars, orange stars. Any color you could name, there were a hundred stars for it. But there were no people. Where was everyone? I was at school; I should've seen people, right?

Wrong.

A terrible idea entered my mind.

What if all those stars *were* the people?

Then I realized my chest was glowing.

White.

I was a white star.

A storm filled my head as those hundreds of thousands of stars of people jumped abruptly. Ringing. I heard ringing. *Outside* my head? In the stairwell. I was at the top. In the doorway. At my seat. The tardy bell's echoes finally stopped.

What on God's green earth just happened to me?

I sat shell-shocked. Nobody noticed or cared. I always stared off blankly in Astronomical Phenomena. I loved it. But not that day, nor that moment. There was no explanation I could find, sifting through the pages of my book when the teacher didn't look, as she taught things I'd read many times already, of what had just occurred in the stairwell. Nothing. Nothing at all. In a class dutifully dedicated to the oddities of the outer worlds, there was nothing remotely close to describing the event I alone had experienced. Nothing.

Then I forgot what I was looking for at all. That's what tends to happen when a terror of your subconscious jumps into reality.

I couldn't stop looking at the caption below a horrid picture:

Double Reaper's Moon. Appearance of blood-staining is due to an extremely rare planet–satellite alignment, in which the atmosphere of the planet bends sunlight in a way that only red light is reflected off the satellites. Superstitious peoples believe that the devil uses these forces of poor lighting as an opportunity to walk amongst the weak, bringing devastation to any he may pass; as such, catastrophic events can be either caused or inspired by this haunting and widely believed legend.

The teacher asked me if I wished to share something, since I'd been obviously not paying attention to the lesson at hand. She seemed surprised that I responded.

"No, ma'am. Just found something I didn't expect."

CHAPTER THREE

FIVE PLUS SIX

"Gah!"

I panted as the banging continued on my door. "Who's it?" I yelled.

"Me, dummy. Who else?"

Ashleeka opened my door and walked in with an air of impatience. "You were yelling random stuff, and you were disturbing the peace," she accused me.

"Nuh-uh."

"Yuh-huh," she retorted defiantly as she clambered onto my bed and threw a pillow at my face. I growled. Time for a new strategy.

"Whose peace? I was the one sleeping."

"My peace. I was the one studying. But I'm done now."

I glared at her. "So why the heck d'ja wake me up for?"

Ashleeka stared at me. Then she hopped off my bed and walked out the door. She was so weird. And annoying. And wonderful. Siblings are complicated.

My back popped a zillion times as I stretched out and batted my stiff wings. My left foot had fallen asleep. I slumped my way out of the room as noises came from the hallway.

"Ash, what are you doing?"

"Nailing this board back into the ceiling where it belongs. It's loose. So unless you want a permanent addition to your facial features, I'm going to keep nailing."

"Whatever," I started, but then I remembered something. Something far off in time and distance, which had finally escaped my mind as I slept. Dang it.

"How long has that board been loose?"

"How should I know? You're the super-genius who notices everything. You tell me, hotshot," she retorted as she continued whacking the heck out of the board above her head. The chair she stood on wobbled as she hammered.

"Hey!" I argued, "Since when do you hate my guts and call me names?"

She stopped and looked at me.

"Ask me no questions and I'll tell you no lies. Deal?"

I said nothing.

"My answer to your previous question, about why I woke you up, is only half true. I woke you because you were yelling, yes, but also because I received a message that all sled riders were to report to the training room at four. So," she paused to check her watch as I grabbed my jacket and shoes, "you have approximately fifteen minutes to get there. I suggest you hurry."

"Gee, thanks," I grumbled. "I sure couldn't have figured *that* out." I grabbed my harness and goggles.

I got to the training room five minutes after four, which everyone knew was ten minutes too late. Coach Wachler was very strict about tardiness, so I was astounded to find that the rest of my fellow sledders were waiting outside the door with great annoyance on their faces. "Why the heck won't he let us in? Geez," someone asked. Others seemed quite unconcerned about their fate at the hands of the coach and broke regulation by sitting on the floor, attempting to go to sleep. Wished I could've done the same, but I could never let myself fall asleep anywhere outside the house. Not me. It was too dangerous.

Suddenly loud footsteps sounded behind the door. The guilty sleepers leapt from the floor and tried to look vigilant as the doorway opened and was filled with the stature of an enormous man. "Good afternoon, Coach Wachler," we all chorused together, praying for mercy. From what we weren't completely sure.

Coach Wachler had the gaze of a ravenous hawk, or an executioner, whichever you preferred. It felt like he could burn a hole straight through you if he wanted to. There were a few myths passed around that anybody who'd ever stood up to him mysteriously disappeared and was found months later rotting in the deep, dank dungeons of the old mining spaces, but nobody really believed them. At least, not in the sort of way that you think is true, but wonder about it, nonetheless, because it's so creepy. Ugh.

We filed silently into the training room. Everything had been removed, which was strange for us. The room felt too big, too open without all the equipment: high-up obstacle courses, weights, and fans to strengthen our wings and increase mobility. I wondered what, then, was the purpose for being here. I soon found out.

"All right then!" boomed Coach Wachler. "Today you are not training in here; today you are not even training! Today," he paused for effect. "You had better hope you are ready, because the High Order has decided to hold the Flight Test early!" An overall groan of dismay rushed over us. "Why?" I dared to ask. Coach turned his penetrating stare to me. A few buddies of mine and I once made a joke that he wasn't really a faery, but a metal frame with an outer shell of man. Like in the movie *The Conforminator*.

The High Order, he told me, had chosen to have the test early because the Watchers of Starglass, the astronomical observatory, had seen a great storm coming our way and had deemed it necessary to test all sledders early for their own protection. "Who knows," he said, as he continued striding in front of his legion, "of what that storm may bring? There are many who say it comes not as worldly weather, but from some kind of conjuror." He watched us for reactions. Nobody took him seriously, and most braved something of a smile.

Coach hinted a smile back. *He wasn't really that bad,* I thought then, *not really at all.*

We had ten minutes to warm up before learning which course we'd be tested on, so we set to doing flying exercises. I found myself to be much stronger than I remembered and more graceful. But what I needed most was speed. Tests were timed and you had to make it before the bell. I wasn't sure if I could. But I had to. I had to pass. I had to.

Flying without a sled is sometimes harder than with it. You don't have anything to kneel on or to rest on. You always, always, always have to be alert and be quick. I sure wasn't the best, but I wasn't too bad, either. I hoped my extra sessions with Dad would pay off. *Will anyone be watching?* I wondered. I hoped not. Too much pressure.

I was stretching out one last time, which I noticed many failed to do, when the coach returned and yelled to get down on the floor again and move it. The others panted and groaned as they ran back to the harness room. I knew they'd regret not stretching. They'd pay for it, one way or another.

Coach led us out into the bright, spring sunlight and cool breeze. We followed obediently on our sleds, all hoping it would be their strongest course they would be tested on, not that one or that one, and please not that one, above all! I drifted along, trying to be unconcerned. *Relax,* I told myself, *relax. Stay loose. Stay ready. We'll find out soon enough.*

My eyes closed.

I saw a storm on the horizon, dark clouds roiling with thunder. It moved faster than the wind can blow, and already it was overhead. Over Skyglass. *No, no, not again!* Rain fell like spears of ice, stinging like hornets in a rage. Thunder plotted destruction over the great tree. *Make it stop, dang it, make it stop! I don't want this!* Flashes of lightning ripped apart between clouds. *Leave, run! Get away while you can! Don't stay to die!* Light like the sun jumped down from the horrid storm, piercing the roots of Skyglass.

Fire blazed uncontrollably like a waterfall pouring over a cliff-side. *No! Ashlee, run! Mom, Dad, everyone! Get out! Run, run, run! You'll burn! Noooooo!* There was no distinguishing between smoke and storm now. All was burning. Flames roared. Every tree, every bush, everyone. Burning. Burning as they flew out windows, like the stones exploding from a volcano. Yes, a volcano...full of heat and fire. A nice home for...what would live in a volcano? Something evil...yes...something scaly...a...a...dragon? A great black creature swept across the smoke-storm, glinting in the firelight of the death it had caused. Wind. More wind. Trying to blow me over. It dove at me, with its sharp, sword-like teeth, calling me to be gnawed on like a toy. I tried to get back...

The river was only a foot below my face when I caught myself. *Don't panic, don't panic,* I told myself, trying to flap fast enough to get up onto my sled again. The water rushed by so fast. *If I just gave up,* I calculated, *I would be swept away and nobody would even realize I was gone for hours...nor would they really care. Just think, Emmaline. No more nightmares, no more bullies, no more pressure...just peace. Forever...*

But not today.

I got back on the sled, wishing the sunlight would stop me from trembling. The mist from the river was cold from the runoff of melting snow. The breeze didn't help much either. But I was there. *And that's what matters,* I thought.

When I rejoined the group, I found myself in an eerily familiar shadow. Panic was thick enough to cut like cheese. The test course was, of course, to be set in the most complex branches and twigs...of the Willow-Tree Market. Talk about accidental déjà vu.

The Willow trial run was the most perilous of all the courses. Everyone knew that. Those brave or dumb enough to try it wiped out in seconds with a bloody nose or a busted arm or worse. Records said only one person had ever made it through successfully. *Ever.*

Coach said that the Willow course was for those who wished to pass at the top of the class with highest marks. If they made it through and if they made it in time. The record was 39.78 seconds. *Eesh.* Even I couldn't make it that quick...right? Then I flashed back to the morning. Shadela's shove. My panicked maneuvers. Making it through. Unscathed. Maybe...just maybe I could!

I volunteered right as Coach was about to send us all off to an easier run. Grumbles, then taunts of being a showoff surged through the group hovering above the rushing waters. Coach gave me an eye of doubtful surprise but asked me to get ready anyway. "You'll have three chances to beat the required time of 45 seconds. If you make it and wish to try for a better time, you may do so. Are you set?"

"Yes, sir."

"Ready," he started.

I unhooked myself from my sled. My hummers sped out from underneath me. I breathed deeply. *Focus. Breathe. Focus. There is nothing but the tree. There is nothing but what is before you.* I practiced what my father had trained me to do. To focus.

"Set!"

There is nothing but the tree. You are alone. Alone in the world with a single tree. That is all that matters. That tree. Stay relaxed, stay focused, and never take your eyes off the tree. Focus. You are alone, with God as witness. With the tree, the only tree in the world, waiting for you to fly its course. You are focused. You are ready. God is watching.

"Go!"

I shot towards the tree. The leafy, green branches parted as I reached them. I followed what I had done that morning. Over. Under. Right. Left. Over over under left over right under roll. Left over under right turn twist under over roll twist glide. On and on. Here and there and everywhere. Branches and wind and leaves surrounding me. For a few seconds that felt like an eternity. I saw the sky calling me home. The light strands drew back like a majestic curtain as I careened out of the maze behind me. It was over. I was through. I was done.

But had I passed?

I slowed, finding my way back to Coach. His expression was beyond me.

"Coach?"

He kept looking from me to the timer he was holding. If he was surprised, he hid it very well. Or not well at all. His face was blank as a white canvas waiting to be painted.

"Coach Wachler? Did I pass?"

I felt panic bursting out of my chest as he wordlessly handed over the timer. I nearly exploded in astonishment.

32.67 seconds. Nobody'd beaten the record. Ever. It was more than extraordinary. It was dangerously close to miraculous.

"Congratulations, Miss Emma," said Coach Wachler without conviction. "You may stay to watch or leave early."

"Thank you, sir," I answered halfheartedly, staring at the faces of the others. They were beyond disgusted.

Heck, I didn't even know how I did it. I wasn't the best. Surely someone else could have done it, too? I was saddened by the lack of anyone else even giving it a shot. *Please*, I thought, *please won't somebody else try? I didn't mean to hurt anybody. I just...can't help it.*

The class dispersed toward the regular trial run in shame and anger. They whispered things, glanced back at me. In hatred.

I'm...sorry...I guess...but I didn't do anything wrong! Why should I have to feel sorry for people when they're the ones blaming me for what they can't do? I was so confused. And angry. At them being angry. At me.

I left early.

I pecked away in the archery grounds later after dinner to try to sort things out. I was surprised the Temple even had archery grounds, given it was dedicated solely to worship and healing.

Whack! Eh. Another inner circle. I'd had better days. And I would have worse nights.

The archery grounds had both field and wooded sections, depending on what you were concentrating on. Now, I just wanted to hit stuff. *Whack.* Middle circle. *Oy.* Keep trying, Dad would say keep trying. Except he wasn't there. He was holding Mom's hand, as the first contractions were starting. *Whack.* Wrong circle. Poop. *A boy or a girl,* I wondered. *Did Dad want a boy?* I didn't know. I had never really thought of asking him. *Whack.* Inner circle. Better. I was surprised when Ash was born, but even Ash was surprised at the idea of a third O'Meern child. *Whack.*

Bull's-eye.

"Nice shot," someone said. I knew that voice.

"Hey, Sam."

Sameela O'Klurn was my best friend. We didn't see each other much, but that didn't matter. We were buddies. And that wouldn't change. She was wearing a favorite blue outfit of hers: tye-dye shirt, sea-blue pants. She wanted to study ocean life. If we'd ever get to the ocean. She had her brother with her. He adored me.

"Hi, Raven. How ya doin', buddy?"

"Good." He bugged his eyes up at me. His name wasn't Raven, it was Yadravn. Raven was just a nickname we'd made for him. Raven was eleven; Sameela was fourteen. He pulled a mutated contraption from his pocket composed of several seeds, twigs, and rocks, and tried to explain to me his marvelous invention. "See, Em-ma-line, this is where the, the rocks, uh, go, and uh, this, this is where the, uh, you pull back the, um, holder things, and this is where you, um, release it to make them fly." He was showing me his latest design for an improved trebuchet or catapult or whatever. I couldn't follow his meaning half the time, but he loved telling me anyway. Heh.

"Heard how you did on the Flying Test," Sameela broke in when Raven was persuaded that I thought his idea was awesome. I grimaced. "Yeah…" I trailed off. We watched Raven load his cata-pult-thing with some pebbles from the ground.

"I don't get why nobody else tried. It couldn't have been that impossible if you pulled it off," she said, trying to get me to say what I thought. I didn't know how much to tell her, so I just told her about my encounter with Shadela earlier that day. She still wouldn't accept my suggestion that Shadela caused me to cheat. "But Emma," she said, "it's not like you knew that was the test route. You just went that way by accident!"

A chaotic sound of thumps diverted our attention. Raven had used my target as his own. Six little stones winked at us with damp-ness from the same marshmallow-like substance that my arrows were stuck in. He pumped his tiny fist victoriously as he ran over to pull them out. Five arrows. Six stones.

Eleven years of haunting dreams.

"Yeah," I protested, "but why me? Why am I the only one who tried, and it just so happened that I had done that route once before in the same day?" I attempted with desperation to hold back the pulsing tears that wanted to spill out of my eyes. "Why?" I sat down on the ground, emotionally drained. All I could do was stare at my feet, my bow heavy and useless in my limp hands.

Sam, Raven, and I just sat for a while, listening to the peaceful quiet of the water in the stream nearby. To the breeze coming in from the windows. To the—

Thunder.

A storm was coming.

I remembered the dreams.

I was so, so sick and tired of those dreams. So tired of getting agitated at every thought of destruction, injury, mayhem. So tired of waiting helplessly for them to come.

Because I knew, whether in a year or a hundred, they would come. They always did.

Sam knew a little. I couldn't tell Raven; he was too young to understand the importance of secrecy. Ash had me figured out, but then, we were very much alike in our abilities. It was like watching a chess match. She saw a single, distinct move on the chessboard. I saw the game from start to finish. And I hated every moment of it. And I liked chess. So that's saying something.

I told Sam what I could say safely in Raven's company then parted ways, heading home, waiting for fate to have its way with me. I knew God was there. But sometimes I just couldn't quite feel His presence. This was one of those times.

I lay on my bed. And waited. Praying for time. Any time. Time for me to be ready, to stop it. But you can't stop an avalanche, nor a flood, nor a storm, nor the dreadful doom of being chased every night by Hell's minions and nobody to talk to about it. So I just prayed.

And waited.

CHAPTER FOUR

EVALUATIONS

A tall, twig-like figure of a man paced around the walkway of the turret he was stationed on. He gritted his teeth as the bitter chill of the storm's wind whipped its way around the tower. A hot fire was all he could think of and a bowl of hot soup. He needed a break from the mindlessness of the Watch, of waiting impatiently for the shift to end. How many hours had it been? His Watch ended at two in the morning.

The man cursed at the idea of how much time he was away from her, how long she had to wait for the stupid bell to sound that meant he was free to come to her side. There was no choice, he had to watch, even if there was nothing to see coming, nothing hiding in the darkness far below, waiting for a single moment of inattentiveness, a moment of failure, to strike its enemy. After all, if he stepped away from his post without order, even for a moment, he would be arrested and sentenced to the dungeons for treason. Treason. For needing to take...a bathroom break.

He sat on his hard, wooden stool and stared out into the darkness. As sleep tempted him, he thought about home, the temporary home, at least, that held his family far below in the massive tree. His oldest, she would be asleep, exhausted from a hard day of school, breathing deeply, resting peacefully. His second would probably be reading or writing late into the night, to be found with a small pen in her small hand and a mess of papers covered in poetry and stories strewn about her. His wife...dang, what was the time? He had to see her soon; he couldn't stand it. What would the cost be worth, the dungeons, how much would he be willing to go through that? *Please,* he pleaded into the wintry night lashing through him like spears in the heat of battle, *let me go, I beg of you! What treason is there in wanting to witness the birth of my third child?*

A sudden noise of the door opening bolted him upright. He felt his joints pop as the shadowed figure in the door held onto his hat and turned to see him in the dimness.

"O'Meern?"

"Yes, sir."

"You have permission to leave early."

"Thank you, sir."

Jolson O'Meern saluted his superior and dashed down the stairs as fast as his frozen, stiff legs could carry him.

Sleep could not reach the mind of Sameela that night. There were far too many troubles bouncing around in her head. That was something else in common between her and Emmaline, besides their reddish hair: once something entered their brains, it was next to impossible to forget it for many, many months. And this had only happened today, so there was no way it was leaving her memory that night—no way.

She rolled over again, rustling her unfamiliar sheets as she did. Sam hated leaving home, even though it was safer to stay in Skyglass. She and her family didn't live in the inner core of NeverSeen. They lived in their own tree on the outskirts of it, close to a small village on the edge of the forest. With nearly everything in and throughout the tree handmade or crafted, the house itself felt like a community of talents and friends, all gathered into one place by a single family. It felt wonderful to be separate from the big city, but at the same time still surrounded with the sensation of living, breathing beings, even when it was only their pieces of workmanship that were really there.

But here, everything was different. There was no community. Only people crammed together in a small space of a single tree, trapped inside with no space to breathe. Just because you were surrounded by people didn't mean you knew them or cared for them. The isolation was astounding to Sam. Never had she felt more choked off from civilization than when she was engulfed by it, suppressing her very ability to think.

Exasperated, she finally sat up, staring blankly at the floor beneath her feet. She replayed the restricted conversation with Emma in her head.

"Wait, so you're saying that you more or less dreamt the end of civilization, of specifically NeverSeen as we know it?"

She'd sighed shakily, replying, "Yeah, pretty much. It was terrifying. To watch everyone dying. And then I think I died, too."

"I've had bad dreams like that before."

"None like this, Sam. You've never dreamt one as bad as this. Ever. And I don't think you ever will..." Emma had trailed off, like she had something more to say, but either couldn't say it or find the words to say it.

"Maybe it'll get better, Emma. Maybe when you're done growing. You know, with hormones and all and stuff..."

Emma stared at Sam briefly. The dead tiredness of her hazel eyes gave her the appearance of being much older than the nearly fifteen years she was, even older than how maturely she tended to behave.

"Sam, nobody's done growing until they're dead."

Sam had tried to think of something, anything, to say to give her friend hope, but she couldn't. Then the seven-thirty bell had rung, the mandatory call to return to their quarters for the evening under the current storm threat. They had hugged good-bye, but it felt more like the kind of hug that you gave somebody you wouldn't see again for a long time, if ever. Like a child clinging to its father before he leaves for the front line.

Why would Emma feel that way? What did she know? What should I know? questioned Sam, almost angry she couldn't help her friend. Sam knew how horribly real dreams could feel, but Emma—she hated herself for even thinking of it—seemed on the verge of being paranoid about her dreams, like somehow they were real. *She's got to be hiding something. Either that or she's nuts, but even if she is, she's no more nuts than Raven or I or anyone else in this dungeon of a tree.*

With that final thought, Sam crawled back into bed and promptly fell asleep.

"Sir, she's dreaming again."

"Well? What is it this time, Grantson?"

"Looks like the same as last time, sir, except it's backwards."

"Record it like the others, and let me know if something changes."

"Are you expecting a new revelation, sir?"

"That is to be judged by the Committee, not me."

"How long until the Launch, sir?"

"I don't believe that's any of your business, now is it, Mr. Grantson?"

"No, sir, Chief Locknut."

"Good. Now shut up and watch."

"Yes, sir."

Ashleeka looked up suddenly from her late-night poetry with a sharp gasp. She tilted her head slightly, staring into space, as if somebody were whispering in her ear. Nodding in understanding, Ashleeka brushed her unfinished rain poem carelessly to the floor and quickly grabbed a new sheet of paper. She paused, waiting, listening to the soothing thrumming of raindrops on the window next to her bed. Then she scribbled furiously onto the page, as if its importance of being recorded were a matter of life and death. But she never quite looked at the page. It was like she was seeing something on the other side of the paper, staring into space as if in a daydream. Line after line she wrote, until a cryptic and haunting poem was before her.

COME SHALL THREE
CHILDREN, SHE.
HARD DAYS OF LATE,
ENCOUNTER FATE.
COUNCIL OF SEVEN:
FOR HELL OR FOR HEAVEN?
DANGER TO END,
BREAK NOT, BEND.
WARRIORS ARISE,
SPEAR OF DEMISE.
LIGHT THE DARK,
A SINGLE SPARK.
ASHES OF SIX
RISE, PHOENIX.

Ashleeka blinked several times and looked back down at what she'd written. She read it, smiled curiously, and let it join her pile of papers on the floor. Before she closed her dark, luscious eyes, she whispered into the vacancy of the room, "Thank you, Teacher. I have much to learn from you. I wonder what...what...they'll...name you..."

The rain pattered gently against the window, and the soft moonlight caressed the young beauty's sleeping face as she slipped off into a dreamless state. For just as Emmaline was trailed in the night by inescapable monsters, Ashleeka was trailed by absolutely nothing.

The smell of wet, mossy earth was overpowering in this dismal place. Murky water formed puddles on the stony floor, and the air was hazy from a lack of ventilation. There was no possible reason that someone in their right mind would have the notion of going down and exploring the horrid, mysterious caverns below Skyglass.

Except one with a strange tip and a stranger hobby.

A cloaked figure stepped cautiously between the dank pools on the ground, taking care not to disturb anything hanging from the slimy walls or the root-patterned roof. The pattern of movement, swift and precise, would give a passing spider cause to believe that it, whatever it was, was both skilled and experienced in the art of sneaking and eavesdropping on certain secret conversations. But the spider did not care, for it was a spider, and spiders cannot eat little invaders of the deep places of the world, and it scrambled away up a hole in the roof. Nothing but the sound of tiny droplets striking chords on the makeshift drums of water filled the lonely cave.

No, wait. There's another sound.

The low mumbling of voices began to reach the ears of the trespasser. The tone was of debate and about something highly important. Searching for any hint of where it might be coming from, the sneak felt the far wall of the deep, winding cave for a crack or scrape, or some other sign of a hidden door. Slender fingers crawled like a creepy-crawly, searching, and found something: a crack, smooth and straight, too perfect to be natural. The muffled noise continued on the other side. Ever so carefully, the nervous fingers slipped cautiously into the space and tweaked it gently open.

Through the gap in the doorway, the spy could see a sparsely furnished room, with a faint light coming from the chandelier above, hanging precariously from a root sprouting through the dirt ceiling. Its walls and floor were composed of compacted earth, some immense roots of the tree overhead, and stone slabs, set up in an attempt to keep out the ground creatures and to hear anyone, however remotely possible, that might be exploring down in the caverns between the Temple's roots. It had quite the opposite effect now: it instead magnified the sound of the argument inside. The dark-eyed scout sat carefully next to the entrance and took note of who was there this time.

...Seven, eight...twelve, thirteen, fourteen...wait, who's that?

The intruder stifled a gasp of excitement and noiselessly pulled a well-used notebook from a pocket and opened it. The conversation around the corner continued heatedly.

"Lark, tell me why," a gruff voice grumbled. "Tell me why you woke us in the darkest hours of the morning in the middle of a horrendous storm? Why not the morning, huh, why not? You're always jumping on the horsefly before you get saddled up!" he blasted.

"I dare say, Senator," a sophisticated and sly female voice crooned. "I do believe that you are merely jealous that you were not the one to witness it!"

"I'll have your head for that, Miss Fritely," retorted the Senator, "but that is not the point of this meeting, now is it? Our job is to watch out, and out watching is what we have them doing so they don't see what's happening under their noses and where their darned noses don't care to go around sniffing in stinking tree roots! So, *Lark*," he growled, "what exactly *is it* that has occurred with Subject 513?"

Somebody young and terrified cleared his voice and reported, "Well, sir, it appears that Subject 513, currently under Class A in the O-B-A-F-G-K-M classification system," he paused a moment to think, "has, uh, well, sir—"

"What *is it*, Lark? Get on with it!"

"It appears she's on the verge of going nova, sir."

The room went dead silent. A pencil clattered to the floor. Tension and fear spilled out of the room and into the cave beyond, thick enough to cut with a knife. The eavesdropper sat breathlessly outside, waiting.

The groan of a chair was heard as the Senator stood up. He popped his knuckles as he leaned forward on the table.

"How long until she reaches class U, Phillips?"

"We don't know. Tomorrow...two years from now..."

The Senator slumped back into his chair. There was a long minute of suffocating silence. The shadow just outside the room leaned in slightly to hear, her fingers tapping impatiently at the moss underneath her.

"Alright, everyone," the Senator sighed heavily, "you know your orders. Track her around the clock, and alert me of any flare-ups. Remember the line in the sand. As soon as she crosses it, she's done."

⇥⇥⇥⇥⇤⇤⇤⇤

When I awoke the next morning, I wasn't engulfed by flames. The tree was still standing tall; the storm had passed over peacefully, if not ruffling our feathers a bit.

And I had a baby sister.

She was named Umala, both for the safe passage of the thunderhead and for her beauty. It was undeniable; she was one of the most gorgeous babies I had ever seen. She had a full head of shiny black hair and paralyzing blue eyes, like the sea after a passing storm. Mom and Dad couldn't take their eyes off her. Neither could I that first week. I was jealous and, though I know it was foolish now, I believed Umala was going to be the perfect child. She would be their favorite from then on. Me and Ashlee, *pff*, we were just "the first two kids."

After all, I was known very well for odd ideas and an upside-down sort of perspective, and Ashlee pretty much didn't say anything to anyone.

So all their hopes and dreams were then laid on Umala, the perfect child, the last chance, the one who would finally fit in, be normal, and live a happy life with lots of friends and have a nice job cleaning clothes or mending curtains or gardening. Forget all the "Hey, Mom, I want to be an engineer and make the world better," or "Daddy, I want to be a novelist and a poet." No, they would have the child that nobody asked questions about, or got teased, or got left alone at recess. I thought sarcastically (and selfishly) that Umala would be so happy to be average in a family of whacked-out kids.

Boy, I should've known. Three, after all, is a magic number, not a normal one.

A month and a half after Umala was born, I was about to walk into my room to hang up my newly arrived "Scroll of Graduation from Basic Education" from the school I would no longer have to attend, and hadn't for thirteen magical days, when I heard a peculiar noise coming from her room. I paused, recognizing that this wasn't just a bunch of baby gurgling like I normally heard, and carefully set my graduation scroll on my desk. I stepped gingerly over to the doorway, which faced mine, and saw through the crack in the door that she was floating above her crib with Ashlee standing on a chair next to her.

"So, this is how you do it?" Ashlee asked and promptly jumped. She hovered for a second and then fell down, toppling on her perch by the crib. Suddenly Umala exploded in a garble of baby goo-goo, still turning slowly in the air. Ashlee paid great attention to her nonsense as I tried not to freak out or bust up laughing at the irony of my long-forgotten jealousy for my baby sister. *So comes the most talented of three,* I thought, *and discovered, she has yet to be.*

Ashlee tried again, but still didn't get it, and asked what she was doing wrong. Umala said something again in baby talk, and I swore then that she was taking the tone of "focus, and stop trying." Ashlee closed her eyes, so dark and deep, and gently pushed off the chair.

She drifted up to the ceiling but didn't touch it. Umala erupted in laughter and clapped her hands. Ashlee smiled as she turned upside-down, and I tripped and blew my cover. On what, I haven't a clue, because I wasn't even moving my feet, so I thought. When I looked up from the floor, they were both sitting calmly, one in the crib and one on the floor, pretending like nothing peculiar had happened at all, besides the way their mouths were twitching in a feeble attempt to not smile, like they were passing secrets to each other. My mouth made weird shapes on my face as I searched for something to say. It finally broke into a wry sort of smile.

"Can you teach me?"

And that was how the O'Meern girls found a loophole in the obey-to-the-letter Code of Flight: it was now possible to fly without ever moving your wings and, therefore, untraceable if you were under the free-flying limit of eighteen. It was rebellious and it was scary and fun and crazy and dangerous all at the same time. But we were good at keeping it secret. Umala was an expert at playing "dumb newborn," and we played along with it, although the scream-ing-in-the-middle-of-the-night-for-no-apparent-reason routine was a bit hard to deal with. Oh well, that's what it costs to have a baby with a huge secret, or any baby, for that matter.

I, of course, had finished school *forever* with, literally, flying colors and was enjoying my summer off with my sisters and parents. I got to be with my friends, and I went on adventures, like everyone should. We dinked around as kids are supposed to do, but every once in a while we'd talk about stuff, usually just the three of us, in the warmth of the sun and the cool damp of the grass. I couldn't directly understand Umala, so Ashlee translated. Ashlee was a short-term telepathic, and Umala "said" she was something like an atmospheric manipulator or telekinetic thingy, capable of changing the effects of the air around her and the granting the knowledge to help others access it. I told them about my terrors, or what I felt they ought to know, and made some use of my time writing stories and drawing pictures. We often wondered how our abilities would be useful, but we knew God had made us to be part of His plan, so we trusted in Him and prayed together.

Over time, and with a stronger faith, I found that some of the scars of the night left on my nerves faded and became dormant. I slept better and had more regular dreams of sunshine and friends and flying and cool story ideas and fun stuff that's impossible, like walking on clouds, and zooming through galaxies, and even seeing a place like Heaven, where you're enjoying it so much you're almost a little bummed to wake up. It was all normal, and it was all good.

Until one night I dreamt of the burning tree again and woke up screaming.

CHAPTER FIVE

DEFINING MADNESS

"Please, Honey, just tell me what's the matter," Mom pleaded softly with concerned eyes. She sat in front of me on a chair with the door shut and everyone else outside it, waiting to see if I was okay. I wasn't.

Some creature that had taken me hostage was shaking me like doll from the inside out. I was, once again, freezing in the heat of the night from sweat coating me like I'd just taken a bath. All I could do was stare unblinking into the space in front of me, my hands iron fists gripping the edge of the mattress, like I might tumble into oblivion if I let go. My hair was plastered to my face and the back of my also-soaking shirt, and I couldn't breathe right. It felt like someone had shoved a rolled-up sock down my throat and I was gasping uncontrollably. My heart was doing jumping jacks and somersaults. I was sure I'd drop down dead from a heart attack any second now.

"Please, Honey, it's okay to tell me, you don't have to hold back—"

"I CAN'T!"

I'd finally lost it and exploded, slamming my hands hard on the bed. Mom jumped back in fear. I'd scared myself too. Running my trembling fingers through my wet, cold hair, the choking hold on my throat finally released enough that I could sob, and once it did, I didn't stop for a long time. It took me a while to realize that she was holding me in her arms, like a child frightened by the monsters under the bed. I needed it. I had needed it for a long time, so long I had nearly forgotten that there was a time I didn't have horrible nightmares.

I didn't remember being put back in bed with dry sheets and clothes. I didn't remember Mom and Dad kissing my soggy head. I didn't remember Ashlee and Umala looking at each other with a sense of knowing and of empathy and quietly waving goodnight as Dad closed the door.

But I still remembered the dream the next morning.

Sunlight was already glinting off the floor when my eyes opened that day. I wondered for a second why my head was cold and why I had different clothes and sheets. I wondered why my arms were sore, what I had been dreaming of piercing with a fine, glinting arrow in Dreamland...

And then I remembered.

My back popped as I gradually sat up. My leg was numb, and my fingers pulsed with pain. I got in the shower and stood there for a long time, letting the sweet, glittering dust pour down my back and drip off my wings. It healed my fingers and arms and let me remember slowly what I'd seen.

I finally got out and dressed in a cute blue outfit of shorts and a tank. I dried and brushed my hair and put it up in a gorgeous, thick bun. I remembered I was hungry and went and had breakfast quietly. I didn't really think about why it was so quiet; I just figured the crew had gone off on an errand and let me be until I was ready. Or maybe they were afraid of me. That was a thought I couldn't bear.

An hour later I sat down and started writing in my dreamlog, surprised to see that I hadn't written in it for months. Sitting back in my chair, I tried to think of how to start. My routine had been broken for so long that I had to go back and check previous entries to see how I'd done it. I finally turned back to where I was and started writing this:

Dreamlog 12, entry 37. 7-14-9042
Intensity: 11
Topic: Skyglass
Perspective: First person
This time it started in an old mine, full of glittering stones, but I wasn't looking at them. All I focused on was a person running away in front of me, and I was chasing him. I never got a good look at his face, but I think it was a boy. We ran down a passageway full of roots and other weird things and open doors with creepy lights coming out of rooms. But we ran past them all and up a staircase made of some kind of metal, but we didn't make any noise. There was a doorway at the top that led outside and it was nighttime. Then I realized I wasn't chasing the person, but running from a fire behind me; there was an explosion or something in the cave we were in.

I looked up and saw the Skyglass Temple against the stars in all its glory—and then I blacked out. The next thing I knew I was inside it, and the whole thing was on fire, and I was trying to find somebody. I had a sword that I have no idea where it came from, and my bow and a weird crescent-shaped shield, and fire was exploding all around me but not touching me for some reason, and everyone was running past me the other way. There was somebody just barely in my sight I was trying to get to, and I think the person had a wand or staff or something, because the figure was throwing fire everywhere. I chased the person to the top of the tree and through the Temple, until we were on the end of one of the highest branches. I don't know why, but I drew my bow and asked, "Who are you?"

The smoke between us cleared a little, and I saw it was a girl in a red dress, with red hair and scarlet wings, and everything looked like it was covered in blood, like she'd been killing people with the black knife in her hand. Then, she started to turn around and look at me, but before I could see who it was, an explosion below us engulfed the branch and she disappeared. I caught fire and screamed. I was falling so fast through the thick black smoke, and I knew I was going to die—and then I woke up screaming still.

My heart was pounding to relive it in my waking world, and I sat back exhausted. I realized I'd been holding my breath for a while and my hands trembled. My stomach growled angrily, and I saw that it was almost lunchtime. I was wondering what to do about food, being alone and having no idea where my family was, when the phone rang. Tripping over my own feet and other objects that seemed to have purposely moved to the middle of the floor, I hurried to catch it before it stopped.

"Hello, this is the O'Meern residence. How may I help you?"

A scratchy and strange-sounding voice answered. "You don't know me. You never will. They're gaining on you. Watch your back, 518. You're next."

"I'm sorry, who is this?"

"517."

The tone echoed on the walls, filling the room with a most hollow and unholy sound. I jumped at the click of the doorknob and the rustling of leaves. The suddenly ominous door swung open dramatically, hitting the wall behind it. Light flooded my vision, and I saw five towering silhouettes engulf the doorway. My knees were on the edge of collapsing.

"Good morning, Sweetheart."

In stepped my father carrying bouncing, black-haired Umala in his bulky arms and my mother holding Ashlee and hauling a long skinny package that was strapped to her back. Ashlee hopped down, somewhat precariously, from Mom's arms, and ran to me for a hug. As Mom and Dad set down their other cargo, she whispered into my ear, "We gotta have a meeting after lunch, okay? It's real important."

I nodded slightly to show I understood, and she released me to go and help with Umala. Rising rather imbalanced, I futilely tried to clear my head from the whirlwind of questions whizzing around. Ashlee carried Umala to her high chair as Mom set the package down by the island. "Did you have a nice quiet morning, Honey?" Mom asked gently as she walked around me to get a glass of water.

"Um, yeah, I guess. Where were you guys?"

"Just doing some errands. Paperwork fun," she grimaced. Something else lurked behind that sarcastic smile, but I knew I'd have to find out from a different source.

"Oh, okay. So what is that, exactly?" I inquired, pointing at the tube she'd brought in.

"It's a set of maps of the city, for Dad," Mom replied, brushing her sweaty bangs back from her eyes.

"Wait, why would he need maps of the—"

"It's *work stuff*, Honey. I can't tell you about it." Dad had jumped in. He gave me one of those I'm-glad-you're-curious-but-if-I-tell-you-then-we-all-go-to-jail looks.

"Ah."

➤➤➤ ◄◄◄

I mindlessly ate my lunch, watching my family. Ashlee moved her food around on her plate to make odd little shapes and trails of gravy, with the chicken and potatoes and peas as little land formations: a plateau, a mountain, a forest. She'd seem to be formulating a story or complex idea about it, and then suddenly she'd stop studying it and jab a piece into her mouth. Umala banged her tiny wooden spoon on her table, sending bits of baby food flying around. Mom and Dad mostly took care of Umala, trying to get her to eat as she successfully acted out I-love-this-food-and-I've-eaten-it-a-hundred-times-but-I-hate-it-now. How strange it was to think that my parents were unaware that their three talented daughters were so much more than that.

Should they know?

And when?

I considered opening my mouth to blurt out, "Hey, guess what, I have nightmares almost all the time about people dying," but Ashlee caught my eye as she was stuffing a monstrous piece of potato into her mouth. She subtly shook her head to call me off. "After lunch, remember?" she thought to me as she tried forcing her lips shut around the potato, resulting in much laughter from all parties. As the moment subsided, I realized with a pang that I was, in fact, not amused at all, but was so used to putting on my mask that it was natural, a habit. How long had I played this game, this illusion of normalcy? Struggling to redeem myself, I thought back as far as I could, searching through the treasure trove of my brain for a memory where I was genuinely happy.

I came back empty.

Eventually, Dad settled down for his afternoon nap, and Mom cleaned the dishes. Umala had been put down for a nap, too, but we all knew better. Creeping like spiders, Ashlee and I snuck down the hallway and knocked gently three times on Umala's door. She answered.

We closed the door behind us. Ashlee pulled Umala out of her crib and sat on the floor across from me on the cute little rug displaying a colorful kiddy version of the city. They looked at each other intently, like they were planning their speech. I waited quietly.

"So, where did you guys go?"

Ash turned her gaze toward me.

"We went in search of information."

"What about?" I started bouncing my knees, not wanting to ask, but knowing I had no choice.

"You."

"Say what?" I subconsciously started turning my lips into a snack.

"We went to the Temple to ask about nightmares, as in how common they are, who gets them, and why. Mom and Dad searched the libraries for a long time but didn't find anything. And of course, in order to see a Mediator, you have to make an appointment, which they didn't believe was necessary at this point. From what they found, it appears to be nothing more than the fluctuating levels of hormones that cause them in teenagers."

Throughout her story, Ashlee was quite casual, even uninterested in what she had to say. By the end, she was examining the fingernails on her free right hand, picking out the bits of dirt that had been snagged there. Umala laid like a bag of potatoes in her left arm, playing with Ashlee's shiny, flowing brown hair.

I didn't buy it.

"What aren't you telling me?" I demanded.

Mom and Dad had been searching on the library's databases for common causes of nightmares. Surrounded by piles of recommended books and paging through virtual articles, Ashlee had offered to take Umala to the much more interesting children's section, merely as a ruse to let them go and find out some things for themselves. One section, as everybody knows, is dedicated to history and legends, and they wanted to see if there was anything about "Drifters," as we called ourselves on the occasions when we practiced nonwinged flight.

They spent a good deal of time, probably an hour, wondering about all the odd tales of water people and star people and of walking mountains and other supernatural events, when they found a book that seemed completely out of place. It was a small, thin, black notebook, stuck between two of the largest and bluest of the *Ancient Mythological Analyses* volumes, as if it were meant to be found. They had pulled it out and on the front found a strange symbol embellished in a silvery ink: a heptagon with lines drawing from each point to a fancy seven in the center.

They gasped in excitement and glanced around cautiously to make sure nobody was watching. Ashlee stole away to a corner in an area where others were reading, playing big-sister-reading-to-baby-sister. They sat down and carefully opened it.

Inside were wide arrays of beautiful paintings, maps, and notes on legends of those with super-faery abilities. There were intricate designs on some of them, like an enchanted portal code of some sort, and on others there were symbols emblazoned with bright colors. It was full of stories, too. There was one about two brothers: one who could drain a lake and the other who could fill it. Several were about girls who could disappear from one place only to reappear in another, and a couple about children who could make objects float around and change shapes. Page after page were these incredible tales, and Ashlee retold a lot of them with Umala's help.

Then, all at once, she stopped telling her story and stared quietly into space. I sat in awe, soaking up all this knowledge, the idea that maybe we weren't alone, that I wasn't alone. Desperation drove me to hear the rest.

"Well? What happened next?"

Silence.

"Please! You have to tell me!" I begged her.

Umala cooed gently to Ashlee from her new place in the crib. Ashlee sighed and continued.

"Then one time, I turned a page and something fell out of it. But I wasn't paying attention to it. I...I couldn't stop looking at the picture that was there." Her face was contorted in an expression of horror, a horror she couldn't name.

"Ashlee...what...what was it?" My heart was pounding with fear of something that I could tell was coming but desperately did not want to hear. It couldn't be.

She blinked rapidly and swallowed. Her mouth made attempts at forming words, but it failed several times. Ashlee finally took a deep, shaking breath.

"Emma, it was a...a Sorceress. A Sorceress in a bloody dress with fire swirling around her. She had a black knife, and Emma...she was surrounded by dead people, and...and a tree the size of Skyglass was burning to the ground."

"Raven, geez! Stop bugging me already!"

Sam was getting irritated at her brother for asking for the hundredth time to come and play a game with him and his stupid catapults. She was busy reading a thrilling novel about a weird, alternate sort of universe, where people didn't have wings and didn't live inside trees, where the insects were small enough to eat or squash and where trees were so small you had to build a house on the outside or simply on the ground. She found it quite thought provoking and was tired of the distractions.

"For the last time, Raven, go away!" She tossed a pillow his direction, and he retreated out the door in a hurry.

Sam sighed. It wasn't really Raven that bugged her. It was Emmaline. They hadn't seen each other for a while, and Sam was getting worried. Emmaline wasn't the kind of person to let a week go by without calling, but she also was probably busy with her new sister.

She'd call if something wasn't okay...right? Sam frowned in concern. Emma would still call if everything was alright. But she hadn't called at all. Trying to let it go, she set to reading again.

As if her wish were answered, the phone rang. She leapt up to get it and bumped her knee on the frame of her bed. Sam rubbed it as she hopped the last few steps to the phone.

"Hello, this the O'Klurn residence. How may I—"

It was Emmaline on the other end.

"Sam? It's Emmaline. I...I need your help. Either I'm going insane, or...or I can see the future." My hand trembled as I whispered into the phone. I felt like some kind of criminal calling for backup before a heist, like on the *Project Improbable* movie series. Finally, I heard her voice.

"I'm sorry, what?"

My lips kept drying out, and I could taste the dried blood. I guess it hadn't helped by chewing on them.

"Sam, it's me. Emmaline. You know all those nightmares that I...I told you about?" My voice kept cracking. It felt like all the water in the world wouldn't quench my thirst. "All those nightmares, those dreams...they're the future, Sam, they're the future."

I shuddered for no apparent reason. Waiting for her answer felt like hours. The loud crackle of the line sounded like cannons firing in a continuous round.

"Emma, are you okay? You sound exhausted. But don't worry, these will go away."

The firmness in her voice did not remind me of the caring shoulder upon which I leaned for security. She continued, "Really Emma, I fail to see what the problem is. Everyone gets nightmares, you know. Besides, escalating the drama of your subconscious to a level of importance as that of predicting the future is sheer foolishness."

I shut my mouth quickly as a succulent glob of spit committed suicide and slopped onto my bare foot. What was that weird accent she'd suddenly picked up? And why would my best friend in the world suddenly become so dismissive of my troubles, after all the years she had stood by me? I was about to interject about it when Sam (*was it really Sam?*) rambled on again in her odd, new vocal pattern.

"Emma, you really must stop this silly act and get on with your life! I truly think you are giving yourself these dreams because you know that you are *never* going to amount to anything important in your future." The exasperation in her voice gave me a spontaneous flashback to somebody I knew a long time ago, somebody that told me as a very small child that I...no, wait a minute, they weren't telling *me*...who were they talking to?

"Emmaline? Are you still listening? I'm not done talking to you!"

I knew that voice. A murky image formed from the smoke in front of my mind's eye: *a playroom, filled with little ones laughing and screaming and running about like wild creatures, just as they should be. In my chubby, little, five-year-old sausage fingers were building blocks, and they were stacked up in front of me on the carpet in the shape of some abstract sculpture or building. Across the room, a sudden commotion arose. A tall and slender lady with a dark ponytail was scolding her daughter for not playing with her dollies. Instead, the little black-haired tot in a worn pink dress had taken a boy's army set and was commanding the faery troops to drop onto the opposing troll hordes from the top of a chair.*

Echoing out of my mind, the voice tsked: *"Della, how many times have I told you to play with your dollies? Your father worked an extra shift to get them just for you!" The lady ripped the army men out of her daughter's hands, sending the child into a wave of bawling, and pulled her off the ground by the arm. She waved her finger around in the child's face, a pouting face with a strangely familiar expression and streaked with well-deserved tears.* "Della, we do not cry. We like what we are given, and we work for what we want. Is that understood, young lady?"

"Emmaline, answer me! If you don't in the next ten seconds, I'm going to tell your parents—no, better, I'm going to tell *everyone* at the next congregational meeting! Do you hear me? I'm going to tell everyone!"

I heard her. But in those precious seconds, I saw in my memory that baby's face and knew what expression it carried and had carried for its whole life: rebellion.

"Oh, I hear you quite clearly. You go ahead and tell everyone at the next congregational meeting, because for your information, *Mrs. Glump*, I know that you won't be there. You'll be at home, desperately trying to care for all seven of your children as your husband slaves away in the mines. However, I must congratulate you on your success of hijacking my call; you must have had granted access by a government official—but that would never be given to a laundress—or you could have broken in with a homemade set of lock-picking tools. Doesn't one of your *many children* have a set like that?" Finding myself sadistically pleased at having turned the tables on my perpetrator, I mirrored her odd accent. "Now, my dear Mrs. Glump, I do believe it's time for you to tell me who you're working for."

Silence. I'd expected as much; the lady was stern and controlling, but it must've taken her hours to rehearse that nice piece. My ability to decipher who she was, despite the fact that I'd only seen her twice in my life, must've cemented the concept that I was indeed able to see the future, if not telepathic, or at least shocked her into trying not to think about who she was working for.

"I see you don't wish to, Mrs. Glump, but I must say, I would *truly* appreciate it if you could pass along this message for me to your employer: get the heck out of my life or I'll *personally* see to it that you are hunted down like the ravenous troll you are and locked in your own special cell *in Hell*. Believe me," I growled, "I have *far* more resources than you're aware of. You're walking on eggshells, Mrs. Glump, and I'll hear you long before you reach me. And now I must apologize," I sarcastically lamented, "because I do believe I called the wrong number. I do hope you have a pleasant day, Mrs. Glump, and your employer as well. *Good-bye now!"*

The false sugar coating in my voice was all I could do to stop myself from continuing my threats, and when I slammed the receiver, I made myself jump. Pacing the length of my room, I let the steam out that had been boiling as soon as I'd realized that I was, in fact, not speaking to Sam. But that was it. That was the trick, an old one I should've expected: they always tap the phone lines and either listen in or play the other end. Dagnabit. Now she knows, and she's going to tell everyone. I always knew Shadela had despised my guts since we were in first grade, but I'd never thought she'd pull a stunt like this. How did she know when to tap in? I collapsed on my bed and stared at the grain of the ceiling.

➵➵➵➼ ⫷⫷⫷⫸

Sam slammed the receiver down with fury. *How could she say that to me! And what was with that accent? Mocking me, are you?* With a rush of adrenaline, Sam grabbed her bow and raced outside, her blood boiling. Raven called to her as she stormed by, but instead of looking at his sand castle, she kicked a hole clean through it, and the rest crumbled into the void as Raven protested. As she passed out of earshot, Sam swore every bad word she knew at Emmaline, both in anger and betrayal.

"You bull snot of a bat-foot, what the heck did I do to you? I've been your freaking best friend for your whole troll-faced life, and you call me an air-headed pixie and the daughter of a dung-beetle? I've never been so insulted in ALL MY LIFE!"

With these final words, she shot three arrows straight in the center of the target, with the final penetrating clear through the spongy material. A fierce, vengeful smile crawled its way across her reddened face, giving the pacifistic, compassionate girl a truly terrifying makeover. "I'll get you back, Emmaline. I'll get you. You just wait," she growled to herself and raised her bow again at a fresh target, visualizing Emma's gentle face in the center of it. She nocked an arrow and drew it back, her eyes glinting with a blue-gray fire that had never kindled until then.

Raven watched her make perfect shots over and over, fueled by a newfound power inside her that she'd never accessed before. Noticing this strange transformation, he considered going up and asking about it, but after a moment, he deemed it better not to. Raven didn't want to risk his neck for information he could find out later with sharp ears.

Tiny feet crept gently over the threshold of the door.

"Do you see, now, Emma? You can't call anyone."

I emerged from the semiconscious state that Ashlee had put me in just after she convinced me to hang up the phone before it connected to Sam's house. To prove she was right, Ashlee gave me a picture of what would've happened had I not done so. Boy, did she nail it.

"Ashlee, what am I supposed to do now? Make some kind of code for us or what?" I thought about what I said in the conversation that didn't happen. Geez, a special cell in Hell? Would I *really* say that, even to my enemy Shadela? Was I becoming that paranoid that I would lash out so fiercely? Was it even Shadela who tapped...who *would've* tapped the line? Who was behind all this?

The cascade of a small, metal chain being placed on my dresser jolted me back to Ashlee's presence. Something shiny was on the end, like a jewel of some sort. Ashlee turned to leave without a comment.

"What is it?"

She turned and stared at me with an expression I couldn't quite read. The way her eyes were shaped made me think of a teacher's expression right before a huge test that nobody studied for.

"It will answer your questions."

I rolled my eyes. Typical of her to answer a question I never asked.

"That doesn't tell me what it is, you know." I sighed when she didn't reply, apparently being preoccupied with staring out my window, the shadows dancing like ribbons across her face. "Fine. *Where* did you get it?"

"It fell out of the book I told you about—when we were at the library. It didn't fit either of us, but it might you," she replied dreamily without looking at me. She seemed to be studying something outside, or maybe something inside her mind, where truth is not obscured by distance or matter.

I stuck my elbows out and sat up on my bed. "What do you mean, it didn't fit? You can adjust them, you know."

Ashlee shook her head slowly. "Not *this* one."

She turned away and left me staring at the shiny thing on my dresser. I sat there a long time. I couldn't tell if it was supposed to be a prank or if she had really gotten it from the book. I wondered if she'd stolen it, but that wasn't her kind of character, besides taking books constantly from the Sunray Elementary school's library. I guess that's not really stealing, but all the same, she could take to hoarding certain things, like rocks, leaves, and sticks. Especially rocks and leaves. Ashlee had done a full-blown arrangement to decorate her room, and to be truthful, it was quite beautiful. Like the glinting piece on my dresser. The sunlight struck it just so, making it scatter light rays about the room. I felt like it was calling me, even though, of course, such an idea seemed unreasonable. But then, so did predicting the future and flying without wings.

Finally, I couldn't resist any longer. In a mesmerized sort of motion, I stepped forward a few feet, then back one, then forward again, and then back. Somehow this moment seemed unbelievably important, but I wouldn't be able to understand it until much later.

It was a necklace with a golden chain and a heptagon-shaped pendant at the end. The gemstone set in it was a marvelous ruby, sparkling like a tiny flame in my hands. My excitement was overflowing. Such a precious gift, a priceless treasure, had found its way to me. It was mine now.

Wasn't it?

Tearing my eyes away from the glistening red star, I turned it over to the metal setting piece on the back, looking for a name.

All I could see was a series of fancy spirals and squiggles along the edges, and lines directing me from each point to the fancy seven in the middle.

"Try it on," Ashlee thought from the doorway as she and Mom walked past to check on Umala.

Enthralled, I gazed down at the treasure in my hands. Fearful of breaking such a flawless thing, I carefully undid the clasp and slid my hands behind my neck. After a few shaky seconds, I'd gotten it on.

It fit perfectly. Actually, "fit" isn't the right word for it. It was more like...it matched not so much my neck as it did *me*—my personality, my soul. I believed that the notion was completely unreasonable at the time, but it felt as if some fragment of me had finally come home, like I was finally a whole being. The sensation was indescribable, but to get somewhere in the ballpark of it, I'll simply say that a piece of Heaven made me overflow with joy, like the Spirit inside of me reached every fiber of my being and made me fearless of everything evil. My soul laughed for the first time I could remember.

I stopped spinning and realized that I'd been Drifting. I dropped quickly, hoping nobody had noticed. As I peeked around the door,

I noticed Ashlee sitting on a chair down the hall with Umala in her lap. They both turned expectantly.

"It fits."

Ashlee whispered to Umala as I walked towards them. She frowned slightly as Umala replied softly in baby garble. "So, what does it mean?" I bounced up and down on my toes as I waited impatiently for an answer.

Ashlee looked up into my eyes.

"We can't tell you yet. It's too early."

"Whaddaya mean too early?!"

Ashlee rose to my height as she Drifted up and back to stand on the chair. "If we tell you now, the chances of you rejecting it are 98 percent, and that would have most devastating repercussions," she explained with scrutiny. Her face scrunched up in thought. It felt like I was being examined by some odd healer.

"Are you sure it's too early, Umala? I think she could handle it."

Umala screamed in protest. "Whoa, whoa, whoa, okay," Ashlee started, but then Mom came flying down the hall, shouting out "What-are-you-doing-to-her" and, "You're-going-to-scare-her-away-from-flying-if-you-keep-teasing-her-like-that" and the like, and stormed away several minutes later with a whimpering baby. We remained, quite stumped.

"So, sometimes even you two disagree?" I wondered aloud.

"Yes." It was unusually straightforward of Ashlee.

I scratched my head. Then I remembered what had caused the disturbance in the House.

"If I don't get to know now, then when will you tell me?" I looked to Ashlee.

She wasn't there. I didn't see where she'd gone, but I did hear her final thought on the matter.

"When you're ready."

CHAPTER SIX
RED ALERT

Nicholas Grantson lazily watched the monitor as he recorded the same dream he'd seen a thousand times. He couldn't fathom the extreme interest of Subject 518; her signatures where nearly identical to all the other 500s, give or take a few: abnormally high levels of creativity, an uncanny sense of intuition, and a concrete moral compass that reached her bones. Then again, he was only the Night Monitor. He had no idea what happened during the day. Maybe he should take a look into it—if they didn't kill him for it.

Nicholas stretched out in his chair yawning noisily and obnoxiously. He dropped his feet on the edge of his desk and considered taking a short nap, when the monitor caught his eye. "Holy!" he blurted, grabbing the phone and punching buttons furiously, glancing away from the screen only for a second. Nick tapped nervously on the desk as he listened to the dial tone. "C'mon, c'mon, pick *up*," he hissed through his teeth.

"What?" was all he got.

"Yes, yes, sir! We've got a, um, situation. You need to get down here. Like right now."

"Fine. Keep recording until I'm there."

The tone sounded in Nicholas's ear, but he didn't really notice as he dropped the phone. All he could do was stare at the rays of light shining out the window on the 17th level.

Dreamlog #: I forgot.

Date: whatever yesterday was

I had another dream. Well, same one, different chorus. This time, it started in a jail cell—who knows where. Everything was blurry, like I'd been hit in the head or something. Soldiers were pacing back and forth down the corridor outside, and nasty water dripped from the dirt ceiling.

In this cell, I was thinking back to a moment before, when I was talking to somebody. It was kind of freaky because I thought the person was Sam, but the voice sounded warped and more like a guy. Whoever it was told me to hide in some secret passage, but I said no, and then there was something random about chickens. Anyhoo, I snapped out of it when a Guard came and unlocked the cell and said we were going to go some-place. He called me "Traitor," and when I didn't move, he pulled me up by the hair and smacked my face so hard it bled.

I blacked out for a while, and when I woke up, I was in some sort of interrogation room, but they didn't ask any questions. On the other side of the glass, I could tell the Guards were showing video footage of "us" running around and rummaging through stuff and messing with some high-level security things. They left me there for a while and then dragged me up a flight of stairs onto a stage and chained me to something.

I remembered when they opened the red curtains, there were a bazillion people in the auditorium and lots of lights flashing. Something kept me from talking and asking what was going on. A metal blade was brought out in the arena, and I was getting really scared, and then there was this flash of fire around me, and something sharp stabbed my back and made me scream, and that's what woke me up.

I sighed as I shut my book and shoved it into a drawer. It was morning, obviously, but once again I felt like I hadn't slept a wink. But there wasn't time to think about it: I had my first apprenticeship walk-through today. I didn't have an interview for another week, but I was still excited. Finally, I could do what I loved and get paid for it!

None of my clothes seemed nice enough for such an occasion, but I improvised with what I could. Besides, it wasn't about the style; it was the substance that counted. I threw on some practical jeans and a simple but elegant quarter-sleeve that I could get dirty in. Combing and tying my thick strawberry-blond hair back, I wondered if I would ever get a nickname at work. Like "the Fox" or something.

Looking in the mirror one last time, I realized I'd accidentally left the ruby necklace on overnight. But, hey, I didn't care because it still matched my clothes. Checking my overall appearance, I stretched my wings out so I could see how they worked with my outfit.

Huh. That's odd, I thought.

"What's odd?" asked Ashlee from the doorway, pushing Umala in a stroller. *What a lazy slug-bug.*

She heard that, responded Ash.

Yeah, yeah.

"Well, I just thought it was weird that the necklace you found is the same scarlet color as on my wings. And my hair seems redder too. Like it's glowing."

"Hm."

I fingered the necklace as I stared at her. "What's this all about?"

"We can't tell you. You have to find out yourself. Otherwise everything will fall apart, and the—uh, *it* won't happen."

Exasperated, I demanded, "*What* won't happen? Tell me!"

"No sprecken-zay Emma." With that, she grabbed Umala's stroller and went racing down the hall. A few baby fun-screams later, I heard Mom chasing after them and telling them to-hush-up-be-cause-Dad's-sleeping-remember?

Shocked at seeing what time it was, I grabbed my bag and headed out the door.

The more experienced man's face was distorted with frustration at being awakened again in the early hours of the morning. His hands were pressed against his face as he stared at the screen at the far end, waiting for the other members to arrive. This moment was urgent and critical in their next move, and they needed to see it unfold.

"Grantson! Where are the others?" he bellowed grumpily.

"Late, sir."

"Thanks, genius, why don't you tell me something I don't already know?" Chief Locknut sank deeper into his chair, growling about "kids these days." Shortly, seven people in sharp, clean suits entered, followed by several more. They sat down at the table and opened their notebooks and recorders as Locknut signaled for Grantson to get on with the video feed. Locknut rose stiffly from his seat.

"Ladies and gentlemen," he grumbled roughly, "you are here to-day to observe the first stage of the Launch of Subject 518. The Launch was initiated yesterday at 1300 hours, in the form of a phone tap on the copilot's side. The pilot, Subject 518, was informed by air-traffic control to not engage the copilot, exposing a classified leak beforehand via a program hack. Also," he paused emphatically, drawing eyes, "we found evidence that air-traffic control has given 518 the clearance code to go nova."

Somebody's pencil hit the floor.

"As time passes, it becomes increasingly clear that Subject 518, along with subsystems 438 and 925, are resistant, even immune, to our defenses. This, if you can recall, is why we planned the Launch. Subject 518 cannot be controlled, and therefore must be neutralized."

Locknut sat back with a huff and nodded for Grantson to bring the video feed on. The members of the High Order leaned forward and fixed their eyes on the screen in front of them.

From a corner of the apprenticeship office, a nearly invisible camera tracked and zoomed in on a figure with a reddish-blond ponytail, straight blue jeans, and a bag over her shoulder as she joined the line for a cue card.

Man, this line is long! How much time will this take?

I shifted my weight from one foot to the other as I waited for the string of people to move up. Pretty much all of my grades' ex-students were here, applying for walkabouts to find the right apprenticeship. I stood up on my toes, searching for familiar faces. Especially ones I knew from the "lunch bunch" the last couple of school years.

The line shuffled forward, and I finally got my ticket. *Joy. Another place to wait and stand.* Bored, I looked this way and that down the lines by me, waiting to get into the engineering and manufacturing department. Out of the six or seven other people stuck with me. Only one was a girl, and I didn't recognize her.

Finally the instructor came and unlocked the door and showed us inside. He said excitedly, "Hi, my name is Mr. Ishfa D'Uno, and I'm very glad to see you all here. We're just going to start with some basics of what's required to have this job."

For the next ten minutes I slouched in my chair, doodling stick figures in my notebook. The guy used huge computer programming words we'd never heard before, and he kept repeating the same stuff like we were two years old and learning to say "da-da." *Mr. D'Uno? More like Mr. I. Dunno.* I drew a corresponding picture for my joke, hiding it with my hand when Dunno passed by.

Half the other kids were almost asleep by the time he let us tour the workshop. He led us through a pair of massive metal doors and down into a huge room where tons of people were grinding, sawing, and melting things into usable items. To minimize danger and hearing loss, each machine was encased in a special glass that stopped noise and couldn't be broken unless a troll sat on it. Or a dragon. But those weren't real.

We paused by one in particular when a tall boy with long black hair asked what the worker was doing. Mr. I. Dunno started elaborately explaining what type of metal the worker was using and that it was a tube for a sink drain, but I soon lost track of the conversation. Something in the back of my mind was pulsing.

I couldn't stop staring at the sparks flying where the man was cutting it. They rose up like a shower, just inches from the man's face. He took the piece of metal and thrust it into an oven, blinding white, where it turned to liquid and oozed. The light radiated to a foreign beat, like the one in my head. The worker contorted the piping hot sheet into half of a pipe, then a whole pipe. Again he cut it, sparks and heat and melting and more sparks.

I searched the wall nearby for a shut-off valve, or an extinguisher, or some kind of protection for this guy. The pulse continued as I watched the sparks and the glowing metal and the oven bathing in heat and everything is hot, hot, hot and imagined how awful it would be if something went nuts.

Suddenly there was an enormous flare, and the guy was on fire, writhing on the floor. D'Uno tried to push us along saying, "there was nothing here to see," but everyone stared at the man burning on the floor, screaming. *Dear God, the sound barrier is way too good! Nobody else can hear him!* I turned to Mr. D'Uno, yelling, "We have to help this guy!" I ran for the control panel to the burning man's workstation. Mr. D'uno caught my elbow.

"No can do," he said calmly, forcing me past me at the torched victim. "That's not our job. The Guards will take care of it."

"*What* Guards?" I demanded, wrenching my arm from his grip. "There aren't any in here! How will anyone know to help him?"

D'Uno reached behind me and grabbed my neck. "*That,*" he hissed in my ear, "is none of *your God-forsaken business!*" He pushed me forward and followed behind the rest of the group, but he couldn't have stopped me with a legion of faeries.

I casually dropped my notebook and turned around like I was going to get it. Instead I sprinted back down the passage to the man's station. I reactivated the control panel and cut the power to his machine as D'Uno walked towards me, yelling for me to immediately halt what I was doing. The walls of the protective case slid upward as I took off my jacket and soaked it in a nearby bucket. I threw it over the burning man, and a plume of smoke erupted from him. I yelled over the noise, "Stay here! I'll get help!" just as Dunno-a-Dang-Thing reached me. He blurted something like "ho-wah," and slumped against the wall, mouth open but nothing coming out. He glared at me as he slid down the wall. I turned to find the other wannabes gaping at me.

"What?" I asked as I ran up the stairs. "He got in the way of my fist."

Assuming the tour was over, everyone else trooped after me up the stairs and out into the intro room, and then out into the chaos. Thinking it was over, I ran to the not-so-helpful Help desk. I was just finished telling them that Mr. D'Uno had allowed a man to be severely burned, when over by the Guard assessment desk, somebody screeched my name.

"Emmaline O'Meern! You pellet-head!"

Marching towards me on the wings of fury was Sameela O'Klurn.

Ashleeka sat in the kitchen, coloring a picture. Umala sat in a high chair beside her, watching the masterpiece emerge. It was simple enough: a picture of their tree, with open windows and oversized birds and bees flying around the flowers in the planters here and there. But the important part was what nobody else could hear their conversation.

So has she figured it out yet? Ashleeka asked.

Nope. But the clues are coming in.

Can you see who it is behind this?

No. Not yet. I'll let you know when I do.

Will you let her *know?*

Umala didn't answer. She scrunched her face up in concentration.

Ashlee?

Yeah?

Put some more red flowers in there.

Ashleeka shook her head in frustrated amusement and grabbed a red crayon.

For the first time in her life, Sam was ready to explode. She'd always been tenderhearted, even when there were jerks at school, but nothing compared to this day. Her eyes kindled with blue-gray fire, and her hands became vice grips, commanded by a force deeper than anger or revenge.

It was betrayal.

Sam rushed Emmaline-the-Enemy, pinning her to the wall. She screamed hateful things into the face of the one she had trusted with her life. Sam dug her nails into Emma's skin, watching her perfectly innocent face be contorted by pain.

"—and now you act so perfect and sweet when you're really a *monster!*"

She stepped back to see Emmaline's reaction. The massive hall was silent, but Sam didn't give a darn. In fact, that's exactly what she wanted: a mass audience of their peers to see the defamation of the Perfect Student. "Try getting some new friends now," she sneered.

Emmaline hugged her arms where Sam had pierced her and moved her wings up and down from being crunched against the wall. She looked at Sam incomprehensibly and asked simply, "What are you *talking* about?"

Seething, Sam screamed, "You, ya slime-bag! You pretend you don't remember, but I do! You called me yesterday and said I was the worst and dumbest person you know and that you hated my guts and you never wanted to see me as long as you lived! Well, too bad! You're lookin' at me *now*, aren't you?"

Emmaline shook her head in dismay, protesting, "I never said that! I didn't even call you yesterday!"

Sam jumped in Emmaline's face again, shouting, "Liar! You liar! You troll snot of a one-armed mosquito! Yes, you did! I don't care what you say—you lie! I hate you! Half-wit of a frog-head!"

She backed away from Emmaline, beginning to hear herself. Milking every last drop of attention, she ordered in a low and ominous tone, "Go die alone in a deep, dark hole."

Sam paced out of the room, hiding hot tears as she weaved between the other empty-headed kids in her way. *Curse you, Emmaline. Curse everyone.*

I stared at Sam's rigid turquoise, gold, and black-striped wings as she stormed out. *What just happened to me? To her? To us? What did I do to her? Or not do?*

My backbone smarted where it had hit the column. Trying to stay cool, I grabbed my bag from off the floor and speed-walked towards the doors. *Jeez, people, why do you keep staring at me? I didn't do anything! I know as much as you do!* But they kept staring as they shuffled forward in line.

I hit the door swiftly, but it was still hard to open. There were a bunch of kids walking around, staring like zombies at their phones. They kept bumping me, glaring like it was my fault they weren't watching where they were walking. I realized quickly that I was breathing in gasps, so I slowed and walked to the railing on the edge of the walkway. Crossing my arms on top of the rail, I stared tearfully out into the forest and at the adults flying by, at one with the world. *Yeah, right. They have problems too. I bet their best friend didn't just dump them for no reason, though. Dear God, what just happened?*

My hair kept flailing in my face—you know—those little wispy ones that you can never get to stay anywhere. I dumped my bag on the walkway and stood there for a while, not sure what to do about anything. I remembered the look on her face, a relentless anger I never thought would come from so sweet a person. *And she was coming from the Guard signup! Why would she be* there? *Sam has never liked conflict, or fighting, or anything. She wants to be an oceanographer, not a mercenary.*

I didn't think I'd ever felt so low. My wings felt like bricks, and they drooped lifelessly down my back. What could I have done to her to make her do that? And in front of God and everybody! *Geez, like I need attention,* I lamented, running my fingers through my thick hair. I stared down at the forest bed, not even trying to spot the deer and the rabbits and whatever else was down there. They let us see videos and pictures of what was there and let us go on a field trip if we were lucky, but otherwise you needed a special pass to go down there, let alone hunt. A few years before, I'd asked Dad why it was that way, but he just shrugged and said, "It's the law, Honey. That's all I know."

Maybe they're hiding something down there.

As if on cue, I heard a familiar voice call out to me from the stream of traffic flowing behind me.

"Myrrh!"

Despite what had happened in the past ten minutes, I couldn't help but grin as he walked up to me.

"Troll face," I replied, turning to see him.

Tracer Mink was one of my buddies from school. His real name was Tryoncore, but we always called him Tracer because he was always drawing stuff, like robots and aliens. We sat at lunch together with some others: Wayk "Earthquake" Liten, Kael "Chain Mail" Farlic, Aiter "The Alligator" Braik, and Falans "Falcon" Cript. Tracer always showed me the new games he'd gotten on his phone. Phone was short for phoney book, made by a company called Sparkpage, because you could go to different places on the screen, but there were no pages. It was used for communication, games, and almost anything you could think of. Tracer and I always debated over who was a better superhero: Batfae or Iron Fae. Think what you may, but I say it's Iron Fae. I like them both, but Batfae doesn't have robots making his coffee and flying suits and saving the world from monsters and stuff.

"Haven't seen you for a while," I said, leaning sideways against the rail. Funny thing about Tracer: he got nervous around me. Now was no exception. He raised one of his thick, post-like arms to scratch the back of his short-haired head, muttering what sounded like, "Yeah, been doin' some stuff. You been doin' anything cool?" I exhaled a sharp laugh, saying, "No, not really. Today's been a complete waste."

Tracer stared at me incredulously and, waving his arms in the air, asked, "Well, isn't that what summer's *for?*" His expression normally would've made me laugh, but it didn't work that day. All I could manage was a small smile and sighed. "I guess. I just don't like wasting time. Even when it's summer." I peered across the vast space of breezy summer air between the tree I was standing on and the next one.

He gently reached his hand out and touched my shoulder, like he always had at school when he wanted to tell me something without interrupting me. I glanced back up at his face to see concern written all over it. "Hey, Emmaline...are you okay?"

I rubbed the back of my neck and gave a wry smile. "No, I'm not," I said, avoiding eye contact with him. He leaned forward on the rail with his hands clasped in front of him to match my posture. I blanked for a moment, trying to put words together in my head, but mostly, I was just trying to accept that what Sam did had actually happened.

"I don't even know what I did," I started, brushing back some squiggly, more blond-colored, flyaway hairs. "One minute I'm talking to the lady at the front desk, and the next thing I know, my best friend is calling me an egg-headed snot-rag." Tracer grinned for a second then realized it wasn't that funny. I stared at my hands. "What am I supposed to say to that? I mean...I didn't even talk to her yesterday! And she says I did, and now everyone on the face of the earth thinks that I'm a total dirt bag. Man, how does stuff like this happen? It's just...ugh. I dunno what to think anymore." I put both my hands on my head and inspected the space between me and the ground, some hundred feet below.

Out of my peripheral vision, I saw Tracer nod his head in understanding.

"I'm sorry," he said, before following my gaze down. A moment later, he added, "I don't think you're a dirt bag. I think...you're nice. Really nice."

"Thanks." I smiled briefly. He fidgeted again.

"Hey, do you...uh...are you gonna go to the big dance next week?"

"You mean the Harvest Festival?"

"Um, yeah," he replied, rubbing his hand on the railing.

"Well, I was planning on it. You know, since it's a tradition. It sounds fun to me," I answered carefully, staying casual as I leaned back against the rail. "I figured I'd just hang out with you guys." I glanced at him. "What about you? Are you going?"

Tracer thought a second and shook his head. "Nah...I don't think so. There's some other stuff I hafta do," he said evasively.

"Aw, c'mon! It'll be no fun if *you're* not there! You *always* make stuff better," I protested and knuckled his shoulder lightly. I wanted him to come. He always made me laugh, and a dance party is no fun if you can't laugh.

He tipped his head down again, nervously tapping the rail with his palm. "I dunno...I don't really like big parties..."

"Will you think about it?"

Tracer shrugged. "I guess so."

What I wanted to do was shout, *Awesome!* What I said instead was, "Cool."

There was a sudden cracking sound by my feet. Before I could blink, I was falling backwards off the edge, flailing my arms. I gave an enormous yelp and found myself staring at a very long drop into thornbushes below. I suddenly realized I wasn't falling anymore. My feet hurt where they had slipped off the edge of the walkway, and there was a huge pressure on my left wrist. Then I saw it was Tracer's hand. He'd halfway followed me over the edge, knowing very well that you couldn't fly without clearance in restricted airspace. I stared at him, calculating that if he let go, I was done for. He stared back at me, strain in his face but strength in his eyes.

I grabbed his wrist in return, and Tracer beat his wings as he pulled me back up. He groaned right before I reached the top, and I pulled myself up with the remaining rail. We stood together and panted, watching the railing splinter on the way down before clunking its end on the forest floor. We stared at each other, astounded, but it got awkward really quick being so close. I cleared my throat and said,

"Thanks," dropping to get my bag and moving away. "I owe you one."

"Um, sure. Okay," he said. I think he was still in shock. The people who had frozen to watch him save me slowly started to move again. I really wanted to bug out of there, but I held back for a minute.

"So, you'll think about it?" I checked. "Yeah...yeah, I'll think about it," he answered, spacey. Tracer focused on my face again. "Wait, you mean the dance, right?"

I nodded, trying not to smile.

"Okay, sure. So, I'll see you later?" he asked.

"Yeah. We're all having lunch tomorrow, remember?"

"Oh, yeah, alright. See ya," he said, waving his hand before he walked, then jogged away. After that incident, I was sure he needed a break from me as much as I did from him.

At least until tomorrow.

Locknut's claps echoed loudly off the solid wood walls of the inner office. The coverage of the first stage of the Launch had been more than successful: it topped everything he'd hoped from it.

"What do you think of *that*, Miss Fritely? What do you think of *that?*"

Miss Fritely nodded respectfully and replied solemnly, "It was well played, sir." She rose and followed the rest out the door, grabbing a copy of the tape as she went. The door creaked closed, releasing an eerie and lonely wail that filled the room.

Yes, the Chief thought to himself, *that's* exactly *the way it starts.*

He replayed the tape, pausing and focusing on cameras 9 and 11, where the copilot's face was contorted with menace. Where the pilot, Subject 518, was defenseless, backed up against the pillar with wide eyes.

Yes. Exactly how it starts. Phase One completed.

Raven picked up his wrench off the floor and wound it back and forth as he tightened a final bolt on his slingshot. The first one could only throw pebbles, and the second couldn't throw much farther, and so this was Mark 3. He was trying more than one sling, too.

He jumped at the sound of the door slamming. Sam's footsteps pounded their way up the stairs, past his room and into her own. Raven crawled to the door and peeked down the hallway.

He couldn't see much, but he saw a shadow of Sam dragging a chair across the floor and standing on it. The fiddling of a leather sheath and something wooden clanked its way against the walls and into Raven's ears. He rolled away from the crack and hid behind the door as Sam's footsteps thundered back down the hall and faded down the stairs.

Raven breathed a sigh of relief. Sam was getting angrier all the time, it seemed, and even though it had only started yesterday, it felt like months. He picked up his slingshot and sat at his desk, watching out the window as Sam attacked her nearly destroyed target. The sound of arrows striking it became a beat, a beat to a tune that only she could hear. *It probably was,* he thought. She'd started taking her phone with her everywhere, like a pet, and jamming the sound buds in her ears every chance she got. The look that would glaze over her eyes when she did was ominous, and he could hear the rock-and-roll music blaring from across the room. He knew well to avoid her when she listened to those songs.

Raven's frustration pulsed harder in his veins, mirrored by the heartache in his bones. What was happening to Sam? Holding back tears, he grabbed some rocks off the window sill and loaded them in the slings. He swiveled quickly in his chair and fired at the target on the other side of the room.

A pair of deep marks appeared side by side in the bull's eye.

The beat from outside changed to double-time as Sam exchanged bow for sword. Without fully understanding why, Raven threw his slingshot on the floor and pulled his knees to his chest, sobbing and rocking back and forth in his seat. His parents wouldn't notice. Dad was away, fixing a light transmitter, and Mom wouldn't be back from the assembly until eight.

He'd have to survive Sam until then.

Only nine hours to go.

My stomach growled as I flew home. It was lunchtime already, but it felt like I'd just had breakfast. Sort of. The morning's multiple incidents had shaken my brains into chaos, so I guess that's why.

Not that I felt like eating. I just felt like now would be a good time to disappear off the face of the earth. My wings flapped idly, struggling to get me home, the home I didn't really want to go back to. *Maybe I'll just grab a biscuit and some fruit and go hunting.*

Somebody had a different idea.

"Dang it, Shades, you goop-headed snail! What do you want *now?*"

Shadela was riding right on my tail, trying to throw me off.

"Finely got yer wings, baby girl? You a big girl now, Emmy? *You a big girl who don't need no stinkin' diapers no more?*"

"Are *you?*" I shouted, banking sharp to the left. She followed swiftly behind.

"You think you so smart, Emmaline! You don't know *nuthin'!* You hear me? Nuthin'! You still a baby who ain't growed up yet! You still makin' boom-booms in yo pants!"

My blood burned like a furnace. I dove toward the ground, with my tail still coming in hot. If she didn't face-plant into the dirt, I'd lose her in the forest. Her brain was nothing but a black hole.

"Eat worms, mole-face!" I yelled, arcing up just before impact. No icky crunching sound followed me. I hadn't expected one. We hurtled as a pair toward the forest's edge.

"Stop, Emmaline! You-sa coward! Run 'way from a fight, you-sa baby, ain't you! Got no guts to face me! You went and got yerself raised by pig slop! Gonna get butchered, Emma-*swine!*"

I oriented myself towards the trunk of a broad tree seated on the forest border.

"Guess what, Emma!"

I didn't wait.

"Your face, prune-head!" I shouted.

I could hear Shadela pause as she realized I wasn't changing my direction.

"Go 'head, Emma! Get yo face ate! It'll help your complexion!"

She was panicking. Sweet.

"Same to you, booger-bug!"

I caught a glimpse of her swerving to the side a nanosecond before I "Shifted" myself through the tree, willing myself to pass through it. The darkness encasing my white star and Shadela's red was not so slow to jump this time: I'd taken to practicing in the target room in the late hours when nobody else was there and in the wide fields and dense forest by Sam's house. Sam. *Oh, Sam. How did I get into this mess?*

I emerged from the other side of the tree unscathed, but I had a weird banana taste in my mouth. Shadela continued to trail my every move but staying a few feet back. I ignored her calls for me. "Emma-line! Stop!" she cried, whacks of branches following her words.

"Go myrrh yourself!"

I ducked as a branch nearly took my head off and zipped across a shaded clearing. A nasty crack sounded behind me, and the tumbling of a body in agony followed. Her groans came in deep gasps, and I thought I'd feel good to have exacted revenge.

But I didn't.

In fact, it felt like landing head-first in a cow pie.

Even to this day, I'm astounded (and thankful) that I had the courage to go back.

Shadela was sprawled out in the dirty leaves and grass, curled up in a ball, face-down, coughing. I hid in the undergrowth, watching as she wormed across the clearing on her arms and knees. Finally, she collapsed with her back toward me, moaning.

I stepped out of the darkness, rustling the leaves of the bushes and quietly made my way towards my enemy.

"Well where'd she go?" Locknut bellowed over the phone.

"Into the forest, sir. She was being threatened by a passenger."

"Well, Carnigan, get eyes in there! Or you won't be a Watcher for another day!"

Locknut slammed the phone down, cursing. *What was their motto? "Wherever they are, we are always Watching."* And that was exactly what they weren't doing. Watching. Trying to distract himself, he pulled out the files on Subject 518 and paged through the dozens of records and notes on her progression. Phase One: completed. Phase Two. What about Phase Two?

Locknut snapped the binder shut and picked up the phone. He needed a projection for Phase Two, and he knew the man for the job.

"Fritely? Get me the Senator."

"Right away, sir."

"Shadela? Are...are you okay?"

I cautiously walked around to face her and was astonished to find her face contorted, not with rage, but with misery. Tears had just started streaming down her face when she looked up and saw that I was there. She sniffed back hard and started wriggling away and against a tree, but she gasped with each movement. Her dark eyes avoided my gaze, wishing to endure alone.

A sudden wave of understanding bowled me over, and I collapsed to the ground. Suddenly I knew why we had hated each other for so long: we were so much alike. In pain, we wanted to hide in darkness, away from others. In anger, we hurt others with words and wished harm on others without doing it ourselves. In joy—*what joy do either of us have?*

My chest hurt all over, like I was being strangled by a boa constrictor, if those still existed. I realized I was crying, crying for somebody I'd always strived to avoid, to not cross paths with as best as I could. I rocked back and forth, my eyes peering mistily over my crossed arms as it hit me: my whole world was falling apart—not just at the seams, but all over. And there was nothing I could do about it.

Then Shadela raised her head.

"I'm sorry, Emma."

"Wuhfor?" I blurted, muffled by my "arms" of defense.

"Making everything you know fall apart."

Behind my tears and wracking sobs, I mumbled, "Whatcha talkin' about?"

Shadela wiped her nose on the back of her grimy hand, pulling her legs closer in. She leaned against the trunk of the tree behind her, sideways enough that we could see each other. She pushed her black, tangled hair back against her head and told me.

"I never shoulda been so hard on you. But I had to. You're too nice."

I stared blearily at her, waiting for more.

"If you're ever gonna make it, you hafta be tough. An' you're not tough enough. Not even close. Not against them." She shook her head, and her dark wings flickered to match. We sniffed at the same time, but only Shadela gave a small smile.

"Who's "them"?" I asked through my stuffed-up nose.

"The gov'ment. You know about the High Order? How they're s'posed to protect the city with the Watchers an' stuff?"

I nodded. "Yeah, my dad's one."

"Mine, too. But anyway, all that's...well, it's a load of turds in a punch bowl."

I couldn't help but bust up laughing at the image. This time it was only me. Shadela's eyes glinted with a relentless fire, reminding me of the fragment in my heart that still told every bone in my body not to trust her. But I still asked her.

"How?"

"They're liars. They don't protect the city from *anyone*. It's all bogus. It's just a cover for their secret programs. An' don't think I read too many conspiracy stuff, 'cause I don't."

I, in fact, did *not* think that she read too much. In fact, until that moment, I'd convinced myself she couldn't read at all. Something clicked and I started spilling the beans.

"No, I believe you. I've always had this feeling of being, I dunno, spied on. The past couple weeks, especially, I've felt like everything has exploded around me. I mean, not more than half an hour ago, there was a railing that broke behind me, and I almost tumbled down into oblivion. And I would've, if, um, a friend hadn't caught my arm."

Shadela smiled deviously.

"Was it Tryoncore Mink?"

"Uh...yeah. And he goes by Tracer. Why?"

"Oh, I was just wondering," she replied.

Sure, you were just wondering.

"Well, *I* was just wondering...why the moose are we even talking to each other?" I asked.

Shadela shrugged. "Dunno. We're meant to, I guess. Personally, I don't believe in God, but...I dunno. Weird stuff makes you wanna talk to anybody you can, I s'pose."

"Yeah...I guess so."

We sat for a while in the shade, smothering ourselves in the cool leaves and dirt. My stomach growled and Shadela's followed. We laughed and fell quiet again.

"So, are you okay?" I asked. "I didn't mean for you to hit that branch. Not on purpose, anyway. You know—"

"What? That we still hate each other? Yeah, I get it. And I'm okay. I just busted my gut in half, but it'll grow back."

"You sound like my dad," I grinned.

"Yeah. I think my dad and yours work together sometimes. Mine's super funny, too. In a weird sort of way."

I remembered my dad talking about a guy at work. Dad said that he was a great guy, and we should meet up with our families, if the Guards weren't restricted from doing so unless they were at a formal procession.

"Hey, by the way," she added, "what's it mean to 'go myrrh yourself'?"

I snickered. "Oh, it's just something dumb I made up. It's the first half of 'maid.'"

She blinked for a second and cracked up.

"I mean—well...bother. At least you get it."

"What, go 'myrrh-maid' yourself? Yeah, I get it!...That'd take some skill to do, since it's impossible to turn into one."

"Or reach the ocean when there's nothing but toxic wasteland beyond the Wall." I laughed.

So did she.

CHAPTER SEVEN
CROSSFIRE

Another day checked off on the calendar. Four days to the festival. Locknut scowled at the days until then, reviewing the consequences if they initiated Phase Two before then. He rubbed his chin and turned back to his desk, checking and double-checking the statistics.

No. It has to be that night.

Chief Locknut sat back in his chair, twiddling his thumbs. The Senator ordered him to wait on Phase Two. If he tried anything, anything at all, the Senator would have him quashed like a mosquito. He had eyes and ears everywhere. Not even his coworkers could escape his gaze. If the Senator said wait, you waited.

And so he would wait.

"Raven! Where do you think *you're* going?"

Raven halted in the middle of the hall, grimacing. He'd tried to sneak past Sam, who was scouring her training book for specialized tactics, but she was far too keen-eyed now to not notice him. Besides, the Harvest Festival was in a couple days, and there were always party crashers looking to smash the giant pumpkins and eggplant.

"Well? *Where?* Use your 'big boy' voice, beetle-juice."

He slowly pivoted around on the balls of his feet, staring at the red-and-blue, plaid-socked feet tucked up on the edge of the seat.

"I...I just wanted to...to test the...the distance on my, um, sling-shot."

Sam waved her hand impatiently. "Fine, fine. Go knock yourself out. But if you really do, don't come cryin' to me. I'm busy."

Raven shuffled obediently down the hall, jammed his feet in his boots, and grabbed his sweater before slamming out the screen door.

"Get back here for lunch! Or you don't get any!" Sam hollered after him, before jamming her ears with head-banging music. "An' don't track mud back in here!"

Raven clambered down the stairs and ran through the misty morning, which was overcast and shadowless. He panted only a little as he ran. He'd been running more this past week—more so than he thought he could have possibly done in his whole life. Dad was still gone working and wouldn't be back until the Festival, and Mom, too, was working late with her apprentices almost every night, so he ran nearly everywhere.

To get away from his own sister.

He reached the target area, greatly expanded and developed in recent days under Sam's control. She'd said she would give him ice cream and stuff he liked to get him to help her, but mostly he just did it to keep Sam from using him as a running target. Even those rubber-headed arrows hurt through the gear.

Raven reached his new campout under the cover of forest and bushes. It was little more than a ready-to-fall-apart pile of branches and leaves, but it was all he had to himself. He slid inside and sat on his heels, weeping quietly. He didn't know exactly *why* it had happened, but he knew that after that last call with Emmaline, something had snapped in his sister. But why? Emma was the nicest person he knew.

I gotta find her and ask what's going on.

The snap of a twig alerted him. He hushed his breath and was still. Raven peeked through a spy hole in his stick house.

A pair of soldiers in camouflage uniforms materialized into view, scanning the forest for movement. They began making their way down the hill, bows half drawn. He heard a hoarse whisper.

"Where's the kid s'posed to be?"

"Some fort he made out here."

Raven snapped his head back in as they scanned his way. They were looking for him. He had a terrible urge to run away as fast as he could, but something held him in place. He was paralyzed and couldn't breathe.

Then he got an idea. A stupid, terrible, awesome idea.

Seeing that they were heading slowly away from him, Raven tied his stealth gear to his shoes: a mere ragged dishcloth to muffle the sound of his feet. He grabbed his pouch of rocks and laced it to his belt. Then he carefully stepped out of his fort, feet sideways to avoid crunching noises, and made his way down the slope. Raven's heart bounced up and down in his chest like it was riding in a bumpy carriage, excited and curious for his experiment.

After all, what better target was there than a few live soldiers?

Sam checked the clock again. It was half-past two, but Raven hadn't come home for lunch. He should be hungry by now, but Sam didn't really care. She just wanted to know if she'd actually have to get up and make a sandwich. She wasn't hungry: she'd just finished off a pack of "magically delicious" soldier gum, enough to keep you going for hours without real food.

Rain started pattering again outside. Typical of Raven to go out and try to do a survival thing out in the wild of the forest, get hopelessly lost and filthy, then come plodding home soaked, hungry, and exhausted in the wee hours of the night. *Fine,* she thought. *I don't care if you're half dead or get lost for a week. You're not waking* me *up in the middle of the night for a warm bath, a glass of milk, and sympathy.*

Sam picked up her practice sword and started to mimic the book's illustrations.

"...and then a robot comes down and goes, '*Wazaap!*'"

"*Pbbwwfff!*"

I sprayed water all across the lunch table when I heard Tracer's imitation of the famed escalator scene. He'd timed it perfectly: I was just taking a huge swig. The rest of the guys "whoa"ed and cheered at the sight, even mouse-like Wayk, and I laughed until my sides hurt.

"That was the best spit-take I've *ever* seen!" exclaimed Kael, slapping the table. Gator pointed his finger interrogatively at Kael, asking, "Or *is* it?" His serious expression quickly melted into peals of laughter as Kael replied, "Well, I should think so! It's definitely better than when Gold Servant freaks out from the giant bat in the gut of the giant earthworm!"

"Dude, seriously?" Falcon peered over the top of his glasses at Kael. "That is *so* not a spit-take! That's just a freak-out-because-there's-a-mega-huge-bat-on-the-other-side-of-the-window thing! Seriously, get your facts straight!" He set back to his drink but grinned in spite of himself.

Gator ordered, "Leave! Just leave!"

"Yeah!" Tracer bellowed, pointing his finger in Kael's face. "*You're not worthy!*"

I bobbed back and forth, barely able to breathe. It was way too good to stop. And no one was about to.

"Hey, man, don't even get me *started* on the *Faetrix*! Think how bad it would be *there!*" retorted Kael, the joy of nerdy competition gleaming in his eyes as his eyebrows jumped up and down.

A chorus of "ohhhs" erupted, and everyone babbled at once, but this is what I caught:

"Think how far the water would go in slow-mo—"

"It'd be like when the rain breaks on Theo's fist as he punches Myth—"

"It would explode in every direction *forever*—"

"No, it'd make a giant water ball, like when Humblebee fights Deathflight in *Faery Potter*—"

"That would take, like, *seven hours* to clean up after it crashed on the floor—"

"Dude, you don't use a *mop* if you have spells or *Faetrix* powers—"

"Even then—and how would *you* know that? Are you really a *cyborg* meant to distract us from an *alien invasion*?"

"Well, I *could* be...but you'd never live to tell about it because *I'd kill you first!*"

"*I* don't even know what we're *talking about* anymore!" Gator waved his hands waved in front of him, empty, like his train of thought.

We all laughed, both with and at Gator. Grinning, Falcon growled, "Shame on you!" Gator's head dropped in mock embarrassment.

"Aww..."

Peals of laughter erupted from all parties.

"Hey!" I objected. "It's not his fault!"

"No, it's *yours!*" Kael retorted.

"Is not! *You're* the one who failed in the *Sky Wars* department!"

"What? Compared to *him*? I'm in the High Order!"

"Aw," said Gator.

Tracer jumped for it. "Actually, you're more like Chewbarka: you only help somebody if they're two seconds from death."

"Uh, Tracer, Chewbarka never saves *anybody*," Wayk pointed out.

Tracer waved his hands in front of him, grinning. "That's exactly my *point!*"

Kael's eyebrows danced up his forehead. "Well, if it were between you and him, I'd leave you both, 'cause you're just too dang ugly!"

I was laughing so hard I couldn't breathe. My muscles ached and right as I started to catch my breath, Tracer slapped the table and shouted something else to Kael. That made everyone go off again just from the way he said it. "Man, you can do really weird things with your voice!" I choked out.

He turned to me and said, "Nuh!" His smile beamed across his whole face. I watched the other guys as they started in on their own mini-fights, and pretty soon I lost track of everything anyone was saying. But that happened almost every time, so nobody minded; in fact, it was almost more fun that way, with everyone laughing at different things. Kael and Falcon started another argument, something random about which game was better, Zeldafae: Guardian of Justice or Dario: Troll Slayer, when everything started to blend together.

Aw, crud.

Of course, *I'm going to phase out right in the middle of a great time.*

It wasn't much, not more than ten seconds, in a blurry grayness of some forest area. I saw a little boy running with a U-shaped, wooden contraption in his hand, looking back at something behind him. His blue eyes were wide open in fear. A second before he was covered by a dark green thing with a shiny inside, the little boy shrieked.

I knew that shriek.

"Huh? What?"

Tracer had touched my shoulder. "You okay?" he repeated. "You kinda blanked for a minute."

"Huh? Oh. Um, yeah, I'm okay. I just, um, I'll be back in a sec."

I felt their vague confusion aimed at my back as I left the table and walked down the path to the nearest phone. Mom and Dad didn't want me to have my own phone for a while. That was fine with me.

Wishing yesterday's afternoon shower would repeat itself, I wiped sweat off my forehead as I dropped some coins in the slot and, against my better thinking, dialed Sam's number. In late summer–early fall, even the shade was just tolerable.

The tone sounded for a while. I figured maybe she was having lunch, but then again, I had no clue what she was doing lately. The last time anyone in my family had seen her out was a few days ago, getting gear for her apprenticeship with the soldiers. Despite everything, I'd hoped that maybe Sam would realize it was all a big misunderstanding, and she'd let it go and invite me over to go swim in the waterhole again.

But I sure as heck wasn't going to ask her right then.

"Whoizziss?"

"Hi, Sam," I replied bluntly.

Her voice shifted to a new gear. "You got fifteen seconds before I hang up, Meerkat."

"I want to talk to Raven."

"He's out."

"Where?"

"You s'pect me to know? He's doing a survival thing, s'far as I care to tell. Yesterday, too. Made up a load of snot about some guys out there. Ten."

"Like what?"

"Pair of soldiers looking for him. Said he whacked 'em with his slingshot and ran back, but, a-course, no one showed up. Five."

"Will you have him call me back when he's home?"

"Maybe, maybe not. S'none of your business what we do in the boonies, towngirl. Call again and I'll set my goon squad on ya."

She slammed the phone on purpose, I could tell. I pressed the inside of my ear over and over to make it stop ringing as I walked back to the table. Tracer watched my face as I sat down.

"Hey."

"Huh? Oh, hey."

He seemed to contemplate asking about it, but he didn't. Instead he asked, "Hey, Emmaline, guess what?"

I faked a grin. "Your face."

"Aww…"

We all laughed again.

Only mine wasn't real.

"Come *on*, dummy! It shouldn't take this insanely long to load!"

I scowled at the library computers, the original version of the phone that you could use to find information from just about everywhere in the books. The progress circle in the center of the screen continued to roll around. My foot tap-danced on the floor. "Geez *Louise*," I grumbled, softer now after a few nasty glances. It finally loaded but with the wrong thing.

"Welcome to Faerykids! Play games, sing songs, and learn fun things!"

Something told me I wouldn't find any useful maps on there.

"Forget this." I cleared the screen, picked up my bag, and walked out of the computer room.

Somebody was waiting.

"Sir, wouldn't this usually clear for access?"

"*Yes,* Carnigan, but Miss 518 is not a usual citizen, *is she?*" Locknut replied, with a contemptuous undertone in his growl. He was getting impatient with all the questions the Watchers had, especially about the High Order. *Soon enough, though,* he sneered, *all their questions will have an answer.*

"No, sir," Carnigan answered correctly, "she is not. Redirecting search now."

"Good. Have your troops hooked the bait?"

"They're reeling it in now, sir. ETA: ten minutes."

"Spectacular. Keep it well preserved until the shark is following the scent in the water. Give it, oh, let's say, two days. That should give enough time for it to track the bait before the frenzy."

"I suppose we're doing an all-nighter for the big dan—er, *frenzy*, sir?"

"You got that right, Carnigan. We're frenzyin' *all night long*."

"Hear yer havin' trouble searchin' something."

From the corner of my eye. Shadela pushed herself off the wall and walked in my direction. "Keep walking," she instructed, looking straight ahead. As she brushed by, something thick and stiff slipped into my hand.

"Didn't you need to go to the bathroom?" Without waiting for an answer, she went to the front desk and asked to check out a book. I got her drift, though: bathrooms can only have cameras at the entrance, to make sure you don't steal toilet paper or soap or something dumb like that.

I shut the stall door and unfolded the packet of paper. Shadela had stolen a map section of the land between the outer edge of NeverSeen and the little outpost of Blue Creek. In surprisingly precise and intelligible writing, she had marked it with arrows and diagrammed the back with something that should've belonged in a multilevel building in a video game.

In the bottom right corner, it read: Emerald Mine Interior.

Raven's breathing was quick and light, verging on hyperventilation. He thought that after the soldiers failed to find who hit their helmets with rocks, they'd shove off and leave him alone.

Boy, was he wrong.

He'd ventured out into the forest, seeking shade for target practice, when he heard a shout from behind him. Even though his wings weren't big enough to do anything, Raven tried beating them together to move him faster, but there were too many to outrun. They chased him through the half of his backyard forest where he didn't have any escapes or tricks to get them off his back. He cried out when he saw a rubber-tipped arrow strike a tree just ahead of him.

"Ahh! Sam! Help! Saaam!"

Sprinting with all his might, Raven realized he didn't even know why they were after him. He hadn't done anything bad, except for maybe stealing a cookie when Sam wasn't looking, but nobody went to jail for that.

Right?

He saw the capture net fly at him, and he screamed in terror as it caught his legs. He tumbled sideways, smacking his wings into a tree trunk. Raven thrashed inside the net, trying to rip it open, but it had a spider-web seal on it, and the more he struggled, the more it pulled his skin and hair. Some got on his face and sealed his mouth shut. He struggled to breathe through the straw of a nose he had left to get air through. Raven heard one of the men ask, "Do we take him now?"

"No, wait until he's out. Then we won't drop him."

"Who cares if we drop him? It would teach him a lesson in not wriggling."

"The Senator cares. This cargo is precious to the pilot. We don't want any, ah, 'mix-ups' before she touches down."

"Roger that, sir."

The shadowy images of the men through the net expanded until Raven could see only darkness. He fought to stay awake, wondering if Sam would ever find him.

That was, assuming she'd look.

He blacked out.

"Snuffagoppleshucks!"

I smashed my head into the headboard of my bed as I tumbled out of the sheets. The little mechanics controlling me from the inside had lost control, and I shook on the hardwood floor, soaked to the bone from my own sweat. *No...no...it can't be!*

I pushed myself off the floor and stumbled around on my feet. My legs felt like jelly in the sun, as I labored to control the hyperventilation. I was being jolted from the inside out by an earthquake no one else felt or could understand. *No. No. No! It's—no! Not! Can't! No!*

I teetered back on my heels near the edge of my bed, and when I looked up, I saw a girl in a red dress with dark hair and fiery red wings standing on the edge of a branch above a firestorm. She screamed at me and fell back.

I hit the bed hard, crushing my wings and smacking my head against the wall again. Gasping for air, I felt ice cubes of tears racing down my face. Some dummy in the nerves department had hit the full-blown panic button. *So this is how a fish feels when it's thrown into the bottom of the boat.*

I curled into a trembling ball at the sound of gentle tapping on my door.

How...no...no...

Ashlee's head peeked around it.

Not...poss...i...ble...not...poss...i...ible...

She tiptoed quietly past me into the bathroom and came back with a towel.

Cold...cold...not...possi...ble...fire...hot...red...fire...not...cold...

Ashlee wiped the slime off my legs and arms.

Nuh...not possi...ble...not...hot...fire...red...hot hot...

She took a corner and cleaned my face.

Can't...no, dress...red...fire...dead...hot...not...possi...ble...dark...

Ashlee left and got some blankets.

Fire red...red dead...all dead...not possible...hot hot...dark...smoke...

I shook uncontrollably as I put on a new set of pajamas that she handed me.

Can't be...not...no...

I laid down on the fresh blanket, and Ashlee put the second one on top of me.

It...can't...be...

Before she tiptoed back out of the room, I found words enough to say.

"Ash...Ashlee...can it? Be? The...the girl? In the red dress?"

She paused. The moonlight glinted forebodingly off her deep and knowing eyes.

"Is it, Ash? Is...is it really? But how can—it's not...is it?"

A faint whisper echoed in the deafening silence.

"Who else could it be?"

"Sir, I believe she's finally broken the code."

"What's that, Lark?"

"She's finally broken the code."

"Show me the footage."

Lark brought the recording up on another screen. The image flickered in static for a few seconds, then erupted into a flurry of other dreams: drops of blood on golden wood, fire licking in reverse down the side of a tree, a dark curtain billowing at the edge of a stage, a shadowy cave wall with strange lights dancing off its surface, a young boy running through the woods. It raced on and on, a remix of all the things they'd recorded for what seemed to be ages, backwards and forwards, faster and faster until it became a blur of light.

Suddenly it stopped.

Lark heard Locknut's hound-like growl. "Wait a moment, sir, it comes ba—"

As he said it, the static appeared and refocused on another thing: a girl in a tattered red dress with a bloody knife, fiery red wings, and dark hair, standing at the end of a branch above an abyss of flame. It shuddered for a moment, then the girl turned around.

All the way around.

Lark hit the pause button. The screen froze, with a few loose feed lines scrolling across.

A devilish smile crawled across the stone-like features of Chief Locknut's face.

"Excellent."

He and Lark stared back at the face of Subject 518.

Jolson O'Meern awoke with a start. He instinctively reached for the knife under his pillow, but when he didn't hear any more distinctive calls, he relaxed and set his head back down. He massaged his wrist: it was sore from yesterday's training during the off-shift.

Checking the time on the clock, Jolson saw it was going to be a long while before the sun rose and baked the earth again, but there was no way he could sleep again now. He pushed himself up slowly, grimacing at his stiff joints, and sat at the edge of the bed, staring bleary-eyed into the stale darkness. It was far too warm outside to open the windows, so they relied on the inner conditioning enchantments to do their work.

Jolson slumped his way into the kitchen, where he filled a glass of water and grabbed his strength meds and hobbled off to his office. It was even stuffier in there, but he closed the door nonetheless. It was Watcher policy.

He sank back into his barely used, tanned-leather chair and stared at the map screen on the wall. It covered every nook and cranny of the areas around NeverSeen that were vulnerable and needed Watching. Some areas they scoured daily for suspicious activity, others they checked only in their biweekly rounds.

And then there were other areas. Territories covered by the High Order, which they claimed to be accounted for and fully cleared. Nobody went in except for the elites of the Watchers: the soldiers and military personnel. There was no concern for their business, and they were never to be asked.

Even though he was barely awake, Jolson began to wonder. He vaguely remembered seeing men taking large crates and covered trailers towards that old mine, the one that caved in a few years before. It was a terrible accident. Right in the middle of a shift change, there was an unexplained explosion. The roof of the main cave collapsed in on itself and trapped dozens of men. Rescue attempts were made, but the rock was still too unstable. Half the men who went in never came back out.

So why would soldiers be taking things in through the back entrance?

Jolson got up and scrolled across the surface of the map until he reached the section with the mine and its surrounding area. He grabbed a stylus and started marking where the cave had collapsed, drawing arrows to show which direction it had gone. Then he drew stick figures to show where he remembered seeing the men with the boxes.

They all seemed to be leading in one direction, towards a small cave near the back of the mine. Perhaps there was an emergency exit there...*but that still doesn't explain why they'd be taking stuff there in the first place. It's impossible to get in. Right?*

Perplexed, Jolson continued to study his diagrams as he popped his meds into his mouth. He swallowed quickly: the Watcher pills were far from an enjoyable flavor. The familiar headache followed for a few minutes; he sat down this time to endure it. *You'd think strength medication wouldn't give you a headache, but I guess it makes* everything *stronger.*

Jolson found he'd dozed off, but only for a minute. He looked up from his chair to find the old mine's map centered in and doodled on. He smiled and shook his head.

That darn Ashlee! Always drawing and writing on everything. Need to talk to her about that again.

Jolson got up and went back to bed.

An old man sat with his crippled legs to his bony chest, staring blindly out the hole of a window that allowed barely breathable air to flow into his cramped cell. He could not see with his own eyes, but he still knew that the moons shone bright and nearly full: Exelor, the lesser moon, was cresting the mountainous horizon, and Trimont, the greater moon, was hovering above the line of treetops. His breathing was labored, and he counted the seconds as they passed. His time was nearly up.

The door at the end of the passageway clicked open, and the jingle of keys made its way towards him. The man in the cell squinted into the murky blackness of the underground jail and recognized the presence of the soldier coming for him. It was the one who had taken him in and who would lead him to his fate.

"Hullo, mister. The time is now, is it not?" the old man croaked through parched lips, which were swollen at one end of his mouth and stretching already taut skin across his sharp cheekbones.

The dark-skinned soldier flashed a sadistic grin at the man, knowing very well that the man could see it.

"Yes, 517, it is time."

Outside the hole, a murder of crows scattered and recircled around, cawing at the delicious gasps of the old man's last breath.

I woke the next morning suffocating from my own pillow. There was only one thing I could recall from that final dream a moment ago, and I put a choke hold on it, lest I should let it slip away like melting butter with the rest of the dream. It was a number, one I'd nearly forgotten. The one before mine.

517.

CHAPTER EIGHT
BAITING TRAPS

The air was stale and damp, and rocks jutted into Raven's tied hands under his back. His head pounded from the landing, whenever that was, and everything was sore from running and yelling and fighting the spider-net thing. He was afraid to open his eyes. He could hear men talking nearby, and he wasn't sure he wanted them to know he was awake.

Sudden hoarse laughter from the men made him jolt, and his eyes flicked open just in time to see their boots approaching. The rock above him made it impossible to see the rest of them without sticking his head out first, and Raven wasn't eager to get his head knocked in again. A pair of boots stopped inches from his nose, and the voice belonging to them high above asked the other pair of boots what to do about this one.

"Check him over an' set him to work with the others."

"'Kay."

One boot reached out and hit Raven's knee. "Out," said the boot. Raven trembled in the rocky bunk bed-style crevice, but he didn't move. The boot kicked harder. "Out!" it said again. Raven wriggled carefully out into the open, trying without success to avoid scraping his tied hands on the ground. As he moved out, the boots grew legs, then a torso, then shoulders and arms and a soldier's head. It felt to Raven that all his little army toys had grown to full size, like he used to always want, and decided to get their revenge on him for all the times he'd buried them in the dirt or tossed them in the sink.

"Get up," the soldier said again. He nudged Raven's legs, and Raven pulled them back, trying to push himself to a sitting position and then up, but his feet slipped on the damp floor. The Guard grumbled, reached down, and yanked Raven up by the arm and started dragging him down the corridor.

Raven tripped once or twice from the roots sprawling up from the cracks at the base of the walls. He smelled the wet dirt and saw water drip from gnarled things creeping down from the ceiling. There were wooden beams supporting the roof, shaped around the main tunnel in squares, and on each side of the tunnel floor a track for something ran each way. Shortly, he knew what that something was: a metal cart, with shiny rocks piled above the edge, raced around a corner, dropping some of its contents by Raven. He paused to look at the rocks' strangely colored sheen, but the soldier yanked his arm again, and they passed the rocks without further inspection.

All at once Raven found himself seated on a metal chair in an office-type room. The walls were finished with cut rocks, and the door was solid wood. The soldier locked it shut and announced their presence.

"Senator, this is the boy as you requested. Shall I release him, sir?"

"Of *course*, Chief Locknut. We don't want our guest to be uncomfortable, now do we?"

The Chief-man cut Raven's hands free and stood at attention by the locked door as the red, leather chair swiveled around. It revealed a man in a striking green suit, glittering faintly like jewels. His hands were clasped together in front of his chin, and one ankle was set across the other leg's knee. The Senator's eyes were a bright, strange, grayish-hazel color, and they stared intently at Raven.

"What's your name, boy?" he asked.

"R-Raven."

"Do you know why you're here?"

"N-no."

"Excellent. You're a bright boy. You have a lot of friends, yes?"

"Wha-what do you w-want with me?"

The Senator's eyes narrowed.

"What do you know about a girl named...Emmaline O'Meern?"

Raven's sharp intake made the Senator grin, not a friendly grin, not even a sarcastic one, but one so horrid and full of large, white teeth that Raven couldn't help but shudder. It made him think back to the pictures of the all-extinct sharks they showed at school.

"Ahh," started the Senator, rising from his seat, "I see that you are, at least, *acquainted* with Miss O'Meern, am I correct? Now, Raven," he continued without waiting for an answer, "I'm looking for Miss O'Meern, and I need your help."

"Why?"

"Ah, Raven," he laughed, walking slowly around Raven's chair, "you really must learn *not to ask questions.*" The Senator's spindly fingers drummed on the back of his chair, and Raven could tell there was far more to it than impatience.

"Now," the man hissed, "this is how you are going to help me. You see," he whispered, coming to a well-practiced halt before Raven, his black cloak billowing out, "I would like *very much* to meet Miss O'Meern, but for some *strange reason* I am unable to find her."

"M-maybe she doesn't want to be found," Raven suggested. He knew that if he had had the choice, he most certainly wouldn't want to meet this Senator guy if he didn't have to.

A resounding smack across his cheek stunned him into silence. The Senator knelt before Raven and locked eyes with him. "You do *not* interrupt me. You do not tell me things unless I ask for them. Is that clear?" he growled softly. Raven nodded.

The Senator's face forced another gruesome smile. "Good," he replied, turning his back. "So, this is how it is going to work: since I have been unable to find her myself, I now have given her reason to come find *me.*"

"How?"

The Senator seemed to forget his own rules about questions as he paced around to stand behind Raven, grinning that terrible smirk. He gripped the ends of the chair, relishing in some fantasy of his devious plans. A moment later, he bent down and whispered the answer in Raven's ear.

"I've got *you*."

Raven shrank from the poisonous voice. "Take him away," the Senator ordered, and the Chief-man at the door grabbed Raven by the arm. He dragged himself, trying to stay away from the door, screaming, "No! You can't do it! You can't take Emma! I won't let you!"

The Senator sneered at him from his desk.

"We'll see about that."

Chief Locknut dug his nails into Raven's shoulders and shoved him down the tunnel.

517. After breakfast, I'd finally remembered that strange call from midsummer. If I recalled correctly, the voice was hoarse, suggesting it belonged to an older gentleman. 517. He said they were after me next, and I would never meet him.

So, that likely means he's dead—probably not from natural causes. And I'm next.

Crud.

I'd already been highly disturbed from last night, not to mention having no word on Raven's whereabouts, so having a target painted on my back didn't help. Dad got up late, which wasn't normal, but his shift was changed all of a sudden, which wasn't normal either. The air was still and stale and sagged with heat. A storm was coming. I could see its scouts peeking over the horizon.

Dad kissed me on the head before he took his pills and stumbled out the door. Mom called after him to watch where he was going and ran to the door to see if he was okay. A carriage had nearly chopped off the end of his nose. Under normal circumstances, I would've run to the door, too, but something else harnessed my attention.

A small shaft of light streamed out from his office door. In his half-awake nature, he'd failed to fully close it before locking it. My gut told me to leap at the opportunity, but just as I moved for it, Mom came back in, sweeping her bangs back on her sweaty head. I put away my dishes in the Kitchen Cleaner and almost tripped over Umala, who was a crawling slug on the floor. She was babbling nonsense for Mom, but I heard her in my head clear as a bell.

Go check it out. I'll keep Mom busy.

I casually made my way towards my room when I heard the cue: a sudden series of screams exploded from the kitchen. When Mom went to pick her up, I darted for Dad's office and shut the door before she noticed.

Nobody but Dad was allowed in his office. He was a Watcher, and nobody could know what they were watching out for—not the secret, super important things, anyway. It was their job to look out for people making trouble and "disrupting the peace" and all that, but I remembered spotting them in weird places before and at more than a few odd times. I knew it was going to be a big deal to go snooping around in government stuff, but nothing prepared me for what I saw.

The whole room was wallpapered with maps: terrain overview, internal layouts of trees, forest areas, and entrances to...*someplace.* One map in particular gave me a déjà-vu. It was scrawled on with Dad's pictures: arrows pointing down on one section of a mountain, and below it in the fields and forest were little stick men. Positions, maybe, of troops...or something else entirely.

Small feet paused outside the door, and small fingers slipped a map under the door. Shadela's map. The baby screams continued on the other side, with futile coos from Mom calling softly. Ashlee suggested Umala was hungry, but we could both hear her whisper, *Yeah, make her shove nasty food in my face. Then I'll get mad for real!*

Hey, I replied, calling the paper to me with my mind powers, *whatever it takes to get me time, right? We need this.*

Fine. Just hurry it up. She's going for the peas and carrots mush again.

I unfolded the map Shadela had smuggled me and compared it to the one on Dad's wall. It was a match, right up to the arrows and the stick men. The flipside, with the multilevel diagram of the interior, had to have a match in there somewhere. I rolled the terrain map back up and searched for one behind it.

I found none.

Footsteps sounded from the living room.

Mom's coming! Shift now! Ashlee called.

A second later I stood sweating in my room, holding a map with no match, listening to Mom mutter things about Dad not closing the door all the way, and "Ashlee-don't-look-in-there-you'll-get-Daddy-into-trouble."

Hiding in what precious shade was left, the members of the lunch table sat around roasting in the midafternoon heat, surviving with possibly the best-tasting ice cream in the known world. I slurped on a strawberry cone, while others savored flavors like banana, pineapple, peach, and orange. Falcon and Kael were arguing about whether pear would be a good flavor or not when I felt a tap on my shoulder.

I tried not to smile at Tracer. He had a few grape-colored, ice cream dots on his face.

"What?"

"I...I might come. You know. To the dance. Tomorrow."

I nodded, trying to hide my joy. "Cool." I turned to the rest of the table. "Who else is coming?"

Kael grinned behind his blond curtain, his eyebrows jumping up high on his forehead. "Well, my mom said no, but I'm going anyway!"

"I can, but I don't have any nice clothes—"

"Yeah, but isn't there a theme? Like, vegetables or something?"

Falcon thought a moment. "No, I think it was flowers for the girls, and...I don't remember what the guys were s'posed to wear."

"Clothes, I hope," I muttered dryly. Falcon snorted into his ice cream, and Gator swallowed a huge bite all at once and laughed despite his brain freeze. Tracer almost did a spit-take with his ice cream and slapped his hand over his mouth, muffling his laughs. He stared incredulously at me. I gave him a subtle but devious smile.

"Yeah, me too," grinned Kael. "But really, do *you* know what the theme is?"

I contemplated for a second. "Well, I think it was about the harvest and stuff. You were right about the girls wearing flowers, Falcon. And I remember the guys were supposed to have something more...I dunno...grains and leaf-ish stuff, I guess."

"Ooh! Ooh! I'll go as a leaf bug!" piped up Wayk, his smile giving himself away.

"No, dummy, you go as a type of *leaf*, not a bug that *looks* like a leaf!" corrected Kael.

"Hey!" said Gator. "Technically, he *could* go as a leaf bug, because they look so much like leaves that no one could tell the difference! It's common sense!" He did his classic waving of open hands above the surface of the table.

"And you're the expert, are you? Why don't you just go and volunteer for the Watch? Obviously, you're *waaay* too smart for us, and you'd catch anyone who tried sneaking in disguised as a leaf bug!"

I laughed halfheartedly. Something dark was growing in my mind. I just didn't know what it was.

"Do you guys hear that?" I interrupted.

"Hear what?" asked Falcon casually, licking the side of his dangerously lopsided ice cream cone. It shifted just a little on its half-melted base.

"That weird noise."

Tracer looked around curiously. "I don't hear anything," he answered with a perplexed expression.

Something flickered inside my head.

Falcon went in for another lick of his cone.

"Whoa!" shouted Kael and Wayk. Falcon's ice cream had crossed the line, and his ice cream slid clean off the cone...

...and onto the plate I slid right under it. I found I was stretched clear across the table, my arm fully extended.

They all stared at me, with ice cream melting down their hands and their tongues frozen in mid-lick. I glanced around, searching for an explanation.

"Uh...I meant to do that." I left the plate with Falcon's melting ice cream scoop in front of him and drew back to my seat. Somehow my cone was still in my hand, undisturbed. I felt blood rushing to my cheeks as their gazes stayed fixed on one thing. Me. I cleared my throat and added, "Saw it coming."

"How d'ja do that?" asked Tracer, trying to take my gaze from the extremely (not) interesting wooden floor. My eyes started watering, and I'm sure when I brought my gaze to his, he must have seen a flicker of fear in them.

"I...um...I'm not sure. It was just...I..." I took a deep, shuddering breath. "Have any of you guys ever got that weird feeling that something's going to happen, and then it happens just like you thought it would?"

A few nodded.

"Yeah...I, um, get those. A lot. Sometimes...sometimes they're really quite horrible. And...and..."

A pressure from inside me was building, like a balloon being filled until it explodes. I vaguely noticed little drops of melting ice cream landing on the table, little pinkish ones. A cold stream of liquid ran down my wrist. A gentle hand touched my shoulder.

I jumped up from the table. My cone crumbled in my hand, and strawberry ice cream dripped out and made a wet splat on the hot wood. The pressure was crushing my head, both inside and out. Tracer and Kael and Falcon and Gator and Wayk all became distorted swirls of glittering wings and sweaty clothes. I brought my sticky hands up and tried to hold my head still. Everything was getting scrambled. A frequency of a freakish metal-on-metal crash racketed about in my ears. I saw two carriages barreling through the sky, and suddenly—

There was a terrible scream of somebody very small and very young.

A little girl.

The world snapped back into place all at once. Tracer and the other boys stood in a semicircle in front of me. Grave concern was written all across their faces.

"There's going to be a carriage crash in four minutes."

"What?" they asked.

"Move!" I commanded. They jumped back in confusion and watched me as I sprinted down the length of the crowded walkway, bumping into people as they ambled along. "Move it!" I shouted. Everyone turned too late and scowled at me as I disturbed their peace. I darted around a flower stand and cartwheeled over a baby stroller (I'm somewhat proud to say the baby didn't wake.). The takeoff ramp was just ahead of me.

Aw, shoot.

I danced up the barely four-inch-wide edge on one side and was jeered at for cutting the long line. Instinct kicked in as I leapt off, air rushed up beneath me, and I arced upward. Just escaping being knocked out of the sky by the racing faeries below me, I circled around and above the walkway, spotting the boys racing down it...in the same direction. Despite the fact that there would be a midday traffic disaster several thousand feet in the air unless I got there in time, I couldn't help but smile briefly.

Those crazy boys are going to follow me!

I flew as fast as all get-out, but the buzz of whizzing wings soon reached my ears. I glanced back to see Tracer gaping at me. He pointed past me.

"Watch out!"

I did a barrel roll down and out of the way of a group of Flight School Trainees, just grazing the tips of their leaf-sleds. Earth, water, and sky whirled around me as I righted myself and zoomed on towards—where was I going?

Tracer caught up to me, and the other boys trailed behind, struggling to keep up. He asked me the same question. "I'm not sure," I answered, shouting over the roar of the wind. "But I'll know when I get there."

Out of the corner of my eye, a carriage rocketed out of nowhere. It flew over our heads towards a wider clearing ahead. This was the one. The wind beat against my already sore wings as I tried to out-fly it, leaving the boys far behind, but a teenage faery against six hummers is no match.

"Duck!" I yelled.

I wasn't sure if it I felt it or saw it darting out from the thick of the woods first. The second carriage racketed about through the air, careening towards the one with the kids. Cries erupted as they saw the second headed straight for them, being pulled by a horde of nasty hornets. It crashed at a sharp angle into their side, with sparks scattering between them where metal met metal. Even in such young minds, they knew it from instinct: they were all going to die.

Not if I can do anything about it.

I pounded my wings faster than I thought I could have possibly done, and later I realized I must have been half drifting or half Shifting to make up for my lack of strength. The carriages banged together again, and the metal rims of the wheels ground against each other. Sparks flew between them, and the little kids inside screamed for their mommies. The hummers and hornets snapped at each other, now having a tangled fight of their own. When they finally separated and the carriages broke away, I got a good look at the people riding in the hornet-drawn sleigh.

They wore dark green suits, black caps, and brown belts, sheathed swords and bows, and their teeth glinted in the shadow of their hoods. One brandished a long, curved knife and waved it at my face out the window. Somehow I'd wedged myself between the two carriages, stuck myself into the frame of the door, and grabbed the handles on each side. My legs screamed continuously as I blocked the incoming carriage with my feet, pushed it away, and had it slam back into me, jerking my knees sideways and twisting my back at a weird angle.

I cried out angrily, and the Guards yelled things to each other, things I didn't understand. We were nearing the edge of the clearing, and I knew I'd only have a few moments to save the kids. The soldiers pulled away again and prepared to come back to squish me like a grape.

The pressure pounding on the inside of my head increased again. I felt time blur, and the world became a watery painting of greens, blues, oranges, and browns. My hands grew hot, like I'd reached for a cooking pot without mitts. As I brought them before me to hold off the next attack, even in the chaos of colors, I could see very clearly that blood was surging down to my fingers, turning my arms a ghastly white. The heat in my hands pulsed stronger and faster, until I thought they'd catch fire.

They did.

Without any idea what I was doing, I brought my hands in front of my face, flames licking sideways, elegantly and steady like a weaving flag, and braiding itself with my hair. I crossed my arms and turned my palms to face me, a bonfire in my skin. I shaped my hands into a bird: thumbs together, fingers out...and blew.

A great ball of fire leapt off my hands and flew across the great, murky space towards the second carriage. The remaining heat and flames retracted into my fingers and transformed my skin back to a healthy peach hue. I watched as the ball crossed over the painted, blurred world. Seconds before it impacted, the ball suddenly spread out and reshaped into a bird, with fiery feathers trailing behind. Its head twisted back, and a pair of bright white eyes looked at me.

All at once, everything snapped back. The carriage exploded in flame, and yells of men followed. The one with the children screaming for their lives, the one I was still clinging to, swerved away to the left and downward as the second was engulfed in flames. Arms and limbs flailed about inside as they tried desperately to get out of the carriage before they burned alive. There wasn't any chance, and I stared as they fell from the sky, tumbling about like a pebble in the rapids. It missed trees by inches as they went crackling down towards a large stream that fed the river and crashed into it, sizzling and breaking apart. Hollers filled the clearing as help rushed in, voices of men trained in combat. Watchers.

The wind buffeted the side of my face as the carriage came to a landing on a tree at the far end of the clearing. I hit the back of my head on the edge of the rack as we bounced to a stop, and the scramble to safety began. Reeling, I fell off the side of the carriage and stumbled to the nearest bench, every step like walking on knives. I breathed in gasps, my muscles burning, as I stared at the little kids clambering off the carriage, crying and running to their mothers.

A girl in a purple-and-pink dress asked something curious. "Where's the Strawberry Girl, Mommy? Where did she go?" Her mom picked her up and said that she didn't know who she was. What did she look like?

"She had strawberry ice cream in her hair, an' it was on her face, too."

"Well, I've never met her. Where did she go?"

"I dunno, Mommy. Can we find her?"

"No, we need to make sure everybody's okay first, and then we're going to see your father. No 'buts' about it."

"But...but...I wanna see the Strawberry Girl..."

The mother stood with her little girl, who had her thumb in her mouth, and looked around at the crowd for the Strawberry Girl.

I made myself get off the bench, wobbling on my weak and throbbing legs, and started walking away from the scene. My heart was pounding a beat into my head, and I couldn't think straight. Footsteps behind me said that my friends had found me, but I didn't slow down. I climbed up a branch reaching through the walkway and stepped off the edge, trying to find a clear view of the wreckage. A small plume of smoke between the trees told me where to look.

"What in Skyglass just happened?" exclaimed Kael, the first to speak. Nobody answered. The buzz of wings laboriously keeping us up was all we could hear in our space of the sky.

"And *how* are you doing that?" Tracer wondered, staring at me.

"Doing what?" I asked vacantly. The image of the fire leaping off my own two hands into the air and attacking soldiers was taking a while to comprehend. *Fire...me...I can control...fire...*

"Doing *that!* Flying without moving your wings!" He pointed incredulously at my back. I turned my head around blankly as cries of men came from the stream.

"Oh. Umm...yeah, they're moving. They're just, uhh...going too fast for you to see. Them moving."

"No, they're *not!*" he smiled in confusion, now drawing on the full attention of the others. "If they're going so fast, why don't I *hear* them?"

I had a hard time focusing on his face and wiped my hand across my forehead. I wasn't sure how much longer I could keep this up, and my shaking hands caught Tracer's attention. My lips searched for an answer when a siren went off. It screamed through our brains, and our group darted for the nearest branch, knowing it was possible to pass out from the chaotic noise. Tracer saw I hadn't moved, and he grabbed my hand and pulled me with him. We collapsed on the branches near the V of two trunks, trying not to fall off into the vast nothingness below. I trembled, inside and out, the epicenter at my heart, clinging to a thin, wavering twig as my wings lay like fragile panes of glass on the rough, crumbling bark.

God, no! It can't—no! I hate fire! I don't want it! I didn't mean to hurt anyone! I don't—God, take it back! Take it back from me!

Guards swarmed from every direction, leading their devious hornets to the crime scene. Their buzz was overwhelming, and I shook at the mere thought of encountering one of those bugs. Everyone knew them well enough to not approach from either end, unless you wanted a large jaw to clamp onto your leg. The stings were deadly. The Watchers who drove them sure encouraged you to spill the beans really quick.

Spill the beans. Somebody would make a bad joke about that right now, if we weren't here. If we were anywhere but here.

The Guards swarmed mostly to the crash site, but a large group landed where the children's carriage had landed safely. They held their weapons down, but I saw their fingers gripping the handles as their leader began asking around. He held out a sheet of paper with a picture on it. I couldn't see it, but I knew who it was.

"Hey! That's the Strawberry Girl!" cried out a small voice. The little girl walked boldly up to the Chief and willingly started talking. He asked her something, and she replied, "Uh-huh. She's the one that stopped the other carriage from hitting us, an' she had strawberry ice cream in her hair. I think she went...um..." She looked around and pointed in our direction. He thanked her and bought her an orange ice cream. She walked back to her anxious mother, slurping at her treat, and they left quickly.

Soldier movement increased. Five stayed, two continued questioning, and five more headed down the mainly vacant walkway. One trailed off and went in the same direction as the little girl and her mother, but I didn't remember that until later. The five coming our way were inspecting everything, like I had left a trail of some sort. Two stopped to ask a shop owner if she'd "seen this girl." All this Conforminator-esque stuff was freaking me out.

"Emma!" Tracer whispered from just above and to my right, "Who are they looking for? Shouldn't we help?"

Fear welled up in my soul like the tears in my eyes as I shook my head slightly. Tracer tipped his head forward and pointed his thumb at the Guards and his finger at me, mouthing, "They're coming after *you?*" I nodded and a tear slipped down my cheek. His expression shifted from that of curious concern to one I'd seen many times in my father's own face, one of stern obedience and protection. He whispered down to the others.

"Guys. Hey, up here. We hafta get outta here. Those soldiers can't find...um, us." He glanced at me. "Anyone got any ideas?"

Kael squinted up through his bangs and glasses. Gator rubbed the back of his neck, and Wayk watched the soldiers from behind the leaves. They were closer now, maybe only a hundred feet, asking a guy selling candy apples if he'd seen the "Strawberry Girl." I counted out the seconds in my head. This had to be perfect to work.

"I got one," I whispered. "When I say 'go,' everyone dives out of here. Got it?"

"Wait!" said Falcon. He stuck his fingers out from where he gripped the tree branches. "Where are we gonna go? They'll be on our tail in seconds."

I nodded. "S'okay, I got it covered. Twice."

Having their escape somehow covered twice distracted them long enough for me to get ready. The soldiers were just about to walk away from the candy apple stand. I spotted the caramel heater resting above a small pile of wood and an oil jug. It steamed with a thick, gooey, gold inside, just waiting to do something.

It would, alright.

There was no way I could hide it this time. But I was done hiding it. I knew Tracer could see a light in my hand as I curled a ball of fire up in my hand and shot it towards the stand, Iron Fae style.

It crashed into the oil jug and exploded. Flaming wood was sent in every direction, knocking the caramel bowl over and spilling hot candy onto the soldiers' feet as they braced for the falling debris. Curses erupted from the boys as they watched the destruction unfold, but only Tracer turned back to look at me. Only one thing was written on his face—dismay.

"Go!" I shouted and fell backwards from the V. They obeyed and some yelled as they fell. My stomach jolted. I'd forgotten that the bases of the trees were laced with thornbushes and nasty insect hives. We couldn't bank away in time. With only seconds, I pulled back and grabbed Tracer's and Gator's hands, and they grabbed Falcon's and Kael's and Wayk's.

Then I Shifted.

CHAPTER NINE
PLOTS AND PLANS

"What in God's name just happened?" Locknut bellowed. He was staring at the static of camera B4-12, where he should've seen the candy apple stand with two of his soldiers close by and the other three scouting the area. There'd been a bright flash and then nothing. His grip tightened on the back of the chair as Carnigan futzed with the joystick and knobs, trying to regain the image.

"Sir. It's gone. There's nothing there."

"That wasn't my *question*, you fool! What *happened?*"

Carnigan stared at the screen. "I don't know...but...I might be able to get another angle...hold on..."

Locknut held on. Barely. Carnigan did his Sparkpage magic and cycled through the cameras along the walkway. Most showed nothing more than debris flying off into the air and a light from around a branch or a corner or—

"Wait, stop! Go back," he instructed. Carnigan shuffled back to camera B4-9, a shot from the far right of the stand, and played back the past few minutes. There were the soldiers interrogating the owner and the other three sweeping the area, then a streak of light from the left and *poof*—no more apple stand. Wood and metal sheets and candy-making mixtures came raining down, the soldiers dodging it to no avail.

Something caught Locknut's eye at the far left of the screen.

"Zoom in on that branch there," Locknut pointed. "Now, replay it." Carnigan did so.

They couldn't see much from this close to the incident, but Locknut was more focused on the branch. Something, or several somethings, was moving in there. Not much, but enough. Suddenly, one of them towards the back moved forward, and a bright light came from it and flew out of the picture. The explosion lit up the branch, and moments later, five or six somethings fell out of the cover of the leaves.

But he had to know for sure.

"Replay and stop it when I tell you to."

Carnigan rewound the footage and played it back.

"Stop."

Little diagonal lines ran slowly up the grainy image. There was a point of light in the darkness of cover attached to something pale.

"Can you zoom into that?"

"I can get it to...there." It zoomed in just a bit more to the area.

Locknut squinted at the pixilated shot. It was a vague outline of an arm, then a bit of a shoulder, and a shaded face...

"That's as far as I can get it. Would you like me to try a different camera, sir?"

Locknut grinned. "No, you won't need to do that. We've got our girl."

***

I screamed as the dark curtain tore back around me. I'd never Shifted with more than two passengers before. Ashlee and Umala insisted I had to practice, but I don't think they'd imagined me needing to take five for a ride. I hit dirt flat on my chest and got the wind knocked out of me. My heart pounded harder as it searched for air and commanded lungs to prove it.

I rolled over slowly. The world was swirling in a kaleidoscope of shapes and colors, impossible to focus on. The beat of blood drummed in my ears, and a mix of voices scrambled themselves in. Guy voices. Yelling.

Where are we? What the *hey* just happened? Hay is for hummers. Oh…hush up, Quake!

"What are you all doing here?"

I sat up on my elbows, my strangulation laced with panic, just enough to see Shadela Glump standing, with a knife belt around her waist and her hands on her hips, at the edge of the hollow.

Ashleeka held onto her mother's hand as they wandered through the heat of the market. The dance party was tomorrow, and they wanted to surprise Emma with a nice dress. Umala wiggled in her stroller, and Ashleeka pretended to play with her. But they were really talking about something critically important.

So she figured it out? asked Ashleeka.

Oh, yeah. No mistaking it.

So what's the plan now?

We follow her lead.

But you told me a thousand times that she doesn't know anything about what she's doing! What she's up against! You said she needed our help!

She will soon enough. But for now, let her follow her instincts. Let her grow into the leader she's meant to be. She's building her strike force. It won't be long now.

Out of the corner of her eye, Ashleeka saw a dress, the perfect dress, flaring out in the breeze. It had a princess neckline, and a gold ribbon around the waist. Tiny white gemstones decorated the front, and it glistened in the sun.

"Mom! Mom! Lookit!" Ashleeka pointed. "Lookit that one!"

"Which one, Ash?"

"*That* one."

"The blue one?"

"Uh-huh. That's the one."

"Well? What are you doing here?" Shadela asked again.

"Uh...that's what we're trying to figure out." It was Tracer speaking.

"How can you not know how you got here?"

I waved my arm weakly from the ground. My lungs caught some air, and I just barely coughed. Everyone seemed to notice where I was finally and walked over. Falcon offered his hand to pull me up, asking, "Are you okay? Do you know what just happened?" I held my hands out to balance as they barraged me with questions. Shadela stared vacantly. I noticed Tracer was just looking at me.

"Uh...Emma? You're doing it again."

"Doing what?" I choked out.

"That." He gestured behind me. "You're off the ground, but your wings...they're not moving." Everyone stopped talking and stared.

Huh, boy.

I set my feet back down slowly. There was no way out now. My voice still strangled, I answered the only way I could.

"It's...it's a trick I learned. From..." I paused. I wasn't sure I should bring Ash and Ume into the mix. Things were crazy enough as it was. I mean, come on, it's hard to keep secrets when somebody's always looking for you. I started again.

"I can do things. Weird things. Like teleporting, but I call it Shifting. It feels more like shifting positions than teleporting." I watched their faces. They all seemed confused. "Well, never mind that. But that's how I got you here. If I didn't get us out, then...the Guards would've..."

Faces of doubt. Disbelief. Even hints of anger.

"Guys...please...don't hate me. I'm sorry if I've broken your trust, but it would be best for everyone if we maybe figured this out later. Right now, I need you on my side. All of you. I've got enough people after me as it is." I nodded to Shadela. "You guys are the only ones I can trust. You've already seen way more than I thought I would ever let you see, and there's way too much that I could tell you, but I can't."

"Why?" asked Kael. He squinted at me between his blond bangs.

"Because the less you know, the safer you'll be. Trust me," I laughed hollowly. "I know a lot, and the more I learn, the tighter everything closes in." My breath shuddered as I looked at their perplexed faces. It's not exactly fun to tell your friends that you're nothing like they thought you were. "Nobody's safe, okay? You *have* to know that. They're after me, and if...if they find out you...you're helping..." I couldn't block the images from my mind. Of what might be if I failed to keep them safe.

"So why should...why should we—"

"Trust me?" I finished bluntly. "Yeah, good question. I mean, we've only been friends for, I dunno, three years. And, of course, I'm the only one who's never told you guys everything, right? Right. So why should that make a darn difference?"

Tracer fidgeted visibly and stared at the crinkling red leaves under his feet. Falcon dug his foot down in the dirt. The silence was thick and dark, like the smoke building on the horizon. Fires in nearby areas had kick-started the season, but I'd forgotten until then.

Lord, I hate fire.

"That fireball that blew up the other carriage...was...was that..." Wayk wondered, gesturing vaguely.

I bit my lip to keep from crying, but I felt tears brimming in my eyes. I looked away at the sky, trying to fathom it all. They knew. They knew it was me. I knew they did.

"I...I was trying...to...to..." I moaned, grabbing my hair in my hands. I buried my nails into my scalp, my heart pounding. Their eyes were lasers burning my skin.

"I never wanted this to happen! Okay? I never wanted to hurt them! But those kids! They were going to die! Those batty Guards were going to kill them! I couldn't..." Anger pulsed through my veins, and I screamed at the sky. "God! Why are You doing this to me? Stop it! *I hate it! Aaaygh!*"

I grabbed the end of the nearest stick I could find, whacked it as hard as I could on the ground twice, and hurled it at the nearest tree. There was a horrible crack as it hit, and the stick split lengthwise down the middle. The two halves landed on each side of the tree, five feet back.

Nobody moved. The air was stifling, and it shimmered in the long twenty feet between me and the stick. The stick I broke. In half. With one throw.

I sighed. Sweat was dripping down my forehead. I was so tired, so hot, so angry. But this wasn't the way to handle it. I forced myself to burn out as I raised my hand.

The two halves of the branch and all the splinters pulled up from the ground and drifted towards me. I put my index finger and thumb together, and the splinters were sandwiched as the branch put the pieces back together. When it was in my reach, I gently touched the middle of the crack with my finger. There was a gust of wind around me, and a light shot down the middle of the stick, sending weird shadows dancing through the hollow. Then it was over, and I had a walking stick floating a foot in front of me.

"Whoa," the guys and Shades said collectively. I wrapped my hand around my stick and broke the connection with my mind. Something was pulling on my hair. I turned to see what it was, and I felt a single hair snap off my head. There was a dot of light on the side of the stick, and the thread of golden-red disappeared into it. Then it went out.

"Ow," I muttered, wondering why the stick had just slurped up a strand of hair like a noodle from my head. But I wasn't really concerned at the moment. The hollow was very quiet, except for the hum of the occasional bee. Sweat laced the sides of each of our faces.

"So...what do we do now?" asked Shadela. She had come to the front of the group, standing to one side with her balled fists on her hips. Her black hair was tied back, and for once I found it rather beautiful.

"We train with Shades," I announced to the others. "If she doesn't mind. I believe she's an expert in tactics and weapons, correct?" Shades nodded with a sly grin. "That is, if everyone's in..." I glanced around. None of the guys moved. I tried not to smile when I noticed Tracer stand a little straighter.

Falcon nodded. "We're all in, Emma." Wayk's grin exploded over his face again. "Let's do this thing!"

"Wait, *what* exactly are we doing?" Gator asked, waving his hands around and looking back and forth between Falcon and Tracer.

"A rescue operation," I answered, "for a boy named Raven. I know where he's being held."

"Alright! Where?" Kael asked.

"In a high-security complex..."

"Okay," paused Tracer.

"...that shouldn't exist..."

"Uh..." faltered Gator.

"...and if we're caught, we're all probably gonna die."

"Oh," said Falcon.

The clunking noises of metal on metal drummed through the chamber. Fumes and vapors swirled around the machines and gathered in the ceiling. And in the middle of the cave, surrounded by Guards, were lines and lines of children.

Raven glanced around at all the other kids in his division. They all wore filthy white suits, and most were his age or younger. He wondered if these were all the kids who had gone missing over the years. They stretched out down the rows of skinny tables, hundreds of them, each having their own job and doing it over and over without fail. It was a mass production line. Run by slave kids.

"Oy! 713! Yes, you!" a Guard shouted at Raven. "Get back to work!" He cracked his whip over Raven's head, and he jumped back to work. His fingers slipped as he tried to screw the bolts to attach the lever to the plate, and one fell to the floor.

"You numbskull! Pick it up, butterfingers!" the Guard bellowed again. Only a few kids around Raven seemed to notice. He crouched to grab it, but once he did, he felt a sharp sting on his back. He cried out.

"That's what ye get when you're a piddly little worm! Now get back to work! All of you!" The whip snapped with authority over the children's heads. They dove back into their worlds, worlds of metal and chemicals and nuts and bolts and screws. Raven's stomach jolted when he saw a boy carry the finished product to a pile at the far end of the assembly line. It was a large cylinder, plated with spikes and dials and a screen with numbers.

They were making weapons. They were making bombs.

I walked out of the hollow, following Shadela close behind, pushing branches out of the way. Someone said "ouch" when one smacked back into his face. "Sorry," said Gator. "Oh, yeah, you're *real sorry,* aren't you? Take *that!*" Kael pushed Gator into a bush.

"Hey, watch it!"

"You watch it, man!" It startled me to think that after everything I'd told them, everything they saw, that they'd still revert back to themselves. It was quite comforting, in a bizarre sort of way. I didn't have to control them at all. I could. I'd tried it on bees and hummers before, telling them to please leave me alone and not get in my face and such. But here, my friends were proving they really did trust me. I wondered if they should as much as they did.

"Hoy! This way, bozos, not that way!" hollered Shades from the front. She pushed past some bushes and led us into a small field lined with targets, obstacles, and wooden dummies. Racks of weapons were lined up, ready for action. I grabbed a bow and tested its strings. Shadela strapped on a back sheath for two sabers. Tracer and Falcon took swords, Wayk and Gator got bows, and Kael fingered a staff. I remembered the one I made and made a note to practice with it later. Shadela glanced around at our crew, geared for battle and standing ready like they were greeting the General.

"Alright, guys. Let's roll!"

"Yo! Chain Mail! Get outta the way!" called Shadela as she helped Gator aim at the center of the target. It was the second rotation of arms, and Shades had us aiming for certain goals. Gator and Wayk were on Accuracy, Falcon and Kael on Strength, and Tracer and I on Reaction.

"Sorry!" panted Kael as he pushed the wheelbarrow out of the target area. Shadela seemed to like bothering us by calling us by our nicknames. Most of the guys didn't care, but I wasn't so sure about mine.

"Hey! Firefox! Watch yourself!"

I ducked as an arrow flew over the army crawl section. Wayk took his turn firing as I reached the end of the course and took off down the path between the bushes. Tracer followed behind and I heard a hefty smack as he encountered a trap.

The goal of Reaction training was to run through a maze and avoid getting hit. If you were, you'd have berry splats as proof. I was bored. I wasn't tired, or scraped up, or dirty. Compared to everyone else.

Tracer, however, was more slime than smile at the end of the third run. I was standing and watching Wayk and Gator at the target range, pecking away at the center, when Tracer dragged himself up and over, panting heavily. "How...do...you do it?" he asked.

"I dunno. Usually, this sort of workout training kills me."

"I wish," he moaned. Half of his face was masked with red juice. The other was slathered with mud.

"I hope not. Besides, you've already got your party mask for tonight."

"What mask? And I thought...it was traditional."

"It's different for us. I found out today that while everyone is listening to violins and doing the waltz, we get a costume party and a light show. You could go as the Phantom Monarch," I teased.

He sat down on a bench and wiped his face with a towel. I was sweaty and dirty, too. I could feel stuff caking my face. But I was bored. Being bored never does anyone any good. If I was going to improve my reaction time, I needed to step it up. The only trick was how to make it harder without risking life and limb.

I was puzzling it out when Tracer got up. "I'm going to try one more time," he sighed. "There's this one section that's driving me nuts."

"Alright. I'll go with you."

I let Tracer get a head start so he wouldn't worry about messing up in front of me. After a few seconds, I started in. First, avoid the swinging arms. Don't fall in the water ditch. Balance on the skinny beams. Hop in and out of the rims, do the monkey bars, practice swing-jumping, push past the dummies without getting punched. Tracer got whacked in the face again, and I laughed when he punched them back.

Then it was back to the field of rolling kegs and pushing wheel-barrows.

Gator was up again with the bow, aiming at the first of the three-target series. I was reaching the middle of the target area, groaning against the weight of the giant keg as my legs threatened to give way. Tracer was ahead, rolling the keg smoothly. It ran ahead of him, catching a good slope, and he hustled after it.

That's when I saw it coming.

Feathers vibrating in the air. The smooth wood of a shaft. Bright blue of the sky...no, of an eye.

A spray of blood.

"Tracer, look out!" I shouted and sprinted as all get-out. He turned at the instant Gator aimed at the third target.

He let go before he realized someone was in the way.

Right as the arrow left the string, I reached Tracer. I was directly between the target and the arrow. The head spun slowly as it flew towards me. There was a slow, high scream, warped by my altered perception. Shadela had seen me move. Tracer started a yell. The arrow split the air, which tickled the feathers on the back, bending them in the stiff force of a gale.

All this happened in a moment.

They'd expected me to fall back dead onto Tracer, with the arrow sticking out of my forehead. Instead, they stared at me as it rotated an inch in front of my nose. It wasn't hard to hold it there, but the gravity of the consequences if I let go definitely made me hold it tighter. And by the way, I wasn't using my hands.

"Tracer," I said calmly, staring down the shaft of the arrow, "You'd best move out of the way."

Gator stood with his mouth agape, still waiting for me to fall down. Falcon didn't move. Kael, Shadela, and Wayk didn't move. Only three things moved. Tracer, as he moved out from behind me, then me as I twisted back and out of that way, and the arrow, which continued at its original speed past me and struck a bull's eye.

"Nice shot, Gator. But, uh, watch for people next time, okay?"

"Uh...yeah...sorry, Tracer." Gator found his voice again. It cracked as he spoke.

Tracer stared blankly at the target. I watched the color return slowly to his face. He looked at me in astonishment. "Thanks," he said.

"No problem. I owed you for saving me from falling off the platform, remember?"

"Oh. Yeah. Right."

The sun was lowering in the sky. It was almost time to head back home, so we used our last half hour making plans. I had Shadela's old map, and we talked through the interior: where was the security room, what were the patrol routes, and how we'd get out with Raven and ourselves in one piece.

As we started to break camp, Shadela came over and asked to speak in private. "These guys remind me of my older brothers," she stated, smiling. "That's how I got so tough. Plus, I had a little sister to look out for."

"Had?"

"Yeah," she sighed. "She, um...she passed away...about three years ago. Got in a carriage accident."

I stayed quiet. We watched as Falcon and Kael started another scuffle over who tripped whom first.

"I'm sorry, Shadela. I...I understand. I have two sisters, and I would never want anything to happen to them. There's nothing as wonderful or as challenging as siblings."

"Yeah."

Tracer and Gator did some slow-motion punches at each other, mocking the *Faetrix*, until Gator fell over and sat on top of Falcon where he lay, trying to pull off Kael's shoe without being kicked in the face. Falcon said something about his glasses, and "Gator, you thick-headed squirrel, get off me."

"Emmaline, do you really think they're ready?"

Tracer laughed as Gator got pulled into the hustle. Wayk stood by, grinning quietly.

"Strength of the mind always beats strength of the body, Shades. They've never been readier."

She nodded, letting the idea sink in. "And what about you?"

My smile faltered. I felt her eyes piercing me like all the times they had before, but with a different purpose. My mind raced to find an answer. Any answer. Anything but the exact, unavoidable truth of the future.

I looked her square in the face. *Execute evasive maneuvers.*

"Nothing will make me change my mind. Nothing. It's worth everything to save someone's life. Even putting your own on the line."

She took it.

Shadela smiled faintly and looked back at the half-grown boys. They'd started wrestling and ended up dog-piling in a giant, laughing mound.

"You know, I never thought I'd hear somebody else say that."

She understood.

"Emma, are you *sure* you're okay?"

Tracer and I walked at the front of the group. Shadela had suggested we break up at different points, giving the impression that we'd just been hanging around the forest the whole time. I highly doubted the ruse would be complete or convincing, and I don't think anyone else did either. We just didn't express doubts for the sake of trying to stay sane.

"Emma?" He said again.

"Yeah," I sighed.

"Are you *sure* you're okay?" Tracer searched my face for clues. I smiled faintly. My walking stick felt heavier than when I first re-assembled it, but I was just tired.

"Yeah. I'm okay. I just want to get Raven out. Alive."

I don't know if he could tell that not all of that was true. He probably could. But he didn't say anything.

"You think they'd kill him? What for? I mean, what's the point?"

"I...I don't know. He's only eleven and only knows about the nightmares. That's all. Unless...unless Sam told him something, but she hates my guts. She'd avoid talking about me at all...I think..."

We walked in relative quiet for some time, my stick tapping the earth gently in time to my meandering pace. The leaves of near-autumn crunched under our shuffling feet. Louder kick-ups behind us told of the leaf wars already occurring between Falcon, Kael, and Gator. I glanced back and saw the three boys stuffing leaves down the back of each other's shirts and hoodies and bits sticking out of their hair. I wanted to match their wide smiles, but I couldn't bring myself to. My heart hurt and I felt myself hunch over more.

"Emmaline?" asked Tracer. I could tell something was on his mind.

"Yes, Tracer?"

He stared blankly at the ground of dry dirt and browned leaves. "How did you know the...the..." He stopped short of the word that almost killed him.

"Instinct, I guess. I just...I saw it coming."

He looked at me again. His bright blue eyes seemed unusually sharp against the backdrop of yellow and orange leaves. I couldn't break away from his gaze.

"Well, however you did it...thanks." Tracer dropped his head, and the moment was over. I found I'd been holding my breath and felt exhausted even though we'd been walking no faster than before. My head spun and I leaned a little more against my walking stick. There was a catch in my throat before I spoke again.

"You're welcome."

It had grown quiet behind us. As we neared the end of the path, and the waning sunlight broke through, I turned around to see Falcon, Gator, Wayk, and Kael staring at us. They quickly found interesting things beside the path, in the sky, and amongst the trees. I smiled faintly and gave them a few seconds to think that I didn't notice.

"Remember, guys," I called back. "Stay cool at the dance. Act normal. When it's over, we make our move. Be ready, and *for Heaven's sake get enough sleep!* Yes, Kael, I'm talking to you!"

He flashed his mischievous smile at me from behind the blond curtain he called hair.

"And you!"

"Aw..." moaned Tracer. "That means I hafta go to bed *tonight!*"

"What, as opposed to o'dark-thirty tomorrow?"

"Uh-huh." He grinned.

I smiled. But mine wasn't worthy of his.

A knock on the door snapped the Senator out of his thoughts. He'd been dropping and catching a small, green ball for half an hour. Every detail about this was critical: one slip and it would collapse like a wet paper sack. He was staring at his map, which flickered light on the dark floor and walls of his underground office, as he evaluated the various entry points and circumstances of Phase Two. Now, Chief Locknut was at his door, ready to report.

"Well?" was all the Senator said.

"All is well, sir. Production is nearly through, but of course, we'll keep them busy, as always."

"And the placement?"

"Already underway, Senator. Is there anything else you need done?"

The Senator bounced the green ball repetitively, like a slow metronome. It was to a count in his head. He had a count for every-thing: the time, the phases, the production—even to the movement of information throughout his network.

"Sir?" wondered Locknut.

"Hmm...yes, there is one thing," replied the Senator, still drum-ming the ball. Drop. Bounce. Catch. Drop. Bounce. Catch.

"What's that, sir?"

The Senator caught the ball one last time and turned to the Chief. "Let's see if we can't add some stress tomorrow. Surely, you know quite well that under pressure, sparks fly quicker...with greater reac-tions."

The Chief grinned. "I'll see to it, sir." He closed the door behind him.

The Senator swiveled back to his map. His machine-like mind set to work, drilling cause-and-effect consequences through the next Phase. He sat for an hour, finding holes in the code of his brilliantly crafted program and filling them with fresh data. And ever on, the steady beat of the ball. Drop. Bounce. Catch.

Drop.

Bounce.

Catch.

CHAPTER TEN
COUNTDOWN

My wings hurt where I lay on them, staring at the ceiling. Once again, there was very little compelling me to go to sleep. I knew too much. And every time I slept, I learned more of what I didn't want to know. So I stared at the ceiling and listened to the wind outside the window, warning of the gradually approaching storm.

But there was more than one storm for me to worry about.

Across the river, through the fields, and under the cover of the tree's branches, Sameela O'Klurn lay in her bed, staring at the ceiling, waiting and thinking. Tomorrow would be her first big assignment. Despite all the things everyone said about it, the Harvest Festival was no laughing matter. Security was top priority, ever since the sabotage several years back had led to the biggest food shortage of the century.

But there was more. Sam's boss, Chief Locknut, had given her a special mission in addition to her normal duties as a Guard. Given the current circumstances, Sam thought it peculiar that the Chief would pay such strong attention to a low-life, pig-headed nobody, as *her*.

As Emmaline O'Meern.

The alarm clock went off. Obeying strict protocol, Sam took her meds, and after the expected short headache, fell asleep.

Chief Locknut strolled around the hall. Workers were everywhere setting up sound systems, cameras, and decorations. It was nearly dawn, and the party wasn't until an hour before sunset, but he needed all the time he could get. When nobody was looking out for anything.

A buzz in his pocket alerted him of a message. He pulled out his phone and answered it.

"Yes?"

A familiar drone on the other end told him it was the Senator.

"Have you got the tackle equipment ready, Locknut?"

"Yes, sir."

"And what of the net? Have you got yours ready?"

Chief Locknut tightened his jaw. He knew there was little time left to be prepared and any delay now could unfold a chain of catastrophic events that, at best, would lose him his job.

"Nearly there, sir, *however*..."

"What?"

"I'm not sure about the equations, sir. From what I calculated, that amount of explosives could make a crater the size of the mountain, if all in one spot. Perhaps we should, ah, give *everyone* their fair share?"

There was a long moment of silence. Locknut gripped the phone tighter in fear of dropping it from his own sweat. He jumped at the eruption of noise at the other end. It was laughter. The sound reminded him of nails on a chalkboard.

"Locknut, you old devil! Yes...that will work very well, very well indeed...giving 'everyone their fair share,' as you put it. Good work, Chief. Reroute the supplies as needed. Report when finished."

There was a loud click and a dial tone. Locknut hung up, refocused on his surroundings, and yelled at a newbie worker for getting the camera wiring backwards.

I sat in front of my mirror, combing my hair. Another sleepless night followed by yet another peculiar morning. Dad had somehow managed to sleep past his alarm and missed his shift. And yet, when he called in to ask for a new assignment, the secretary said he wasn't the only one to do so. In fact, nearly the whole platoon had done the same. He took his meds as normal and left.

Mom had a similar puzzle. She'd been told by the Festival Committee to come very early and help with decorations and confections, but during breakfast, before Dad got up, she received a call saying everything had been handled and her services were no longer required. She seemed to think nothing of it and set off to buy groceries as normal.

Except nothing about it was normal.

There had been news reports all evening and morning about the carriage incident and the seemingly coinciding vendor explosion. No accusations were being made, and no definitive evidence of who the culprit was. None at all.

So why did I feel like I was being Watched?

I glanced up, for what felt like the seven-hundredth time, from my maps and diagrams scattered across the floor. This had to be perfect. I had to get Raven cut. That was another thing bothering me. Actually, it was closer to driving me mad. There had been no reports of a kidnapped child at all. Mr. O'Klurn wouldn't be back until this evening, and Mrs. O'Klurn was working hours so late that I think she just assumed Raven was already in bed when she got home.

And of course, Sam didn't give a darn about anyone or anything anymore.

There *had* to be something else going on. Nobody just *forgets* that a person exists.

...Right?

Either way, I was pretty sure I'd find out soon.

As in the coming evening.

After that...

After that was a whole different problem.

Raven panted under the weight of the cart. It had wheels and was rolling down a slick track, but it was still obscenely hard to push for a kid his age. Some of the younger ones had to do it in twos or threes.

After they'd finished making the bombs, the kid workers had been told to take them to a different section down a long, narrow, winding path, and deposit their loads in the hollow there. It was full of giant roots and mud puddles, so it was very difficult to find sturdy, dry ground to set stuff.

Raven ducked as he zipped under another root on a sloped section of the track. This had to be at least his fifth round. He couldn't remember the last time he'd had food. Water was sparse and gross, and they only rested an hour at a time in shifts. As he slipped again on the increasingly damp dirt, Raven realized he didn't know whether it was day or night. All the soldiers seemed wide awake and not in the least bit naturally.

Another stringy root reached for his head and reminded him of something else. He shuddered at the thought of the man with the whip: he'd gotten snapped at least a dozen times in the past few hours. Raven's ankles hurt where they'd been lashed, and his back ached with every breath.

He sighed with relief when he saw the cave appear around the corner. Raven pulled out his load, found good ground for them, and started pushing his empty cart back to Point A to start over.

Just think: only three more hours to go.

"Do you *really* think it looks nice?"

"Emma, I *told* you a hundred times...you look *wonderful*," replied Ashlee. Umala cooed her consensus.

I was standing in my bedroom, wearing the dress they got for me. It was beautiful, unlike any dress I'd seen before. Most were extremely traditional, with high collars, itchy lace, and heavy arm drapings, but this...this was light, bright, and flowed in the air. I caught myself wondering what Tracer would do when he saw it.

Oh, please, I told myself, *don't get all mushy. He's a guy friend. You don't date guy friends that can barely look you in the eye and are too shy to say you look nice.*

And yet, it felt compelling. But I'd never had a boyfriend. My relationships were strung out as it was. I couldn't risk trying, inevitably failing, and having awkward silence at the lunch table until one of us left, as that would just ruin everything.

So, we were stuck until one of us figured out what to do. If tonight went as wonderfully as it possibly could. Which it wouldn't.

"Aww, *Mom,* do I *hafta* wear this? It's stupid!"

Tracer fidgeted again as his mom straightened out the frock coat. He hated the way it looked: it was dark green on the outside, and the bowtie was light yellow. He was supposed to be corn. Tracer hated corn. At least looking like it.

"Moooommm, this is *stupid*! Why do I hafta wear this? It's *ugly*."

His mother stopped in front of him, still adjusting his suit. Tracer knew she didn't mind his protests, but it still hurt him when she smiled, stood on her toes, and kissed him on the cheek. She told him he looked like his father, and that all the girls would think he was handsome.

He thanked her for lending him the suit and watched as she left his small room. The house was very quiet despite the fact he had a younger brother obsessed with obnoxiously loud video games. He was getting ready, too, with their mom's help. But even in the deep quiet, his mom wouldn't understand if he called after her now to say he only cared about one girl to think well of him. The first reason he didn't was because there was no way on God's green earth that he would let his brother hear that. The second was that his mom wouldn't understand anything he said at all.

She was deaf.

"Oh, Honey...you look wonderful!"

I spun around for Mom a few minutes before we had to leave just as Dad walked in. He'd been taking a nap after a long shift, and he stared at me for a minute.

"Am I still dreaming, or is that my little lady?" he asked.

I laughed as Dad shook his head in mock distress and left to put on his suit. I heard him mutter, "Can't leave the house," as he shut the bedroom door.

"Emma! Emma!" cried Ashlee, racing around a corner with Umala giggling in her stroller. She slammed into my leg and sent Umala doing doughnuts down the hall, stopping abruptly in front of a door. Mom, of course, ran to see if Ume was okay, and right as she reached the stroller, Ashlee tugged my arm.

"We won't have another chance to speak. When the time is right, give this to the little black bird. *Don't lose it.*"

She slipped something into my hand and skipped away, her little pink, white, and brown-flowered dress billowing out behind her as she landed. Dad came out of the bedroom in a dapper, green-striped suit and a black-spotted red tie. If it wasn't obvious enough, he said he was a watermelon. Mom laughed and took his arm, her daffodil dress sparkling with dewdrops. I couldn't help but smile, too.

As everyone got in the carriage, I took a peek at the thing in my hand.

It sparkled red.

The ride was nice enough, but it was slower than normal: we had to avoid the smoke layer over us. It had really bogged down yesterday, so everyone was hoping it would clear up tonight when some of the storm's headwinds blew through. The air was very still at the time; nevertheless, I had to check my hair every now and then to make sure it wasn't exploding out of its bun. When it was, I just told it to fix itself and it did. But I fussed with my hands to hide that. Sometimes I wonder if I'd gotten *too* good at hiding things. Even from myself.

We heard the music in the air long before we landed. Far beneath us, in the open field on the island splitting the river and housing Sky-glass, lights twinkled in the growing dimness. Tents had been set up all over for food and drink and games and crop contests. Kids could go on bunny rides and race through mazes. There was vegetable carving, and carnival games, and even miniature roller coasters. But the big prize was the dance floor, lined with spiderweb trellises and illuminated by fireflies.

That was for everyone else, though. The teen party was in a small, stout tree within earshot of the main Festival. The path leading the way was traced out with colored lanterns, and shadows danced around the entrance from the disco lights inside. Of course, the final touch for the outside of the tree was a huge balcony for couples who didn't want to weird anybody out by kissing while inside.

But, there weren't a lot of those kinds of couples. Way too awkward.

We had a smooth landing, and we wandered as a family a bit through the festivities. Ashlee and Umala liked the jugglers and the candy apples and candy corn and cotton candy and all manner of sweets and the stands with brightly colored toys. Animal rides, the Hall of Mirrors, and a few small roller coasters provided more entertainment, stuff I'd enjoyed for years. For adults, there was the Hammer Smash, the arm-wrestling competition, and pie-eating contests. Giant carts displayed food and crops, especially squash, including a pumpkin that had to be the size of four carriages put together. It was all good fun, of course, but I'd seen the likes of it every year. Now that I was fifteen, I wanted to go have a "big kid" party with kids my age.

With friends.

Finally, the hour came when the dances would start. I could sense a growing tension in the atmosphere, something I couldn't see. But I got permission to head off to the teen party, which I readily looked forward to, but not for the music. Most of the stuff my peers loved was pretty awful, but some of it was decent. Besides, music with bad language or ideas was banned from being played publicly under any circumstances a few years earlier. Worst-case scenario: I'd hate everything, not find anybody nice to be with, and leave early.

And face the next big crisis of busting into a high-tech jail and getting out of the night alive.

No pressure.

I followed a darkly dressed couple down the lantern-lined path to the tree. The night made everything seem very lonely. Eighty degrees was far from cool, but I got goose bumps looking at the storm. What a night it would be.

Up ahead I saw a gathering of others in the path surrounding the entrance to the dance. Most were overdressed for the heat, but there were costume regulations. There were two security officers and one ticket person. I waited my time in line, occasionally hearing jeers by school jerks from behind me, but I ignored them. The only thing I cared about was getting inside without having my head lopped off by the guy whirling ninja stars around in front of me.

I forced myself to relax as the ticket guy took mine, and the Guards looked me over for security. I swear the smaller one of the two watched me walk in, and it felt like the kind of stare I knew too well. But I shook it off, attributing it to their creepy helmets, and attempted to act natural and look like I was having a good time.

The hollow under the tree was enormous, spanning at least the size of the cafeteria back at Moonbeam Academy. There were different colored lights flashing from the ceiling, some spinning back and forth, and a strobe that came on once in a while when the music called for it. It was all a blur of shadows in dresses and costume suits, all bouncing around to the beat. Everyone looked the same, and I kept close to the walls to make sure I was actually getting somewhere.

Somebody bumped into me and yelled, "Watch it!" I kept my head low and avoided eye contact. Though everyone was staring at each other or the floor or at the blur they made by shaking their heads back and forth, it felt like I was being watched from all directions. It was like an itch you can't reach. I searched for any break in the continuity of the sea I was trapped in.

There was a cluster off toward the side I thought I recognized. I worked my way ahead and found what I was looking for.

A colony. A nerd colony.

"Did she say she was coming?" asked Falcon. He stared out into the sea of masqueraders. Tracer, Kael, Wayk, and Gator had just barely managed to find each other about fifteen minutes earlier, even though the party had only just started. The lights reflecting off the walls were hypnotizing and made it almost impossible to recognize anybody in the room. It had been particularly hard to find Wayk: he was dressed as a black jaguar. Besides the fact that nobody could have possibly heard him under normal circumstances, he disappeared in the darkness. There was a lot of darkness. Sometimes Falcon forgot Wayk was right beside him.

Like right then.

He jumped when Wayk replied, "Yeah, she did. Remember at lunch?"

"Uh, Wayk, about a billion-and-a-half things happened around lunchtime that I can't even *try* to explain, so, *no, I don't* remember!"

"Oh. Right. Fire bombs, teleporting, and"—gesturing to Tracer—"nearly getting your brains shot out of your head."

"Shut up already!" growled Tracer. "Don't blow our cover!"

Kael scowled. "I'm pretty sure you already did with that costume, man! That thing is *ancient!*"

"Oh, shut it. I didn't have anything else to wear, okay? Are we *sure* she's coming?" wondered Tracer. He looked around the crowd again, peering over heads for anybody not bouncing up and down. It was dark and hazy from the fog maker, and lights blinded him in every color. The people flashed like an original motion picture with the strobe, pulsating its ultra-whiteness. Tracer couldn't stand it anymore and looked away to the side, where the lights swept the edge of the room and lit the gaps around the massive, pillar-like support roots.

Then he saw someone. Someone he thought was more beautiful than the sun or the stars or the jewels in the earth.

She was wearing a deep-blue, daylily dress, with indigo springing up in bright streaks from the bottom. Across the top were splashes of dark purple and blue, flaring out like tiny petals. A gold ribbon circled the middle, fluttering in the air. Down the center to the waist was accentuated with sparkling, white gems, and the funny little strands in the center of the flower laced over her shoulders and crossed between her wings. Her reddish-blond hair spilled over her right shoulder like a waterfall, tied by a sprig of multicolored feathers. Just below her neck sat a dark, swirly pendant on a brown-beaded chain, and her eyes...

In the few seconds it took for Tracer to take in all the beauty of this girl, she had walked almost all the way over. A white light flooded around her from behind, but he didn't blink. He couldn't.

"Hey, guys!" said Emmaline.

Even though the heels on my shoes weren't exactly high, I felt a lot taller as I walked over to my friends. Just as I predicted, Tracer stared unblinking for a second, then quickly dropped his gaze, either unwilling or unable to speak. It wasn't often I dressed up. There was too much to focus on at school. But now, I didn't even know how I was going to get a job after that encounter with Mr. D'Uno. Beating up a potential boss to try to help a potential coworker generally doesn't help your chances of getting accepted. In fact, I hadn't bothered to go back and try again for any job. Something was closing in on me, a foreboding future. *Not now.*

"Wow, you look great, Emma!" said Wayk, melting out of the darkness as a light passed behind him. It wasn't often he said anything, but when he did, he was gracious and kind.

"Yeah, you look really nice," added Gator with a slight bow, as was his manner, followed by Falcon's agreeing comment of "Yeah." Kael nodded his head as he cleaned his glasses on his coat. He'd managed to pull off a rather convincing potato with a mix-up of the raggedy, dark-colored clothes he usually wore. Tracer glanced at me once or twice but didn't look me straight on when I looked back.

"Hi," I said, waving my hand. "I'm here."

"Uh...I know. I saw you."

I nodded. "Just checking."

Everyone shifted nervously as the song changed. "Fudge, I hate this song," grumbled Tracer. The song "I Kissed a Squirrel and I Liked It" blared through the speakers as red lasers started zipping through the air.

"Anyone seen the Shadow?" I asked, breaking the not-so-silent silence. As we looked around our island cluster of solitude, I spotted an odd figure darting around the crowd. It was dark and small and raced through the middle to one side of the room. A Guard.

"I'm right here."

My heart froze for a millisecond as we jumped. Shadela stepped out from behind one of the many support roots of the tree. I shuddered: her gothic dress made me think of a great black spider, wrapped up in her own web.

Her eyes glinted in the dancing lights of the room. The way she blended into everything else, even with the lights flashing over her silver-lined dress, freaked me out, besides the fact her mask was black lace and shaped like a web. I had despised her for my whole life, and she made it hard to not continue to do so. Not to mention the fact that her favorite creature was the black widow.

"Well? Whatcha all starin' at?"

Right. We're still supposed to hate each other.

"Your face," I muttered. "Now that you got a mask on, the mirrors stopped breaking."

She gave me the Evil Eye. I couldn't tell if she was still playing or if this was real. Had any of that stuff, the good—well, not good, but better than the troll snot before—had any of that actually happened? Had anything changed? A pang struck my heart as I remembered Sam. *Lord, I miss her friendship.*

Shadela slid by me, bumping my shoulder. "Freak," she muttered. Then she vanished into the sea of arms.

Ouch. So she's still a mean girl. Or pretending really well.

I tried to forget that word. Freak. That one word that I feared was true. Actually, I knew it was true. What else could I be?

"C'mon, guys," I said without conviction. "Let's party."

We all acted relatively happy and excited, but I knew none of us was really thinking about the dance as we vanished into the crowd.

The sea's waves continued, and light glistened over the surface.

Raven collapsed on the ground. He could finally sleep. It was his off-shift now.

But what sleep was there? All sorts of horrible noises reverberated in the corridors and echoed in the chambers. He barely managed to sleep before, but now it was pure exhaustion that put him under. Raven breathed deep and sound. He hadn't even reached his crevice of a bed.

All the other boys in his shift were copies of him. A few older ones held little ones in their laps, in an effort to produce some kind of comfort level worthy of rest. The bangs and pings of metal being hammered and shaped rang down the passages, and the crack of the whip over newly awakened heads filled the dreams of the sleepers. They twitched and moaned in unison, and there was no peace in their dreams.

But they had to sleep. They had to rest. They had to be ready.

Ready to face it all over again in fifty-seven minutes.

The dance was chaos. With flaring lights, booming bass beats, and the continuous swaying of people, it added to the perfect scenario for hypnosis. I couldn't have survived suffocation in that crowd for more than ten minutes before I stumbled off to the side and leaned up against a root. I phased in and out, again and again, seeing wisps of fragments of things I'd seen a million times before: a girl on a gray hillside, unmoving; a red curtain billowing in the breeze; drops of blood trailing down a hall; a hallway of mysterious lights and doors; the girl in the red dress holding the saber knife above the firestorm.

Then a small boy in dirty clothes on the floor getting kicked in the ribs by a boot.

My head pounded. The air was stifling, and I couldn't see straight. I got a horrible pain in my side and I started panicking. I slipped away to the very edge of the room and followed the veined wall to the nearest door to the balcony.

The air that spilled over me felt like a cold shower. I needed that. Bad. It was hotter than Hades in that mosh pit.

The balcony rails were suspended by thick ropes of ivy that reached to the top of the not-so-tall tree. I grabbed one of them as my knees buckled, trying to stay on my feet, and looked up. One moon flew high in the sky, the other grazing the mountaintops. The stars glistened at their brightest that night, and I could see part of the galaxy in a great band of blue and purple and pink across the sky.

My breath found me again, and my muscles relaxed, regaining their stability. The air was cool and damp with river mist, and the breeze teased the blond highlights that had escaped my brush. My hair drifted politely into view and floated about, calm and unworried about the coming insanity. I breathed deeply and closed my eyes, listening to the music of the violins and harps of the Festival and the wind in the trees. I could imagine Mom and Dad spinning around, laughing, and Ashlee and Umala looking on from the side, clapping their hands. The Spirit cloaked me in peace.

Footsteps alerted me of someone else. A boy in a dark green suit stumbled out of the doorway, and a chorus of raucous laughter bellowed after him. His face was deep red, and he curled his hands in and out of fists. The noise level died back to normal, and the boy, after starting back in and coming out again several times, forced himself away from the door and walked to the edge. He bent over partially, flexing his grip on the rail, and breathed heavily with foul wishes for his offenders hissing between his teeth. I knew that feeling: the internal pressure of trying to choose between running back in to pummel someone or getting out of there entirely and heading for the hills.

He stayed like that for about ten seconds before he noticed he wasn't the only one on the balcony. I knew that face. He waved.

"Hey, Emma."

"Hey, Tracer."

He released his grip after a moment, but seemed embarrassed to be caught like that only a few feet away. I felt the same. The moonlight washed over us, and as we meandered closer to each other, I could see the refractions of the gems on my dress making tiny points of light on his suit.

"Are you alright?" I asked gently.

Tracer shook his head, looking off to the side. "Ah...no, not exactly." His face flushed red again, and I noticed that the yellow bowtie was gone, and his shirt was ruffled up. "There were just, um," he waved his hand back towards one of the doors, "there were just some jerks saying a load a' dung beetles about...stuff." He thumped his fist on the railing, and I could feel the anger he was controlling in the pack it carried.

"They're stupid," I reassured. "They think it's funny to hurt other people. It's hard not to want to hurt them back." He glanced at my hands as my knuckles popped. I glanced back at the party and did a double take.

"What?" he asked, following my eyes.

"I...nothing. I just thought I saw...somebody over there. Someone I saw running around earlier. Never mind. I'm just going crazy. But I guess you know that already, huh?"

He half grinned. "What, you mean with all your superpowers and stuff?" he asked, gesturing wildly. I grinned for real. "Yeah, 'cause it's totally normal to set your own hands on fire without the benefit of matches, right?" We snickered for a moment then stared out into the golden lights of the moons and the stars.

"You think it'll work?" he asked, looking at me. I stared down at my hands.

What am I supposed to say?

"Emma?"

Tracer wanted an answer. I fidgeted and gripped the railing harder. "It has to work."

He nodded, glancing at my hands. I realized I was white-knuckling and let go.

"Are you alright?" he asked me, watching my face carefully. Over time, I'd learned that Tracer was just as observant and attentive to detail, not to mention as caring, if not more so. His bright-blue eyes reminded me of my dad's: deep and understanding.

"I...uh...I'm fine. Fine. *What* am I saying? Of course I'm not. You can't be fine when the world is swirling around you and all you want to do is the right thing. Aw, geez, I can't think, I can't sleep, I can't stop acting like everything's okay...Lord knows how much I wish it would all just *stop* for once...what I wouldn't give..." I gave a small laugh, but only to keep the tears in. My hand shook as I pushed a strand of hair back. Tracer watched my face for a long moment. I finally looked back and gave a shaky smile. "I'll, um...I'll be alright. Once it's over."

We looked away at the same time. The air was cooler than I thought it would be; it had to be part of the system coming with the storm. I stared at the tall grasses rustling around below us, trying not to glance back every time Tracer glanced at me. He drummed his fingers on the railing. It was desperately quiet. It made me think too much. And the more I thought, the closer I got to going nuts.

My hands shook so hard, they made my arms shake, too. I remembered a girl in a red party dress stood on the brink of a ledge, staring down into an abyss of fire. I remembered how the smoke was made of screams, and the saber knife glinted scarlet, made of the red liquid that kept us alive. I remembered how there was no life in the dark-haired girl, or in the wings flaring out in flame and darkness...

Something touched my hand.

"Emmaline. It's going to be okay." Tracer looked into my soul.

I nearly lost it then. He had no idea. I already knew the outcome of this night. The thought came to me that perhaps these visions were self-fulfilling. But then, I still had freedom of choice.

Right?

I took a shaky breath and smiled. "Thanks, Trace." He smiled, gently let go of my hand, blushed, and dove into some deep thoughts. We watched a charm of hummingbirds fly by on the way to get nectar from the river flowers.

Tracer glanced at me again. "That's a cool necklace."

I picked it up. "Thanks. It's one of my favorites from my dad; he got it on a business trip. It's an ammonite fossil, some kind of snail creature from the dinosaur times." I realized I was rambling and shut up.

"Am-min-ate?" he repeated.

I smiled. "Am-mon-*ite.*"

"Am-man-ite," he tried again.

"Close enough." I grinned. He nodded, said "cool," and lapsed into silence again. The seconds were years. The breeze rustled the leaves of the vines, and the starlight twinkled through them. I watched them and the wisps of cloud drifting by, trying to keep calm and my heart from exploding out of my throat.

"Hey," Tracer started, coming out of his contemplation, "I wanna show you something." He pulled out his phone and started swiping the screen. "Remember how I got that game the other day? I showed you at lunch."

I grinned wryly. "You mean that one where you use some kind of bug to kill off the city?"

"Yeah, Mega-Plague 4. It's got, like, a million upgrades for everything, but I'm almost done."

"I thought you just got that a few days ago."

He grinned. "I did."

I stared, dumbfounded. "Is that *all* you do during the summer?"

"What? *No!* I do other stuff too."

"Like what?" I watched as the game loaded.

"Uh...*it doesn't matter! Stop asking questions!*" Tracer loved getting fake-mad at people. He made weird voices when he did. I smiled as he started playing and then panicking when a city region would notice and start making a cure.

"No! Stupid scientists! Die!"

Tracer loved talking about video games. It was the one thing he could talk about without getting nervous. That and superheroes.

"...see, now that most of the area's infected, I can make it start doing stuff without them fighting it off. See, I can make it cause heart failure, paralysis, respiratory problems, organ failure..."

"That's nice," I commented sarcastically.

"...and one more symptom: sneezing!"

My face exploded and I laughed my head off. I clung to the railing to keep from falling over. He grinned widely to see such a turn-around. "Didn't see that one coming!" I choked out. He made the game double-time. Red lines zipped across the screen and regions turned dark red, then black.

A wave of murkiness overcame me. It was dark. I couldn't breathe. I was wet. A tank. They were shoving my head into a tank. Of water. My heart pounded, starving for air. Red. Red around my face. They pulled me up. Air. By the hair. Gasping. Water. Red. Running down my face. Gasping for air. Water. Underwater. Couldn't breathe. Screaming. Up again. Screaming. High.

A young boy. Screaming. In a cave. Dark. A tank of water. Guards. Yelling.

Tell us what you know. Tell us right now.

A young boy screaming in a dark cave. Guards. A water tank. Couldn't breathe.

Raven.

"Emma! Emma! Hey! Snap out of it! Emma!"

I was crumpled against the vine column when my eyes refocused. Tracer was shaking my shoulder, his expression one of terror. His touch was delicate enough to suggest that he was afraid I might crumple like a rose petal underneath it.

Heat surged up my face. That was before I saw the faces crowding the window. Snickering, commenting, speculating. I stood up quickly, brushing leaves off my arm. "I'm fine, Tracer," I said hollowly, walking to the door. I pushed my way past the people standing in my way and became surrounded by jeering faces. Tracer followed behind at enough of a distance to prove we weren't officially together. Somebody wolf-whistled as I pushed through. People pressed in on us. Someone called, "Hey, Emma, you know that meerkats and minks are *related*, right?"

"He asked you out on a date yet?" another catcalled.

I knew we were both red in the face, but I don't think mine was so much from embarrassment. Somehow I got pushed into the middle of the room where there was a huge circle. They had made a dancing arena and were trying to get us in there.

Not. Cool.

Nobody could see it, but my blood was getting very, very hot.

Tracer felt fear. He just didn't like to show it. But when Emmaline started breathing weird and her glazed eyes darted around, looking at something that wasn't there, Tracer got freaked out. *What do you do when somebody has a vision?*

He was afraid to touch her. Would she lash out like a sleepwalker or think he was trying to hurt her? They were good friends but not too close. Theirs was one of his most valued relationships. He didn't want to lose it, but he had to help Emma. She still held onto the rail, but her arms were twitching, like she was trying to fight off something.

"Emma? Hey, Emma! Are you okay?" Tracer tapped her shoulder, ever so lightly.

Emmaline was almost coughing, like she was choking. Her head jerked back and forth, but not in a head shake to say no. She made funny noises, like her mouth was covered by something, and her eyes squeezed shut. She slipped sideways, falling into the railing. He caught her by the shoulder as carefully as he could.

"Emma! Emma! Hey! Snap out of it! Emma!"

Her eyes opened suddenly, and he could tell she was coming back. She shook under his touch, and when she met his gaze, her face flushed a deep, strawberry pink. Then she looked away, and when he looked back, he saw half of the kids from their old school staring at them through the window. Jeering. Sneering.

Ah, nuggets. Now they're gonna think we were gonna kiss. I hate crowds.

Emmaline slipped away from him and headed straight through the crowd of peepers. Tracer realized with great chagrin that there was only one way out, save jumping off the balcony. He followed after her at a distance.

Just as he reached a more open spot where he could see both Emma and the door, Waximitt St'ail stepped into his way. "Hey, T-man, you goin' somewhere? Tryin' to get back with yer girlfriend?" Wax moved closer, always grinning stupidly. He loved to bug people, but this was torture and intrusion. And Wax knew it.

"Get outta my way, moron," growled Tracer, disgust written across his face.

"Or *what*, T-man? You gonna hit me, you big showoff? Huh? Huh?" Wax shoved him back. Tracer realized he was stuck in a big circle of partygoers, most of them sneering.

"No. I will."

Wax turned and found Emmaline in his face, wings flared up in multicolored splendor. Tracer wanted to tell her not to fight Wax, but the look on her face told him to keep his mouth shut. He'd only seen it once or twice when he had insulted one of her favorite superheroes, Thunder, and it had scared him then.

"Sorry," scoffed Wax. "I don't fight girls." He glanced at Tracer, and if it was possible, an even more devious grin crawled across his face. Wax added, "Especially the *pretty ones.*" He reached for Emma's face.

Tracer lunged for Wax, but his cronies grabbed his arms. It took four or five of them to keep him back. He struggled to get away but relented when he saw the calm, stoic expression on Emma's face.

When Wax's hand was just inches from her face, Emma said, "Touch me and you're dead." Her wings twitched ominously, hands curling.

"Zat so, babe?" He glanced deviously at Tracer, his hand suspended in midair. He looked back at Emmaline, drawing closer and reaching again, this time for the back of her neck. Emma didn't blink.

He's going to try to kiss her! Tracer surged unsuccessfully, trying to escape the grip of Wax's minions just as Wax drawled, "Why not just *one little dan—*"

The crack of Wax's nose made everyone flinch, but what followed made them gasp. He didn't stop sliding through the crowd until he hit the sound equipment, leaving a streak of red behind him. The room was filled with silence, and his curses reached every crevice and hollow where people were hiding and making out. Everyone's attention was on the arena in the middle, shifting slowly between Waximitt and Emmaline.

"That's right, turdface," retorted Emma. "Why don't you go wash up in a toilet?"

"Hey!" whined somebody. "Don't be mean!"

Oh, dang, that was so not the right thing to say, thought Tracer. He tried wrestling his way out of the grip of Wax's henchmen, but they stayed firm.

"Oh, so now *I* can't be mean?" yelled Emmaline, her face contorting in unmatched fury. She turned slowly, facing each area of the circle. "So I don't get an excuse to be ticked off? I can't stand up to people, huh? Like you guys were all nice to me!" She laughed coldly. It sent shivers down Tracer's spine.

"Shut up, Emmaline! Nobody cares what you think, Teacher's Pet!" called Wax, wiping his bloody nose on his black sleeve as he stood up.

"Unless you want quick answers to absurdly easy homework," she jeered back. Tracer wondered if she was really herself. This wasn't the Emmaline he knew. But then again, there were a lot of things about Emma he didn't know until the day before.

"Get over it, nerd girl! You just study all the time because you don't have any friends!"

"That's a lie and you darn well know it, prunehead! Now shut it and let us out before I give you another!"

Wax grinned a mouthful of shark's teeth. "So you are together, aren't you? Yo, T-man, you asked her out yet? Huh? C'mon, man, she's *right here!* Ask already!"

Someone started chanting, "Ask her out. Ask her out."

Tracer's face grew hot. He could tell they wouldn't let either of them out until he did.

"Ask her out. Ask her out."

He glanced at Emma. Her face was turning red, too, but from more than embarrassment.

"Ask her out. Ask her out."

He struggled to find words, angry to be trapped like this. How was he supposed to say it when he didn't want to? Not in front of *these* people.

"Ask her out. Ask her out."

Tracer watched Emmaline, silently begging for ideas to get out of it. Her hand curled.

Boom.

The strobe light blew out, and sparks rained down on a screaming mob of teenagers. A multicolored globe exploded and then a set of hypno-lights. They went out like metallic popcorn, spraying gold light everywhere, until only the emergency lights from the door remained. Girls screamed as their hair was burned, and the fog maker spewed smoke. In seconds, the room was a dark, smoky whirl of adolescents running to get out and to get air. Tracer coughed and with his captors gone, he searched for Emma. He couldn't see anybody until he ran into Falcon.

"What's going on?" Falcon choked, leaning up against a root. "I couldn't see anything!"

"I dunno. One second she's there, next second all Hell breaks loose!" yelled Tracer. Kael, Wayk, and Gator melted out of the chaotic crowd. "Where's Emmaline?" Wayk repeated. They stuck their heads around the group of roots they were pinned by. "I don't see her!"

"Up here!"

Emma dropped down from the ceiling. Tracer noted again that she didn't move her wings. She grabbed his hand and Falcon's, and the rest instinctively grabbed each other's. He saw her glance at the ceiling, and as a new wave of people jostled by the root wall, she Shifted.

CHAPTER ELEVEN

AMBUSH

Shadela smirked as she watched Emma's reactions. It still gave her a thrill to watch Emmaline get annoyed. That was why she'd done it to her so much in school. It was insensitive, rude, and downright stupid. But she couldn't help herself. Emma's response was always priceless, the "perfect princess" of good against the forces of evil.

Masking her voice, she started the chant of "Ask her out" just to see what Emma would do. Shadela knew that Tracer would never have the guts to ask her, even if he meant it. She saw Emma's hands curl, and then the lights exploded.

Typical. If you can't win, cheat.

Shadela loved cheating.

Trimont and Exelor were soaring in the night sky, and their light made double shadows of every bush, every branch, every member of the ragged-around-the-edges party.

"I'm getting too old for this," moaned Wayk, rubbing his head where he'd clocked it on the ground.

"Dude, you're *fifteen.* If you call that old, what do you call young?" asked Falcon. "And don't say *your face,* 'cause that just doesn't work."

"Fine. I won't," replied Wayk. "But someone else will."

Tracer slogged out of a tributary of the river. His suit had seen better days, but it didn't look beyond salvation. He tried rubbing water off his face but rubbed it back on with his soaking sleeve.

"Yo, Tracer!" called Kael, always ready for an argument. "Whatcha tryin' to do, morph into a fish or something?"

"Oh, shut your face," he growled, plopping onto a rock. Water oozed out from his clothes. "Ha!" said Wayk, grinning. "Told you somebody would say it."

"He didn't even say that to me!" protested Falcon.

"Hey, man, how do you think *I* feel? I'm the one tryin' to getcha all through the space–time continuum without rippin' you all in half!" Emmaline groaned and sat promptly on a nearby wall by a rock pillar, her head tipping back and forth like she was dreaming. She reached back to rub her head, felt something, and brought her hand in front of her.

"Oh."

Attention turned to her vaguely at first, then quickly with alarm. Emmaline's hand was covered in a shiny liquid, and dark streaks ran down her arm.

➤➤➤➤ ⟵⟵⟵⟵

"Dear God, what did you do to your hand, Emma?" cried Falcon, who stumbled over to me, despite his twisted ankle.

I felt lightheaded. I wasn't afraid of blood as much as my mom, but Shifting on top of that didn't help. "Anybody have a bandage?" I murmured blankly, leaning back onto another rock. Why did my head bother me so much?

"Wha's goin' on?" asked Tracer, slipping off his rock. Kael and Wayk started dragging themselves over. My head hurt more.

"Emma split her knuckles when she hit Wax."

"*Emma hit Wax?*" exclaimed Kael.

"In da face!" I gestured gleefully, swinging my hand out to punch the air. "Ow." More liquid ran over my hand. It fell on the rock and made little colored dots. My head swirled again.

Falcon looked around at the disoriented crew. "Anyone got a bandage of any sort?"

"I think I do," said Gator, as he fumbled around in his brown, scaly suit. Tracer struggled to untangle himself from a bush. "Dang it!" he muttered. "Now my suit's soaking wet *and* covered in leaves." My vision was distorted, and it felt like I was looking at the world from outside of my own head. Falcon said something about keeping my hand above my heart.

"Hee, hee, lookit Tracer. He looks like a mermaid," I apparently said. I don't actually remember saying it, and I don't even *know* where it came from. Maybe it was because he was soaked. The dark stuff tickled as it trickled down my arm.

"Hey, good thinking, Tracer! Go get water from the stream. We hafta wash this off," hollered Falcon.

I heard Tracer mutter, "Aw, *man*..." before he turned around. He grabbed a bucket hanging from a nearby tree. I couldn't see straight.

"Why does my head hurt?" I asked nobody in particular.

Gator tripped over a rock on his way over. "Here's a handkerchief."

"Did you use it?" glared Falcon.

"Yeah, Falcon, I'd give you a used, goobered-up handkerchief to wrap her hand with!" Gator looked peeved. I smiled.

"Thanks, Alligator. Heh, heh, ali-gator. Lee-gator. Leg-eater. Heh, heh, you're a leg-eater..."

My head hurt again, and I shut my eyes.

"Why is she saying random stuff?" I heard Gator ask.

"Dunno, maybe it's a side effect of, uh, whatcha call it, Shifting. She said her head hurts, too. Hey, Emma, keep that hand higher. I'm going to check your head, okay?" said Falcon.

"Okay," I sang. I set my elbow on the rock and watched red drops have a race down the track of my arm. "Pretty colors..." I murmured. Falcon gently tilted my head from side to side, inspecting. I'd forgotten his mom was a doctor. I'd also forgotten to keep my hand up again. Falcon stepped back, shrugging. "I don't see anything. Maybe she got a concussion or something."

Tracer dripped his way back from the river with the bucket. Wayk had finally made it over from the rocks by the river, a moving shadow in his costume, and Kael offered to take the bucket from Tracer.

"Nah, I got it."

"Well, too bad, I'm helpin' ya!" He grabbed another part of the handle and towed it along. "Geez, you don't hafta be so mean about it!" said Tracer, half smiling. He glanced at me and his smile disappeared.

"What's behind her ear?"

"S'called hair, Tracer." I didn't know why I was slurring, but I felt stupid. I sounded like I'd had one too many at the pub or something.

"Not *that*," he said, kindly ignoring the slight. "The gold thing."

I reached back with my good hand to investigate as Falcon got the handkerchief wet. He took my arm gently and held it over the pail.

"Kay, Emma, this is gonna hurt like—"

"—a mother's monkey!" I finished. Everyone looked at me like, "Say *what?*" I laughed at them. Falcon said, "Ohh-kaaayyy..." and squeezed water onto my right hand just as I pulled the thing out from behind my ear.

"Oh...so *that's* where I put it! Plum forgot," I said, staring at a red and gold star in my hand. It almost seemed alive as the water ran over my hand. Falcon glanced at me. "Doesn't that hurt?"

"Uh...no." My head felt clearer from staring at the red diamond in my hand.

"Where'd you get that?" asked Tracer, enthralled.

Falcon rinsed my hand off and wiped down my arm.

"The library. Well, not exactly. I don't know. It was a present. Sort of."

"That's weird," said Falcon. "I don't see a cut anywhere." He turned my hand back and forth, glittering from the moonlight. It was a tad red, but otherwise fine.

"Huh." I pulled my hand back and checked it out. That just didn't sound right. It had been throbbing just moments earlier.

"Man, Emma, you must'a really clocked 'im!" Kael grinned his approval.

I nodded, not agreeing on the inside. "Yeah, it felt pretty good."

"Not good, Emma, *epic!*" Tracer made an evil face, but his dramatic expression quickly gave way to his naturally enormous smile.

I took Falcon's hand and stood up. "Thank you for your doctoring, sir!" I mock saluted him. The smiles breaking across the faces of the other boys showed my efforts to diffuse the tension were successful.

"Uh, sure, but I'm not a doctor..."

"Don't bother me with facts, man." I squeezed out Gator's handkerchief. "Sorry to get it all grody."

He nodded. "Eh, it's okay. It's just a handkerchief."

"Well, thanks anyway." I patted his shoulder and wrapped the gold chain back into my hair. I'd hidden it in the band of feathers holding my ponytail.

"So, we're still on?" asked Wayk from the back. He'd been forgotten again.

"Yeah, as soon as we find Shades. Did any of you guys see her again?"

Nobody had.

Sam watched the party from a corner, keeping an eye on Emma. Though it was her duty to keep the partygoers in check, she found it impractical to break up the circle they pushed Emma and her friend, Tracer, into. Something ticked on when Wax reached for Emma. *Pow.* Emma punched him in the nose and sent him sprawling. Despite her protocol to never side with the enemy, she thought, *Nice hit, Emma.* She smiled briefly.

Then protocol flew into her mind, raging about the consequences of even a minor slip-up like that. Sam forced her face back into a blank slate. She was invisible, unmoving, staring between the roots against the walls. Sam was a Guard, not a referee. She remained there until the lights exploded and lost sight of Emma in the rushing river of teens.

⤜⤜⤜⤜ ⤛⤛⤛⤛

A few of the guys looked around to see if Shades would melt into view like last time.

"Do you think she went ahead? To get ready?" Falcon looked perplexed.

I shrugged. "I dunno."

A twig snapped in the bushes. I held up a finger for quiet, peeked over the rock, and realized I'd dumped us on the far side of the multilevel, kiddy, hay-maze fortress. The wind rustled some grasses nearby, and some groups of moving black ran by down the pathway, the last of the stragglers.

Nobody moved for almost a minute. Maybe Guards were searching the area as we breathed. The air was very cold.

"C'mon, guys. It's getting late. Let's head off." I nodded towards the path, but that was too boring. We made some fun out of it by jumping up onto the bales and hopping across the tops, which was quite a feat in heels. Not surprisingly, Gator was the first to slip.

"Aw, dang it," he moaned, landing on the second layer of bales below him. Tracer laughed at him, then tripped and fell down, passing him and hitting the ground. "Quit jinxing people, man!" he scolded, pointing at Gator.

"Get away from my face!" Gator swiped at Tracer.

"You get outta *my* face!" Tracer retorted.

"I was never *in* your face! How can I get out of your face when I was never in it in the first place?" Gator conjectured wildly as he crawled up and over to another wall. Wayk and Falcon grinned as they silently tagged behind.

"Hush up! You're confusing me!" said Tracer, avoiding Gator's query.

"Guys! Will you *chill out*?" I protested. "*Honestly*, you're all going to drive me—*agh!*"

I waved my arms, trying to not fall. Shadela's spidery form stood impatiently around the corner.

Sam stood at attention before the Chief.

"Now, explain to me, Private O'Klurn, why did our fish leave without its tail?"

"Sir?" Sam wasn't experienced to the ever-shifting code language that came with Guard duty.

"Explain the events of tonight, Private. Your job was to tail her. Why did she escape your view?"

"There was an incident, sir, resulting in the majority of attendees fleeing the vicinity. I lost sight of her in the chaos."

Sweat trickled down the sides of her face in the heat of the poorly ventilated office. Security regulations cut office air supply to the Watcher section. No eavesdroppers on the other end of the vent. A fan with a bad blade wobbled back and forth, clicking on the corner of the Chief's desk, feebly waving more stifling air in her direction.

The Chief sat back in his chair and stared at her, his fingers laced in front of his face. Sam tried not to fidget under his gaze. Click. The door creaked open and shut behind her, but she didn't move an inch. The fan wobbled as it blew more warm air towards her. Click. Click.

"Well, I guess it's time we made arrangements for a transfer, isn't it, *Senator?*"

A familiar drawl made the hairs on Sam's neck stand on end. The fan turned to see the newcomer. Click. Click.

"Of course, Chief. It's about time we raised the stakes for our new...*employee.*"

Sam snapped her head around to see a man in a snakeskin suit with glinting gray eyes and grinning with a mouth full of horribly white teeth.

Click. The fan stared at her, trembling. Click. Click.

"Why do you always have to jump out like that?" I gasped, glaring at Shadela.

She smirked deviously. It reminded me of a similar smile that belonged to a guy named Wax who currently had a bloody nose. "They don't call me the Shadow for nothing, you know. Gotta keep up my reputation."

I wanted to say, "With whom, the other goth pixies?"—but I knew what it was like to be stung with that unholy accusation. Instead I said, "Well, we're not them, so you can cut the scare-the-snot-out-ta-ya act and head back home. Change of plans. We're not gonna move until two, okay?" I nodded to the guys. "C'mon, I'm bushed. Let's hit the hay for a few hours."

"Hay is for hummers," Wayk muttered from the darkness.

"Oh, shut your mousetrap, Earthquake!" scolded Tracer. "You've said that a billion times already!"

"Said what?" replied Wayk, one eyebrow raised.

"'Hay is for hummers, dummy!'"

"Well, now I'm not the only one."

Tracer finally added two and two. "Dang it!"

"Fail!" said Gator. Everyone else laughed. Except Shades. She cackled like an old lady.

But I could only smile, rueful of the nightmare I would meet in sleep and of the nightmare I would face when I woke again.

Raven gasped in pain as he reached for the next pipe. The soldier had kicked him three times in the side, but it felt like a hundred. He was so tired.

He yelped when someone jolted his line from below. A couple of bully Guards walked away, snickering. They said something about screams and a girl. Raven released his grip on the rope, trying to move as little as possible. The pulley system suspending him from the ceiling looked precarious enough, besides being rusted over. Occasionally when he reached for something too fast, Raven felt tiny particles fall on him from above.

Afraid he'd be caught not working and get his rope yanked again, Raven took the pipe and placed it carefully in the hole before him. Then he took the trowel and stuck it into the pail fastened to his belt and plastered the stuff around the pipe. He poked the wire into the hole at the end of the pipe and threaded the cork over it to plug it. Another would come around later and tie it and all the others to a long cord.

Some pebbles loosened by a nearby wall-worker hit his head. They weren't given helmets. They were "dispensable." Raven thought he knew what that meant, but he wasn't sure he wanted to be right. Nothing about this was right. None of it added up.

Especially sticking twenty-five pipes into holes in the wall.

After I found my parents waiting around the open-carriage station, I apparently fell asleep on my dad's shoulder. I don't remember any dreams. Just the cold night wind washing around me. Just the light of the fireflies guiding us home. Just the peaceful presence of content and sleepy family members.

Getting ready for bed shortened because of the hour. No reading. No late-night snack. Just a quick shower and into pajamas and into bed. It was pointless for me, of course. I was going to be up and fighting in a few hours, and who knew how dirty I was going to get doing that.

As I tried to fall asleep to the snuffling snores of the hummers outside my window, I heard Mom singing a lullaby to Ash and Ume. It was my favorite, one I missed from childhood when I wasn't plagued by nightmares of death and horror and evil things happening to people I loved. The lyrics followed me into my dreams, guarding me from the demons seeking to drive me beyond the brink.

"You are my Sunshine, my only Sunshine. You make me happy when skies are gray..."

Tracer lay on his bed, listening to the clock tick. He wondered if it was better to be deaf. His mom never complained about the noise when his brother and he made a huge racket. She never noticed when he desperately beat the piano to death. But somehow she could tell when she did one song wrong. It was always her favorite, and she could remember how it sounded. He'd catch her humming it perfectly, despite the fact she couldn't hear it herself anymore. She told him she could feel it in her voice.

Restless, Tracer got up, went to the living room, and sat down at the piano reflecting the moonlight onto the ceiling. For a long time, he'd stopped playing, but he had a new motivation, a secret motivation. He practiced it again to stay awake, knowing his brother wouldn't hear or care. He was too immersed in his video games, or had fallen asleep playing them, and would complain in the morning about the magic being run out.

Tracer didn't need to look up at the pages anymore. He'd memorized it. One day he'd play it perfectly, and that would be the day he would tell her. He sang quietly.

"You'll never know, dear, how much I love you...please don't take my Sunshine away..."

I awoke with a start. It was time.

All my stuff was hidden in the closet and under the bed. I figured if we were sneaking around like ninjas, I should probably dress like one. So, I had black pants, a black tank, a black jacket, and dark boots. Then came the weapons. I loaded up with my bow, my staff, and my hunting knife. I put on the arm and shin guards Dad gave me when we first started training together, admiring the mystical engravings weaving down the sides of them. Not that the armor would do me any good in the long run; it was just for buying time. And some courage, I guess.

I redid my hair into a bun, held tightly by pine needle pins. I put in more than I needed; Pine needles served as decent distracting tools. They hurt as much as a knife without being as deadly. Especially when stabbed between highly susceptible laces. I found that out by accident when Dad wore his boots into my room once and I enthusiastically jabbed at his feet.

Once.

I slid on my helmet, carefully avoiding the pins that I could only see with moonlight. I couldn't turn the light on or somebody would notice. There was a strict no-lights rule, especially before a storm. Nobody wanted a magic shortage when it came to injuries and tree repair.

I paused a moment, looking at myself. This was more like something from the costume party I was just at, not the suit of a warrior. Sure, I had armor and a helmet, but nothing would keep me safe from what I was going to face in the coming hours.

I was fighting my fate. I had seen it. It was inevitable.

And I was doing it anyway.

Maybe you could call that reckless or foolish. And maybe you'd be right.

I called it faith in the One who made me.

Though it may help you to know that I still felt reckless and foolish all the same. You tend to feel that way when you're walking straight into your own death trap.

I waited for about ten minutes after I'd sent the hummers home. I needed to keep my strength up for whatever was going to be inside the mountain, and I'd rather risk getting spotted on a sled than Shifting there and getting my energy cut in two. Frankle and Studbum weren't exactly thrilled about me hitching a ride at two in the morning, but they perked up after some nectar. I kept the sled and hid it in a hollow tree and sent them home back to their nice, warm perches by my window. It hurt to say good-bye. I wasn't sure under what circumstances I would see them again, if ever.

I fingered the feathers at the back of the arrow, ready to draw as footsteps approached. They were cautious and amateur in the art of stealth, but I couldn't take that as proof. I heard the birdcall and whistled back. Out of a dense cluster of bushes came Tracer. He looked exhausted.

"Didn't you sleep at all?" I asked, doing my best to mask a yawn. I unfastened my staff from my pack with my free hand and put some fire at the top for light.

He blinked. "Ah...no, not really. I couldn't. I practiced the piano instead."

"In the middle of the night?"

"Yeah, nobody minds." Tracer finally leaned up against my tree to keep from falling over. "I've been trying forev—" A massive yawn broke his sentence. "—ever to get this one song right."

"Which one?" I was mostly trying to stay awake. Talking helped. Besides, we wouldn't be talking a lot during a full-fledged assault on a heavily fortified military base in the middle of a caved-in mine that everybody knew about and nobody thought to look in for suspicious activity.

Tracer rubbed his eyes. "Yourmuhshungshinagh," he yawned, tipping his head back against the bark.

"Sorry, what'd you say?"

He looked at me. "You Are My Sunshine," he said flat-out, rubbing his eyes, then stared at the moss pile under his feet. "I know...it's kinda stupid."

I was shocked. "Are you kidding? That is *not* stupid! It's one of the most wonderful songs ever written. Mom always sang us to sleep with it."

He smiled disbelievingly. "Really? Mine, too!"

Somebody said "ow" and there was a sound of a body crunching through a bush. After some muffled groans, there was another birdcall. I whistled back. So did Tracer.

There were stomping sounds, and Gator plodded around a tree, sticks and leaves sticking off his clothes and out of his hair. He didn't look in the mood for jokes. Neither of us offered any. Mostly we talked about sleep, reminiscing the sweet softness of our sheets and the warmth of our pillows and if only we could be back in them.

Over the next ten minutes, Falcon, Wayk, Kael, and Shades showed up. As expected, they were all hashed. I wasn't quite as much as them. I was used to being awakened in the middle of the night. Shades didn't seem too daunted either. I wondered what sort of mischief she did when everyone else slept soundly.

On the way through the forest, we found a Guinolia fruit tree, reminding me of the math classroom with Mrs. Plumbottle and extensionals. The fruit was well known for being jam-packed full of vitamins and energy, way better than any sugar cocktail that kids were addicted to in school. We ate some and felt much better off. It was weird: you could smash it with a hammer and not leave a dent, but if you grabbed it in both hands like a football and pulled lengthwise where the laces would be, it opened without any resistance whatsoever. Wackadoo.

Bleariness chased from our brains, we set forth on our mission. Shades led us through the forest for about ten or fifteen minutes and across a meadow of tall grass. At first I thought maybe she was lost, the way she looked around every minute or so, but after a while longer, she pointed out the back entrance from the grove we'd hunkered down in. The door had a very convincing appearance of being unattended and left for rot and ruin, as would be required to deceive the people and keep them from asking questions. A few interesting rock features and plant formations indicated otherwise.

"Camouflage," Shadela confirmed. "I literally ran into one of these guys once before I realized he wasn't a log. Barely got away alive." Half a minute of planning and a swift attack rendered the Guards unfit for duty. Wayk, Falcon, and Tracer helped Shades hide the Guards in the bushes. She took their pass cards and weapons, hand-ing them to Gator and me, and tied them up with some of Kael's rope. Since they just had a shift change, they wouldn't be expected to report in for at least an hour. We didn't need longer than that.

Gator took one of the passes and waved it in front of the door. A light appeared, flashed the card, and disappeared. The door *ka-chunked* open from the inside. Kael grabbed the door handle, motioned a countdown, and opened it.

Inside was a dark staircase leading down a passage we couldn't see. I readied my bow and crept around to the bottom. A strange rolling noise echoed in the hall. There was nobody down the hall, though there were some odd cracks in the wall.

I waved with two fingers to come down, and we moved down the hall. Kael shut the door behind us, but made sure not to close it all the way in the event we should lose the pass cards and be trapped in there. The cracks in the walls, we discovered, were actually openings to rooms, but the rooms just had odd materials in them. We checked them out one by one. Shadela had taught us "the ways of the Order" The Guard order, anyway. She'd picked up more from her dad than any of us had from ours. All guys had to have some form of military service to be a contender for any other kind of work.

I told my head to shut up and focus. My heart pounded inside my chest. My hands were covered in sweat, and my fingers twitched involuntarily, ready for some kind of target, anything, that would alert me that this was it and after that nothing else. I couldn't stand waiting in the darkness, but we couldn't afford anything more than the torch at the end of the tunnel.

The rolling sound came back, and a little kid in a brown suit driving a metal cart full of metal stuff went by on the track. He was small and dirty, but I couldn't save him right then. I was looking for Raven, but however many more there were, I would do my best to save them, too. They had a future. I didn't.

Another kid with an empty cart rolled past much faster. We understood. It was a constant cycle of bringing, dumping, and taking back. If we timed it right, we could follow the track back to the start and look for Raven.

The first boy rolled by again with an empty cart, not even glancing in our direction. I motioned towards the opening. "Must be an enchantment or something," I whispered. "Disguises the tunnel as part of the wall."

They nodded. "Do you think we'll be able to find it again?" worried Wayk from the back.

I nodded. "Don't worry. I think I can take care of that."

Suddenly, the blare of an alarm shattered the chilled air. We all jumped, cowering in the shadows where nobody could see us. The echoes of a Guard bounced down the passageways. It was a shift change for the kids now.

"Quick, let's move. We can slip through unnoticed." I hoped Shades was right and her memory was strong as she led us down the middle of the tracks. "Keep your weapons ready," she ordered unnecessarily. *As if we were just going to stroll in like guests at a party.*

Light broke around the edge of the tunnel. We backed into the wall as a horde of kids and Guards went by, a jumble of cries and whimpers and bellows and orders. It seemed very quiet afterwards.

Shades counted us off, and one by one we rounded the corner. It led to an enormous room full of strange equipment. There were beakers of all sizes and giant pots and cauldron-sort-of-things holding steaming liquids. The chemicals had left pockmarks on the assembly counters. It looked to be a production line for a kind of weaponry, but what kind of magic they were meddling with felt far from friendly. The very scent of the stuff reeked of lies and malice. I knew the others could sense something, too. Shades, as usual, seemed completely and utterly unconcerned with the matter. She seemed preoccupied trying to remember which way led to the slave rooms.

We went down a series of tunnels, narrowly missing Guards multiple times and getting turned 'round and 'round until I couldn't remember which way was out. Realizing it was a network of grids, I began doubting Shades's confidence as being her ego. "You know," I whispered, "if you're lotht, you can jutht athk." (Saying the "s" sound makes an audible hissing sound that will betray your presence, so we made the "th" sound instead.)

"I'm. Not. Lost," replied Shadela, glaring at me. *Great. We've just ended up in another room.* It split off into at least eight other big, dark tunnels from where we stood.

Shades's confidence didn't look quite the same. She squinted, her finger tracing a map that only she could see. Down the hall we came from, boots sounded softly.

"C'mon, we need to go…" I sang nervously. The boots grew louder. It was too loud for there to be just one pair.

"Wait, hang on. We went there and there, and now we go…" Shadela's forehead scrunched in deep thought, her eyes shut. The feet were loud now. It had to be a whole battalion.

"C'mon! We gotta go!" I said a little too loudly. A passing light from one tunnel suddenly stopped, and a man appeared in the doorway. He looked back into our room.

Didn't want to do this, I thought. The arrow hit his shoulder, enough to put him out. A yell followed, but not from him. There were others in that hallway. "Shadela!" I screamed as the organized march of boots broke into a stampede. Torchlight flooded the hall. Her eyes finally flew open.

"This way!" she shouted and sprinted towards a tunnel on the left. Shouts followed us as the Guards came around the corner and found me. I fired as I backpedaled, nabbing three or four before I turned and sprinted for my life's worth. Which wasn't much.

We ran down the tunnel into another room. Somehow the Guards were already there, staring down a tunnel opposite us. Gator, Wayk, and I fired at them from behind while Shades, Falcon, Kael, and Tracer ran behind us to another tunnel. We followed that one and ended up running into more Guards, some of them wounded. It only took me a second to realize these were trick tunnels.

"Guys!" I panted as we ran back the other way with a Guard hot on our tail, "we're going in circles! These don't lead anywhere!"

Kael paused to throw a knife as I ran by. "So which one's right?"

"I dunno! That wasn't my job!" Shadela glanced back at me. "Well, *sorry* for not being perfect," she growled.

We found the room again, the one we'd just left, with still more soldiers. Arrows whizzed past our heads as we ran back. We slid to a stop in the middle of the tunnel where there was a small bumped-out corner room used as a storage area. Wayk and Kael fell back against some rocks, panting.

"You know this is useless, right? They're going to try to close in from both ends!" shouted Falcon. Boots came from one end, and Guards appeared around the corner.

"Not if somebody covers 'em!" Gator answered, shooting one in the elbow. Another tripped over him and hit his head on a rock.

"Guess he surrendered." Tracer smiled wearily, drawn sword wavering from exhaustion. He leaned back against the wall to look around the bend. His head suddenly vanished into the rock, then the rest of him.

"Where'd he go?" asked Wayk. He stared where Tracer had been standing not seconds before.

An arrow whizzed past his ear and vanished where it should've hit the wall. There was a muffled cry from inside the wall. It sounded like, "Ow, marshmallow," or "No, don't follow." I couldn't tell which, but we had no choice.

"It's another enchantment! C'mon, let's go!" I said, feeling the wall for the edge of the door. I found it, and the rock in the wall became a murky gray color under my fingers, an obvious spot to jump through.

We jumped through the door and fell screaming about ten feet on a curved metal slide. I rolled straight over somebody's legs at full speed. Falcon spun around, scraping Tracer with his quiver. Shades, Wayk, and Kael all ran into each other. Gator jabbed himself in the gut with his own sword hilt. A collective grunt followed the brief silence.

"Sorry for hitting you, man," Kael apologized. He'd grazed Tracer's nose on the way down. Tracer just sighed and stared at the ceiling. His sword was half under him.

"Any broken bones? Anyone dead?" asked Shadela, wiping blood off the corner of her mouth with her arm guard. It was engraved with red snake skeletons and gave me the willies.

"I think...I just...coughed up...my spleen," wheezed Wayk. There was barely enough air in his lungs to be heard.

"Sorry." Falcon rolled off his back and groaned as he crunched onto metal. "My wings almost snapped in half, but otherwise I'm good. You, Em?"

"Yeah. Tracer?"

Tracer covered his eyes. "Why didn't you listen?"

"Listen to what?"

"I said *not* to come through!" moaned Tracer, waving his arms feebly. He continued staring at the ceiling. Little red dots raced over his chest.

Aw, son of a bug-eating lunch monkey...

On the metal walkways above us stood forty soldiers, all with lasers at the end of their weapons.

"Didn't see *that* coming, did you, Em?" Shades asked gracelessly.

I shut my eyes. "I'm not perfect, either," I whispered.

The Guards enjoyed searching us. We gave up every last weapon. Every arrow. Every blade. Every stick and stone. Not that there were many left in the first place. And not that we could actually fight off an army from the inside of their fortress. For once in my life, I had no idea what came next.

I only knew that, at best, not all of us would be getting back out.

They cuffed us and pushed us along the passageways with an iron grip. A pair of soldiers to each of us. As if we could fight off one without getting shot by another.

Shadela tipped her head in the signal, asking to attack all at once. I shook my head. No words were safe and neither were actions. My heart pounded. They had metal weapons that I couldn't name; nonetheless, I sensed they were called "guns."

A poke into the brains of one of the soldiers walking me confirmed it. Connected thoughts included "bullet" and "trigger." The soldier glanced around, like there was a fly buzzing around his head. I retreated back into my own mind, disturbed to think that this technology was present without our knowledge. It definitely turned the tables, and I didn't like where they were going.

The next room we entered was massive, and on ledges and walkways stories high, Guards stood at the ready. In the center was a dais with a large desk in the middle. A man sat behind it, facing the chair on the opposite side while looking at something on his desk. Once he saw his new prisoners, he jumped up.

"Ah! So these are the brave warriors, ready to fight to save their friends!" He clapped his hands and rubbed them together as he walked around the end of his desk. "No, wait," he paused. "You're not warriors, and there's only one friend. And actually," he sat on the end of his desk, pointing at us, "only one of you knows him. How intriguing."

He passed his eyes over the group and landed his gaze on me.

"Miss O'Meern! Or may I call you *Emmaline?*"

The man walked down the steps of the dais. "Oh, it's so wonderful to finally meet you!" he exclaimed, smiling, arms open in welcome, like an uncle or an old friend. His hand waved at the Guards. "Come now, we mustn't keep a guest waiting! Release her!"

The Guard whose mind I'd probed put his thumb onto the side of my handcuffs. There was a whirring noise, and a light passed over his thumb. The cuffs came off on their own, and both the soldiers stood by, their expressions as blank as a certain flying coach's face I'd known.

The man with the shark teeth offered his hand to me to climb the stairs. I didn't move. "Well, then," he said, "shall we have a nice chat over a cup of tea, hmm?" The sugary sound of his voice made me want to stab him through the eyeball. The sudden and violent thought startled me, and I wondered from what dark part of my brain it had come from, if it had come from mine at all. Already I was praying I would never have to meet that other side of me, even in broad daylight.

"As opposed to what?" I answered his rhetorical question. "A nice chat over a couple of dead bodies?"

I followed him up the dais to his desk, watching as they brought my wordless warriors to the side of it. I wish I could've seen stoicism and resolve in their faces, but I did not. Instead I saw faces reflecting my own: confused, angry, and scared even as their cuffs were removed and they were led into a giant metal cage at gunpoint. There was space enough for a hundred people. The hinge to the door wailed at an earsplitting frequency.

I sat down in the chair opposite the man. "Can I get you anything?" he asked.

"Yeah. Your total surrender and Raven O'Klurn or letting all eight of us go free. You pick."

He smiled as he poured glasses of hot water. "I'm afraid that cannot be arranged for quite some time. See, there's a lot of protocol needed to authorize a personnel transfer like that."

"Then get started."

"Ah, I forgot! Senator's the name." He reached out his hand. I didn't move. He didn't deserve handshakes from anybody with the operations he was running. The Senator retracted his hand with a smile and continued to make our tea.

What kind of game are you playing? I thought.

"Excellent question!"

He grinned at the look on my face and waved his hand over his desk. It was made of glass. Pictures were appearing on it. It was like the computer was built into the desk. But how was that possible? I'd never seen that kind of magic.

Nor did I understand how he could have answered my silent question.

Nobody could have heard that. So did he just read it out of my head? My head went 'round in circles.

"I've been waiting to show you this," he said, still staring at his screen. "Here it is." The Senator slid the pictures over to my side of the desk.

"What's going on up there?" whispered Wayk. Emmaline was sitting at the desk, talking with the very guy who had thrown them in here. Whose side was she on?

"Don't worry, she's got this." Shades nodded confidently at the boys. A cry from the table snapped their attention back. Emma had jumped from her seat and was sliding the virtual pictures all across the desk. There were tons—some she slid out to make bigger. "No, no, no..." Emma's fingers flew across the glass then stopped completely.

"Oh, dear God, no..." they heard her wail.

Emma fell back in her seat and covered her eyes with her hands.

"Emma, what is it?" called Kael. Emma didn't answer.

The Senator sneered. "Shall we enlighten your companions, Miss Emmaline?" He drew the pictures back to his end of the desk, picked them up in an odd little square of light and threw them into the air.

Reaching to the ceiling and grazing the edges of the walkways, dozens of pictures and videos appeared. Movies. Cartoon shows. Advertisements. All kinds of mass media.

"Hey! Those are news reports!" Falcon exclaimed. "How did you get those out of the televisions?"

"Why are you showing us these? We already know what's going on. You can't surprise us," said Gator. He leaned against the bars of the cage. Sparks zapped off them and he jumped back. Everyone moved away from the sides.

"You guys really believe everything you see, don't you? Nothing unusual at all?" The Senator picked up a glass tablet and tapped some buttons. All the pictures abruptly stopped, reversed, and played over at quarter speed.

Tracer squinted at one. There were some strange-looking feed lines zipping across the screen. They flickered in odd patterns. It made his head feel weird, but he felt like he'd seen them before. He suddenly felt like he should go chill out someplace nice and forget everything.

"Didn't you ever wonder whenever there was some kind of major catastrophe and a call to action shortly after, why nobody chose to do anything?" The Senator looked at the kids in the cage.

"Subliminal messaging," Emma scorned. "You put hidden codes into the programs."

"Exceptional as always, Miss Emmaline. How long have you known?"

Emma sighed. "I didn't. But I had a hunch."

"But why?" asked Falcon. "Why would you do that to the people? They have the right to think freely."

The Senator waved his hand dismissively. "Oh, please," he replied impatiently. "You know what people are like. They're offended by the media. Don't deny it. They're shocked by what they see there and all the horrific things other people do. We make a vow to dramatically change the systems, to fix all the problems. We chant, we record videos and news specials, we march and protest on the walkways.

And yet..." He zoomed in on another picture. It showed a scene from years before, when a lightning strike hit a kindergarten. Rubble and wood splinters were everywhere, and a rescuer was carrying out a little girl with a bleeding leg. She was screaming.

"...and yet we choose to do nothing. And you know why? Because we *like* to be offended."

"That's not true!"

Everyone's eyes snapped to Wayk.

"We do fix stuff! We want people to be safe, 'cause once something goes wrong and people die, it can't be fixed, not even with magic—"

High-pitched laughter stopped him short. The Senator sat back in his chair, rocking. "Magic! Magic! Did you hear that, boys? Ho, ho, ho! They still believe...in magic! Woo!" The soldiers didn't respond. Nonetheless, he continued chuckling for several seconds. He subsided and looked at Emma and the cage, smiling.

"There is no magic. Only a perfected illusion of divine control and guardianship."

Emma shook her head. "That's not possible! God gave us magic! It heals us, it shelters us from the cold and the heat, it runs through every branch and knothole, anywhere anyone lives. It keeps us alive!"

"And who, Miss Emmaline, told you that?"

She paused to think. "Well...everyone. My parents, the teachers, the—"

"No, no, no," he said impatiently. "Who told *them?* Where is the origin of the information?"

"Well, the Elders, of course. They said—"

The Senator laughed again. "The Elders! Really, Miss Emmaline, I thought someone as bright as you would've put all the pieces together *long* before now!" He grinned deviously, waiting for an answer.

Tracer felt sweat sliding down his temple when he heard Emma's shuddering breath.

"The Elders are lying?"

"*Now* we're getting somewhere! Tell me, Miss Emmaline, how many times have you seen the Elders? Five times? Three? You've never seen them *at all*, have you?"

Tracer couldn't believe this nonsense. He wasn't exactly big on the idea of God, but the Elders were always right.

"Nobody sees them. Just their messengers. You know that. Nobody is allowed to speak with them when they are in the Hall of Silence," she murmured, lowering her head.

"And of course, what other than faith would tell you that they really there?"

Emma snapped her head up. "They must be. It's where they listen to God. He tells them what to do. They've warned us of every storm, every flood, every danger we've ever had to face." Her wings twitched and she leaned forward, hands gripping the chair arms. "They have always kept us safe! And they can't lie! It is forbidden!"

"Too much faith, even in reality, however stable you think it may be, will lead to your destruction, Miss Emma." The Senator laced his fingers over his desk. "Guards! Would you please release our little friend?"

From a door in the darkness came a torrential squeal. In the grip of two massive soldiers wriggled a small, pale boy, dirty, and skinny.

⋙⋙⋙   ⋘⋘⋘

Sam watched the footage of Emma and her squad entering the room. It played through without stop. There was no audio, but she knew very well what was going on.

"What is the purpose of capturing her?" she asked the Chief. "Is it some sort of effort to contain her influence?"

The Chief smirked and crossed his arms. "Quite the opposite, Private—pardon me, *Specialist*. The purpose of capturing her is to exploit her influence, not withhold it."

Sam nodded. A tiny figure appeared on one side of the room. "Who is that?"

"That is no concern of yours, O'Klurn. My, it is getting late, isn't it?" He squinted at his watch. "About time for some coffee, I think."

Chief Locknut's assistant brought over two cups. He handed Sam hers and watched as the curiosity on Sam's face melted back to the lifeless mask of a Guard.

"Emma!" Raven screamed. His feet slipped on the stone surface. Tracer's stomach jolted at the sight of massive bruises all over the little boy's body.

"Raven! Thank God you're alri—*gyaughh!*"

Emmaline fell back into the chair. Clamps hidden in the back of the chair had snared her wings. She groaned, breathing through her teeth. Several voices called her name.

The door of the cage opened, and little Raven collapsed on the floor, scrambling to get away from his captors. Most of the boys shuffled their feet, some saying, "Hey, are you okay?" Shadela stood by looking on, with little interest in her eyes. Tracer thought he saw her smirk.

To their surprise, Wayk stepped forward and got on his knees. They heard him whispering things—things a brother would say.

"Hey, it's okay, Raven. We'll keep you safe. I won't let them hurt you."

Above the quiet murmurings of Wayk and the cries of Raven, a voice rose up, both confident and cold.

"Well, now that we have things established, you will learn everything you want to know, but not from me." The Senator looked around the room, as if searching for something. "Well, what do you think, men? I think it's about time that we welcome home our Shadow!"

There was a loud click. A Guard opened the door and Shadela walked out.

⇢⇢⇛⇛ ⇚⇚⇚⇠

I'd never felt so stupid in my whole life. Of course she was working for them. Even in the agony of having my wings nearly torn off, I'd thought the enemy of my enemy was at least an ally. Instead, the "enemy" of my enemy *was still an enemy.*

"You monster!" bellowed Gator, his usually mocking joke for once exploding with genuine fury and conviction.

"Traitor!" yelled Tracer. He ran towards the cell door, seething. Sparks exploded from under his hands. But Tracer held tight. Falcon, Gator, and Kael grabbed him and pulled him back. "Not the best time to try and kill yourself, man," muttered Falcon. Chest heaving, Tracer stopped and turned back, digging his nails into his head. "Stupid, stupid, stupid!" he accused himself.

Shadela glanced back, drinking in the despair. She cackled just loud enough for me to hear. Her boots tapped to the beat of her princess-like stride.

"Now, Agent Della."

"*Shay*—della," she corrected. Her black eyes narrowed.

"Pardon me, *Shadela*. It is nice to have you back on board. Now, would you like to tell our guest about your work?"

"With pleasure."

Shadela stepped onto the dais, boots tapping, and stood beside the Senator, smirking. The screen in the air shifted to a single image.

I stared in disbelief. "No..."

"This is what runs everything you know. Anything that lights up. Anything that turns on and off. Faucets. Phones. Medical equipment. It's called a "power plant." Oh, I know it doesn't look like any species you've ever seen, despite your obsessive investigations. That's because it's not a real, organic plant. We made it. It's concealed in the one structure everyone was too blind to search and where it was needed most. Skyglass Temple." Shadela stared through me. "What you call a divine warning, we call weather forecasting. What you call magic, we call electricity. You call it what you do because that's what we told you it was."

My muscles tightened as she walked slowly around my chair. "What do you mean?" I asked.

Shadela stooped down next to my ear. "Don't you get it, you pathetic worm?" she hissed. "There are no Elders. *We* are the messengers. The High Order controls everything and everyone. The Guards, the politicians, the nurses, the priests, and even the teachers in your very schools. Faith, law, and media convince people that it's in their best interest to obey and not ask questions. We tell them that life is fair and is as it should be. They don't know the difference. We made sure of it. Nobody can fight us. We have dominion over all life in NeverSeen."

She slunk away, wings glittering black and red. I wanted to be furious. I wanted to be doubtful. I wanted to be ready to jump up and fight. But there was no effort inside me. A great cloak of hopelessness had wrapped around my soul. I fought the desire to drown in my own sorrow as Shadela walked around the edge of the dais.

"Except," she continued, "there are the odd few we couldn't put under our web. Immune to our tactics, they saw more of the world for what it was. More than they should have. And the rocks that impede the flow of a stream must be removed or pushed away."

No. You didn't. You couldn't!

"Strange how many bright, special people are suppressed by society or disappear at such a young age," Shadela murmured thoughtfully. The screen changed again. It flickered through hundreds of photos of children. Raven gasped as he recognized someone.

"You kidnap them?" My stomach felt like a worn punching bag.

"What better way to recruit an army of workers?" the Senator reminisced. "Let's take a look at their progress, shall we?"

He stood up, ordered his Guards to bring the "guests," and walked towards the back of the dark room. I was lucky enough to be escorted by Shadela, her voice hissing curses into my ear. All the worst ones she'd ever told me, all at the same time.

"You are worthless. Everybody hates you. Nobody is good enough to talk to Miss Teacher's Pet. You think you're so perfect. You're nothing but a pile of rotting flesh, wasting space in the world and making it reek of pride. Anyone who encounters you wishes they were dead. You don't belong anywhere and you know it. Don't you? Of course you do. You're too smart to know otherwise. Right, Emmaline?"

As she ranted on and on, a second voice echoed in my head. My own disappointment.

How could I have ever thought you were really going to help us, to help me? I was dumb enough to hope for you. And now everyone I care about will pay because of my mistake.

Someone yelled behind us. Gator had tripped and a Guard was kicking at his shins, yelling, "Get up, you useless scum! Get a move on!" He kicked again.

"Back off!" Tracer ran at him, struggling under the grips of two soldiers. He got near enough, though, to make his point. The Guard walked on. Gasping, Gator got to his feet with the help of many hands. Prods made them move forward again.

The giant doors at the end of the room swung open. An enormous, strange facility flooded our view. More metal than I thought was in the earth was piled in blocks, bricks, pipes, and boxes.

"This is the manufacturing facility. Right now, they're working on our new line of weapons." We watched the machines working in the pit below us. The clanging of metal on metal rattled my brain.

"Guns?" I blurted.

Fingernails dug into my shoulder blade and shoved me towards the only room with a window at the far end.

"You're having a bunch of eight-year-olds who can barely do multiplication make guns? Are you *mad?*" I screamed.

The clamor below us relented when the door shut, but the hustle of both man and machine continued at a breathless pace. Workers below us didn't turn from their labor, on pain of...well, pain.

Shadela snickered. "I'm assuming that's a rhetorical question. However, I think we can say something a bit more definite for yourself. It's not every day that you can teleport a half a dozen people without a device of any sort."

Oh, no.

"'Oh, no,' is right, Miss Emmaline. This is our security system." The all-hearing Senator waved his hand around the room. Thousands of black-and-white videos were displayed across rows of computer screens, cycling through on the biggest one at the front of the room.

"We have cameras stationed in every nook and cranny of every store, playground, and public place in the whole city. The Watchers are just a guise of protection. They don't even know they've been robbed of their jobs since before they first laced up their boots. We are the true Watchers. We watch everyone and everything, and we wait."

"For what?" I asked. The boys were thrown into a new cage, smaller than the first. Raven banged his elbow on the door before it shut and was shocked.

"For those suspiciously talented and young, such as your little pal Raven,"—a gasp sounded from the cage—"to let slip of their unusual...powers. We start tracking their behavior, and if they get out of line, we make them disappear."

"Then why has it taken you so long to get me? Don't tell me you were scared of me," I scoffed. The appearance of looking relaxed is about impossible to pull off when you're chained to an interrogation table.

The Senator crossed his arms, looking out into the room of computers and video feeds. "We weren't scared. In fact, we could have taken you out anytime we wanted. It only takes one shot in a deserted area, say, near your friend's house. The news would reveal it as a terrible and tragic accident."

I swallowed and glanced at the cage. The boys stood petrified and wide-eyed at the thought that I could've vanished from memory long ago. Raven's face was streaked with shimmering lines. Despite the growing knot in my gut, I managed to speak.

"So why did you wait until now?"

Shadela grinned. She made me think of one of those creepy skull masks kids wear for the Harvest Festival.

"We needed a catalyst, a person everybody both admires and hates. It will be such a great shock to the world of faeries to discover that the beautiful, perfect, genius Emmaline O'Meern is convicted of High Treason."

My body trembled around me as she shoved me down onto a hard metal chair on one side of a hard metal desk. The boys ran to the side of the cage, yelling profanities. One was louder.

"You blood-sucking, worm-eaten corpse! I'll rip your face off and—"

Tracer forgot about the electricity running through the cage bars. He flew back and crashed into everyone else. They banged into each other, collapsing in a crumpled pile of legs and arms. Their eyes glinted from the shadows like a ravenous wolf pack.

"Now, Emmaline, I'll make you a deal," offered the man on the other side of the desk. "Your friends are free to go."

I blinked. "On what condition?"

He leaned in over the desk, sliding a piece of paper. "You stay here."

Raven's cry was abruptly hushed. Wayk was kneeling, whispering to him. Raven shook under his hands and stared at me.

"Or you can watch them die."

My knuckles popped. "For all I know, you could get both if you wanted. You don't give a fish carcass what happens to people. I do. That's why *they're* not afraid of me." I glanced hopefully over at the boys in the cage.

The Senator scratched his head and sighed. "Well, that is a bit of a disappointment, but you are wrong on one thing. They *are* afraid of you. And so will everyone else be once they see what you *really* are." A video of me making the fire bird lit up the room.

"That's a load a' troll snot, Emma! Don't listen to—ow!" Kael waved his hand in pain from a zap from the cage bars.

The Senator continued as if there were no interruption.

"You know you can't escape us, Emmaline. There is nowhere you can run to that we can't find you. We're going to get it from you one way or another...along with that beautiful necklace of yours."

I glanced down. *Shrimp nuggets.* "It's just a necklace. Why should you care?"

"Didn't *they* tell you why it wouldn't fit them?"

Ash and Ume.

"Why does it matter?" I was getting sick of this game of questions.

"It's your Life Crystal," Shadela answered, breaking out of her unsettling silence. "It's a flawless gem crafted into a heptagon, the only known shape capable of absorbing the powers of a—"

"—person with capabilities such as yourself," the Senator butted in. He glared at Shadela. She nodded grudgingly and backed away.

"What she's trying to say is that the stone on your necklace absorbed your powers. If you are injured to the point you can't take care of yourself, it will use its power reserve to save you. Like the batteries of any electronic device, it can be drained only so far before it is useless. It must be recharged."

Shadela snickered. "And if something were to happen to it..." She came over and snatched it off my neck.

"You heartless old hag. I *never* should have trusted you." My blood burned.

She played with the chain in her fingers. "Really, you just figured that out now? My, you *are* as slow and dull witted as I first thought." In one swift motion, she set the necklace on the table and drew her knife.

"No!" Out of the corner of my eye, I saw six of the bravest young men I knew run towards the side of the cage.

Shadela brought her knife down swift and hard on the red stone. A great light erupted between them, and a force like thunder threw the three of us back from the table. The window turned to shards, and the Guards fell to the floor. Amongst the glittering fragments of metal on the black marble, a speck of red caught my eye.

I made the power fail, and the room went dark. The Watchers started yelling orders. At the exact same moment, Tracer, Falcon, and the others rammed into the door of the cell. The lock snapped under their force, no longer reinforced by the electric field. In the flickering of the emergency lights, the necklace flew into my hand.

"Run, run, run!" I yelled, pointing back towards the door. I Shifted and, in midair, spinning-side-kicked the Guards outside. On intuition, we divided up: Falcon and Gator, Tracer and Kael, and Raven, Wayk, and me. We ran as a pack, jumping down into the work area, ducking under swinging metal arms and through the grid of tunnels and walkways, fighting surprised soldiers with our bare hands and booted feet. I found our little sticks and stones. Bow strings laced across chests, weapons rebelted. Raven got his slingshot back. A Guard caught us there. He fell with a blow from my stick.

We ran harder when alarms blared overhead in the immense caverns. We stumbled upon a weapons room, sheathed our meager toys, and grabbed the slave-made, factory-new guns straight off the racks as we raced by.

I told them telepathically how the guns worked. "Here's some ammo," offered Falcon, tossing a few cartridge boxes to Kael and Tracer. They loaded them as they ran, dropping half of the bullets on the way.

We shot and fought our way through another network of dimly lit, jam-packed, bad-guy tunnels. I wasn't thinking at all. I just ran. Raven screamed at the gunfire. His grip on my hand was like iron.

Through the commotion, I saw an elevator up ahead. I made it come back on, zapped the Guards with their own Electrifiers, and slid in. Tracer, Falcon, Kael, Gator, and Wayk all made it within seconds of each other, and the doors shut just as soldiers rounded the bend and fired. Rapid-fire pings sounded off the steel outer doors and slowly faded as we went up.

The silence was deafening. It hurt to hear the sound of our own heavy breathing. We looked around at each other, checking to see everyone was accounted for and managing to stay alive. Some stood; others leaned on each other or the railing. I put my forehead on top of my walking stick. Tracer's face was drenched in sweat, and his head was tipped back against the wall. His cheek was smudged with dirt, along with a purple splotch of a bruise.

"Hey," I panted, "are you okay?"

He nodded breathlessly. It was quiet for a long, horrible minute.

"Emma...you don't think all that stuff...that what's-his-face said...was true, do you? I mean...there is a Hall of Silence, right?" wondered Wayk. Battle-mania seemed to have influenced his speaking capabilities. Raven was making my arm go numb.

I shook my head. "I...I dunno. Just becau...because somethin's there...doesn't mean it's not empty. Half of it makes sense, doesn't it? I mean...why d'ya think kids can't stop playing video games? They're being hypnotized...to ignore the world...and the truth." I coughed violently as dust fell down from the ceiling. My face felt wet and the red beads of blood tickled.

We started when Kael dropped his gun. "Sorry," he muttered and reached down to get it. His bangs were plastered like noodles against his forehead. A considerable bruise was forming behind them.

The sounds of another level passing us grabbed our attention. Five to go.

"So, what's the plan?" Falcon wiped his forehead on his shirtsleeve, his glasses crooked. "Do we even have one?" The cut on his cheek smeared red. "*Please* tell me we have one."

"Well, we have guns. Maybe we can shoot our way out," reasoned Gator.

"But which way is out? We haven't exactly got a map of this place." Wayk's voice was laced with apprehension. Raven whimpered and I lost feeling in my fingers.

"And how are we going to hide? They've got cameras everywhere!" Tracer's armored arms flopped back down to his side. Four levels to go. Up a creek without a paddle.

I phased out in thought. It was hard to see straight. My own mind was fighting against me. *Stop it!* I told myself. *You have to get them out of here!*

There's no way you're getting them out of here, Emma. Not alive.

I jumped. Shadela was in my head.

CHAPTER TWELVE
PHASE TWO

Ashleeka stood at her window, letting the breeze flow through her eight-year-old hair. She wasn't tired. She never was. Not really. She just went to bed to seem normal. But she never had dreams. Never. Sometimes she considered exchanging her powers for the ability to dream. Like right then.

But as she looked out the window and saw the moons Trimont and Exelor glowing in the sky and heard the trilling of crickets and the bubbling of the brook that ran around the base of her tree, she remembered what Umala had once said to her: there was no other worthy of what she could do, just as there was no other like Emmaline or Umala herself who was worthy of what they could do. They could not give in to false hopes of a normal life. They'd never have one, anyway.

Especially now that *she* had Regenerated.

Ashleeka wondered how long the Darkwielder would wait.

You really thought you were the only person in the world that could "speak your mind"?

My temples pulsed with a sickening pressure. Like somebody was trying to squish my head between their hands. Or break out from the inside. My stick wobbled under me. I grabbed the handrail, trying not to fall over. Three levels to go.

What are you? I demanded, hoping she couldn't hear my thought-voice shaking.

Shadela's poisonous voice melted through my head again.

What I am doesn't matter right now. You and every last person in this valley will know soon enough. But not yet. You have a little job to do for us first. And believe me when I say this: You will not live past another sunrise in your precious city of NeverSeen.

"I know."

"You know what?"

Falcon was staring at me. Kael was staring at me. Wayk, Gator, and Trace were all staring at me. Raven looked up at me with his wide, blue eyes, brighter than the sky at noon.

"I...uh..."

One level to go. Everyone shifted their feet. Fingers flexed and gripped their weapons. Eyes blinked. My chest pounded. I swallowed, trying to stay calm.

"I have a plan."

The elevator came to a halt. My heart pounded in my throat. The stick felt hot and rubbery as I shrank it to fit Raven and handed it to him for something else to cling to. I stared at Tracer. He stared back.

"Run like Hell's going to scramble you for breakfast," I remember saying.

There was a clunk of machinery, and the doors rumbled open.

Don't worry. She's safe.

How is she safe, Ume? She's just purposely sprung her own trap.

Exactly. She's accepted it for what it is. She is safe because her heart is still her own.

They were shooting from the rafters. Gunfire rang on the metal and stone of the elevator. Emmaline sprang out, lifted air, and whirled it into a massive invisible shield. Bullets and arrows froze mid-trajectory.

"Run!" she screamed, beads of sweat already running into the drops of blood on her brow. "Run!" The shots made them deaf again a hundred times over. *The movies had huge battles*, thought Tracer, *but they only had bows and swords. This is worse.* Main characters in the movies couldn't die. They weren't in a movie. This was real. And they were going to die.

Tracer summersault-dove around the corner. He shot back, startled and empowered by the thing in his hands. *Bang. Ratta-ratta.* Guards swarmed on dozens of walkways, ferocious ants ready to bite. The gun stomped them out. They dropped like flies. Emma danced forward and back, covering them from the sky as they shot at the ones on the ground. How Tracer wished he were a ninja.

Guns everywhere flashed. Rapid fire. Chaos. Screaming. Raven screaming. Jumping. Ducking behind machines and into passageways through the stone pillars. Tables for shields. Fire back. Down one passage and another, into one mini-room and another, always watching the skies and shooting from the ground. The room was so very long.

Bang, bang. Kael grabbed Gator's shoulder and shot behind his back as they ran. Falcon went sideways shooting, Wayk and Raven running behind him, hiding behind rocks and machines. They became too spread out. Emma couldn't cover all of them anymore. Bullets embedded themselves into metal sheets just inches from their heads. Soldiers jumped out from behind everything. They shot at them and swung swords, and red spilled on the stone floor. They screamed without thinking. Raven cried. The room was very long.

Twang. Bang. Bang. Ping. The rain of arrows flying towards them became too much for Emma's hands. Her arms paled and the air turned to a shimmering globe. Arrows came. They vaporized. Ash particles drifted through the air. The room was very long.

Ratta-ratta. Pow, pow, pow. Emmaline stood in front of them, holding off the attack, running ahead with one hand while guiding them down the narrow halls to the tunnel at the far end of the massive storage area. Tracer's teeth rattled in his head, little bits of ash landing on him. An arrow missed his head and struck a pipe stretching up to the ceiling. It spewed a blue mist on the soldiers jumping out behind him. They fell to their knees, screaming.

Still turning and running and stopping and turning, Emma's arms shook, hands rigid. The onslaught poured on her. Bullets, arrows vanished, deflected, combusted, melted. The ground surrounding her ever-shifting feet was littered with hot remnants of metal and wood. Beads of sweat trickled down from her hairline like rain on a window. She wouldn't last much longer. The end was so near: a tunnel in the far wall, their way out. No Guards. Not yet.

In a spontaneous moment of genius, Emma made metal tools fly up to the catwalks and knock soldiers over, whacking their guns from their hands. One got hit in the face.

"Nice one, Em! Right between the eyes!" Tracer couldn't help but grin as Emmaline glanced back at him. Her skin glowed and a faint smile formed in her eyes. She backed towards him, shielding them without fail. Tracer thought suddenly, *We might actually get out of here!*

A concussive silence engulfed them. Tracer could hear his own thoughts again. Emma paused in her dance of defense down the row of metal racks and machines, hands still sculpting the air. There was nothing but his heartbeat.

Then he heard it. A faint whizzing noise. Wings.

The hornets. The hyper-bugs.

They came in a rolling cloud of thunder of glass wings and yellow bodies. Their growls and screams echoed in the chamber like bats in a cave. Tracer saw their beady black eyes narrow on their targets.

"RUN!" Emma sprinted past him, grabbing his hand and yanking him along. They barreled into the others and ran as the hornets zeroed in on their position. Every corner got in their way, and the hornets came. They looked back and the hybrid insects were already on them. Emmaline flew sideways, a hand out behind her, repelling the bullet-shaped bugs. They bounced off her shield again and again, snarling. In the midst of shooting at them, Tracer caught a glimpse of one frothing at the mouth. Its saliva hit a shelf, the green stuff fizzing eerily and eating a hole in the metal.

Without further ado, Tracer blasted it to smithereens.

Stalactites forever pointed accusing fingers at them from the ceiling. Still they ran, on and on they ran, towards nowhere and everywhere. The hissing of the terrible hornets rose and dove like a demented orchestra of vibrating wings.

"Watch out!" yelled Wayk. Out of a hidden side passage, the bugs bombarded them, snapping and waggling their stingers. They fired back at the swarm, trying not to shoot each other in the process. A swift blast from Emma blew the bugs away into corners and metal and stone. They circled above them, like a conspiracy of ravens waiting for the weaklings to die. "Go!" she screamed. "I'm right behind you!"

"Here! Here! This way!" Falcon waved his hand frantically. The tunnel swallowed him up as he led their troop down into it. Tracer finally caught up with them, panting like a dog, and realized he was alone. The way behind him was vacant.

"Emma, come on!"

His heart pounded. Why were the hornets backing off? Where was Emmaline?

Tracer stumbled his way back around the corner. The buzzing of wings was a chorus of off-key violins.

"Emmaline?"

The Senator watched the machine mending the cuts on his arm where glass shards were embedded from the blast. The anesthetic was highly effective, but he was far from relaxed.

He watched his wall screen as the cameras played back footage, news reports, and all manner of shows to be run tomorrow. The algorithms were very successful at convincing people that what they saw was real time, with neither flaw nor fault of any sort. That was how the system had been designed all those years ago after the Great War, the war to end all wars, across the planet.

And here he was, hundreds of years later, carrying on the same, mundane mission as the fifty-some-odd men and women of the generations that had come before: the same old, same old of keeping the people happy, blindly happy, and happy to be so blindly happy. Happy, happy, happy.

He hated happy. There was too much happy. There had to be an opposite, a negative, a neutralizer of happiness. Anger. Hatred. Fear. That's why he needed them. That's why he needed her. Her and the other. Shadela.

That girl was far more dangerous than he'd first conceived. Perhaps they should have done more screening before choosing her as next in line.

A rap at the door snapped the Senator out of his semi-trance. "Yes, Chief? I hope you bring good news."

The Chief shifted his feet. "Well, sir, yes and no."

The machine had done its work. Only faint scars were left from the incident. The Senator rolled his sleeve back down, turning towards the man in the doorway.

"Well? Are you going to elaborate? I thought you were trained for this job, Locknut, not simply dropped in from elementary school."

The Chief cleared his throat, eyebrows slightly raised. "*Yes*, sir. The good news is we got her."

The Senator glared at him. "*And?*"

"And the bad news is, the one that got her wasn't a Guard."

Tracer hadn't blinked before Emma sent the shockwave. A field of yellow and black flowers blew up towards the roof. His heart pounded in his throat as Emma sprinted past, snatching his hand for the second time, and darted down the passage. They ran past the others, who soon gave chase, and followed the curve around and down and down and around. Light from yet another massive cavern zipped past them as they bolted across a narrow stone bridge, avoiding the straight plummet to certain death.

They entered a short tunnel with a stone island at the end, full of torches and mine carts, with a sheer wall on their left and a shaft plummeting down to infinity on their right. Luck was theirs in that nobody was there. A large metal door left ajar sat at the end of the tunnel. They stumbled through the doorway and turned to shut it behind them. It took all of their energy combined just to make it move. The door closed with an ominous rumble, and the bolts groaned as Kael and Falcon locked it shut.

There was a long silence. The atmosphere, stuffy from lack of sufficient airflow, put them in an exhausted trance, teasing them with the rest they so desired and could not afford. Without a word, they looked around, doing mental buddy checks and searching for hidden areas where at any second, a soldier could jump out, open fire, and kill them all. Emma stood drenched in sweat, hands on her hips, struggling to breathe.

Their wounds were in more need of attention than before. Wayk had a nasty gash on his forehead, Kael and Gator had several cuts on their arms and legs, Falcon could hardly walk from the surplus of vicious blows to his left knee, and Tracer was almost certain he'd dislocated his left wrist. When Kael heard of Tracer's discomfort, he walked over and set it back in place.

"Ga-ah-ah! Frog mother!" The horrible sensation of his sore and blistering fingers returned with a vengeance, and Tracer cursed under his breath for several seconds. Raven stared, eyes wide, from his perch on an edge of the rock wall. Miraculously, he'd managed to go nearly unscathed.

The boys set to treating their injuries. Gator hissed between his teeth, clenching the area around the slice in his thigh. A trickle of water ran out of a hole in the rock face, providing a way to clean their injuries. Falcon knelt beside Gator, pouring water over the wound, talking to him, not saying much, but enough to keep them both sane as Gator writhed under Falcon's grip. Kael and Wayk tended to themselves nearby with shirt rags and water, keeping an eye on Raven, who sat rocking back and forth, breathing quickly.

Tracer, comparatively alright, stood in the middle of the shelf, tracking the mostly destroyed cart rails with his eyes across the chasm, looking for a possible way out. Out of the corner of his eye, he spotted Emma wandering toward a dim, blocked-off passage, one hand against the wall, the other on her side. Something struck a chord.

"Emma!" he called, voice wavering. "Where are you going?"

Emma stopped and turned her head to the side, glancing back at him.

"I know the way out," she replied vacantly. Despite being secured to a solid surface via her hand, she swayed slightly into the wall. Her feet were spread in an odd stance, and her knees were bent.

Falcon looked up from his work on Gator's leg. "Emma, what's wrong? Are you hurt?" All at once everyone was looking at Emma, with her brilliantly colored wings and her ash-covered hair.

Emmaline didn't answer. Her arm buckled, and she gracefully fell in against the hard rock wall and sat down on a boulder. The color in her wings was muted by the dust falling down from above, and the darkness of her shirt had a strange, even blacker, shimmer by her right side.

"Dear *God*, Emma, why didn't you say you got stabbed?" Falcon leapt up from the ground and raced over, pursued by Wayk, Kael, and a hobbling Gator. Raven jumped to his feet and ran to her side. He gasped when he saw her.

"Not stabbed," corrected Emma between uneven breaths, face paling, "stung. One of the darn buggers got me."

Falcon cursed. "Make that twice." He pulled away the side of her jacket to show a second, rapidly growing stain on her black tank top.

Raven shook visibly, lips trembling in speechless agony. Breathing was hard and heavy.

Emma turned her gaze. "Hey, s'okay, Raven. S'just a...just a scratch." She swallowed, sweat beading on her neck. "God help us," said Tracer, unaware of what he was saying. Emma moved her eyes towards him, but already they were glazing, and her skin was turning gray. The venom was swift to take its toll. In a few minutes, Emmaline would either be unconscious or...

They jumped. Bullets on the door. Guards were here. They were trying to shoot through. *Ratta-ratta. Ping, ping. Blang.* There was a shout: "Get the RPG!"

"Grenade missile," whispered Emma, staring at the door. "You guys gotta go."

"No!" retorted Kael.

"You must leave."

"This is like Hell, Emma. We're not going anywhere!" bellowed Falcon.

Bang. Bang. Bang.

"You have no choice."

"We aren't leaving you here to die!" shouted Tracer in anguish.

"They don't want me dead."

The shots continued. The door had dents all over it. Emma looked each of them in the eye. "They could care less about you."

Bang. Ratta. "Where's the RPG, dagnabit?"

"But you can't just stay here!" Gator cried out.

"Yes, I can. They want me for something. They'll keep me alive."

"Yeah, for how long? How long, Emma?" Wayk failed to conceal his trembling chin.

"Long enough for you to come back and bust us out. Me and the rest of them."

"RPG's coming!"

"Emma, don't let them hurt you!" cried Raven. "Don't die!" He grabbed her tight in a bear hug, like he could be a shield from the very things he was most afraid of. Emma's eyes shut in anguish, but she said nothing to stop him.

"Raven, look at me."

Raven looked up at Emma, tears streaming down his face. Tracer recalled with a start the same look on his brother's face the day they found out Dad wasn't coming back from the border Watch. He couldn't breathe.

"I need you...to keep this safe." With trembling fingers, she reached her hand out, and he put the sparkling, red star around his neck.

"RPG's here. Get it loaded!"

Tracer's heart wasn't in his chest. It *was* his chest. It was a giant drum, beating its way out of him into the terrible night. "Emma," he stammered.

She didn't hear him. Under great strain, Emmaline O'Meern pushed herself up from the rock and leaned against a pillar. She swirled her finger to get them in a circle, nearly all color gone from her face.

"RPG ready, sir!"

Put your hands on Raven's shoulders, they heard.

"Three."

Shaking hands lay on Raven's tiny, starved frame. Their minds were racing with so many things to say that the thoughts piled up exponentially, and like a bird that goes straight up too high, they stalled. Nobody could speak to the fading beauty, the flower struggling to stand tall as the breeze threatened to push her over.

"Two. Fire in the hold!"

Tracer's face was wet. Emma stood before him, wings spread for balance, a rainbow in the dark dankness of the cave, of which there was no time to find a way out of or to say good-bye. She was looking at him. Right into his soul.

Take care of yourselves.

"One!"

His mouth moved. "Emma, wait!"

Emmaline reached out. A wall of air hit them, and when they looked down there was no more ground beneath their feet.

"Fire!"

A globe of energy surrounded them as the rock wall collapsed, but all of them watched helplessly as Emmaline crumpled at their feet. Before they could scream her name, she vanished from sight, and they fell down the chasm. Air blasted their faces. They couldn't open their eyes or take a single breath. The seemingly bottomless pit proved otherwise, and a millisecond before they'd have turned into jelly, the wind was knocked out of them as they hit the damp, leafy ground in the middle of the forest. The moons were overhead, still deep in the sleep of the dark sky, and the sun didn't rise for many long hours.

She was almost comatose when they found her just beyond the blast area. They injected her with antivenom, put her on a stretcher, and escorted her back into the recesses of the winding, underground stronghold. For the time being, they left her in a cell in the darkest, deepest level of the cavern, surrounded by rusting metal and decay.

She could do no damage there: the Life Crystal was far from reach, and the very walls had forces of their own.

It isn't true, the Senator thought as he watched the clouds moving from the observatory at the top of the mountain, *that there is no such thing as magic.* There was merely the ability to choose power, to make things bow to your will. Some people used speech. Others, art and storytelling. Then, there were those like Emmaline O'Meern who were born with the inclination to have certain things in the natural world respond to their thought, their stimulus. If you were lucky, you could control the response. If you were lucky.

If you weren't, somebody else could teach you. And if you were very unlucky, somebody would take you as an apprentice and teach you all the right things for all the wrong reasons.

Someone like him.

The Senator wondered if she would change her mind.

Being thrown in a dank, dark jail cell in an endless, disorienting military facility gives you a lot of time to think. Especially about regrets. Like not being a better sister. Like not loving others as I loved myself. Like how I didn't shut myself up in one way or another while I still could. Before this. Now, everything was screwed up because of me.

My mind kept swirling back to one memory, the best I could remember. It was Worship Day, and the whole city was raising their voices as one in the Temple, the indestructible symbol of community and peace. I couldn't recall what the songs were, or the message, or even the dancing praise we did, but crystal clear in my mind was the colored glass glittering like the river in the morning sun, and the cool, autumn breeze flowing through the sanctuary, and the sweet, gentle harmony of voices, all singing to God and praising His name.

Perhaps it was this very day, many years ago, when I ran with Sam through the meadows and waded into the creeks, showing baby Ashlee all the teeny fishes and frogs and all manner of creatures. Maybe, this same night, as an eight-and-a-half year old, I roasted marshmallows over a campfire, watching and waiting in awe as the stars crept out in the indigo sky, and pointed at the constellations. All those days ago, in the times of wonderment and innocence, when I fell asleep in my father's lap, and Mom looked on lovingly as Dad carried me gently to bed and tucked my stuffed hummingbird under the covers with me. When I slept under the watch of the angels, peaceful and quiet, with bubbling hope for a brand new day.

Now I had none left.

My head pounded still from where they'd "accidentally" knocked it against a rock as they set me down in the cell. My body was hot, and it felt like I'd swallowed fire, hotter than the hottest cocoa you'd ever drunk by mistake. My chest continued to burn for hours, and I couldn't taste any of the moldy bread they tossed down for the rodents. It was the first time I saw a real, live rat. They're unbelievably hairy and disgusting. At least compared to what I knew. Everything I was used to seeing was shiny and scaly: insects and fishes and tadpoles. Most other animals we heard about were in schoolbooks and movies about the times before the Great War, when such creatures still existed. Actually, that's where the majority of everything I knew came from: several hundreds of years before even my great-grandparents were born.

To what extent had they blinded us? Just how many things had they thrown out of sight beyond the Wall? They said the Wall was made for protection, and the Watchers stood guard, looking out for trolls and wild creatures in the bleak, outer country. Nobody went past the wall. Nobody wanted to.

What was out there? I'd always thought it was to keep bad things out. Maybe it was the other way around, and they just kept us happy where we were so we wouldn't get curious to find out about what was out there and come back and start talking. The last time some-body tried that, they went crazy and drowned in the river. That's what the news said.

I blinked and forgot to open my eyes.

When Ashleeka woke up in the morning, she already knew that Emmaline was not back in her bed, comatose from a night of total chaos. She knew Umala was deep in thought, watching the cell with their sister trapped inside, encased in enchantments far outmatching any of their own. She knew that Mom and Dad would wonder for a moment where Emmaline had snuck off to during the night, then get very nervous and try to call her over and over on her phone that was still in her room. They would drink their coffee and take their med-icines, then become very distracted as they abruptly remembered all the work that was left to be done about the house.

"Come on, Leeka-poo, we have to fix the door and the shelf and water the flowers and do the laundry, and don't forget to do your homework. You have Faith School tomorrow, remember?"

"Yes, Mommy. I remember."

Ashleeka always remembered.

The light of late afternoon was filtering through the dark orange and red leaves of the canopy. Tracer blinked his sore eyes a few times, staring into the sky above. Then, recalling the previous night, he bolted upright and hit his head on a low-hanging branch. He got bark stuck to his forehead and was in the process of picking it out when somebody sat up next to him.

"Hi." Gator gazed blearily at him and yawned immensely. He rubbed his face then grimaced as he rediscovered a sizable bruise just above the corner of his right cheek bone. One by one, the young, semiconscious warriors woke from a stiff and thoughtless slumber, making fog clouds in the cold, fall air and waiting for somebody to come up with what to do next.

They hadn't been exactly sure of where they were in NeverSeen, but with the help of moonlight and surprisingly still-agile legs, Wayk, Kael, and Gator had scaled some trees and found a good lookout.

Emmaline had Shifted them to the far southwest region of the city, where the brush was thick and there were fewer housing trees. The pale glow of Exelor and Trimont showed them the towering structure of the Wall below the edge of their valley, a hanging valley staring out into the great waste beyond it.

But exploration was out of the question. They flopped down in a circle in a nearby clearing. Before they had even pulled their coat hoods over their chilly heads, they were asleep.

Now, they were awake in a terrible new morning with no idea what to do.

But food was a good start. They found the biscuits and fruit they'd packed, just in case they needed proof of a camping trip, and ate them. They were not very interested in food, but their stomachs were. Raven's eyes lit up like sunbeams at the sight of bread and for several seconds did nothing but stare at the gold in his hands, savoring the smell and the feel and the very fact he had it at all.

"How long have you gone without bread?" asked Falcon, gnawing on a piece of his own.

"Since last week," Raven answered through a mouthful. He didn't seem the least bit troubled by the slightly stale nature of it. "They gave us gross mush-meal stuff mostly. It tasted like burned toast and asparagus."

They lapsed into the cool, rustling silence of leaves in the trees and under their feet. Kael and Tracer were lucky enough to score a rock to sit on. The others sat on the equally cold and damp ground. They knew not to start a fire, no matter how cold they got. There wasn't anything dry enough for the smoke to go unnoticed.

And smoke meant death in any circumstance. Smoke meant fire. Sometimes they were more afraid of smoke than the fire itself. Even if they were left untouched by fire, the smoke could choke them in the valley and clog their flight patterns. The chaos was often more troubling than the destruction.

Tracer ventured at length, "So, what do we do now? We're supposed to go back and...um...you know. Rescue her. Somehow."

They nodded. Falcon scratched his head. "Ow!" he started.

"You okay?" asked Kael.

"Forgot about the sore up there. I'm fine." He wiped his stained fingernails off on his already filthy pants and sat with his arms lying over his crossed legs. "But about that. Obviously we have to get back somehow. Or find a shortcut."

"But there are Watchers everywhere! How are we supposed to get all the way across the city floor without being caught?" challenged Wayk.

"Well, maybe there's a cave network we can find. There've been rumors of tunnels going back behind waterfalls, but people have nearly drowned trying to find out," said Gator, stroking his chin.

"You dumbsicle! Everyone knows the only waterfalls around here are right next to the Temple! That's where they'll be concentrating the most. They don't want us running in and yelling, 'Hey-ey, look at us! We found this giant conspiracy and we're gonna tell you all about it before they shoot us down as Traitors!'" Kael scoffed, waving his arms about dramatically.

"You got a better idea, dipstick?" growled Tracer, leaning forward.

"Yeah, shove your head down a rabbit hole, and get your face eaten off!"

"Shut your face, pinhead! You don't know anything!"

"Wanna bet?" Kael jumped off the ground, knuckles popping. Everyone else but Raven pushed and pulled themselves onto their numb feet, all protesting and arguing and threatening each other all at once, not listening and growing louder and louder. Fingers pointed inches from faces, and they pushed at each other, some trying to break others apart, and others ending up right in the middle by accident. Punches readied.

"STOP IT!"

Everyone froze. Hands remained clenching shirts as the boys turned and stared at Raven. He stood on top of a log, Emmaline's staff in his hand, huffing and puffing as if it were him and not them who had been in the middle of the scuffle.

"Stop it," he said again. "If anything around here is going to happen, then we gotta shut up and think." He glared at each of them, enough to make Tracer look away at the ground.

Raven pointed back to where the very top of Skyglass could still be seen. "Emmaline's just spent the whole night and half a day somewhere in the mine. We dunno what they've been doing to her, but they want her alive. That helps us." He hopped down from the log and walked to the center of their flop circle. "Last time we were in there, we got lost and trapped. We can't have that happen this time. If we're going to get Emma out, we hafta get in the main entrance. That's where they'll have the controls." He drew in the soft dirt with the staff.

"Now listen carefully, 'cause this is what I can remember."

For the next hour, Raven talked them through what he'd seen. An hour after, they had a plan, and an hour after that, as the sun made long shadows across the forest floor, they recited their missions, who they were teamed up with, and what to do if something went wrong.

And as they waited for the sun to set, they sat thinking, sometimes talking about something, and other times nothing, as they rechecked their quivers and sharpened their swords. They watched as Raven ingeniously tied his slingshot to the top of the staff Emmaline had given him and shot a few pebbles into a knothole.

And when it was dark, they set out very carefully across the suburbs. If somebody had been close enough to notice, they would have seen a small, red star bobbing up and down in the darkness.

I was half awake in the darkness. There was no sun, no moons, no stars, nothing to tell me the time. In and out of consciousness through the whole day or night or whatever it had been since they put me in here.

I kept my knees to my chest, my wings drooping like melted glass onto the floor beside me. There was no light to make them sparkle, and I didn't have energy to spare to move closer to the pale, yellow lamp dangling from the cave ceiling. The hornet venom had knocked most of everything out of me, and now I could tell just how much I needed that silly necklace.

But if I had it now, it wouldn't help. They'd have it, of course. *Can't let her get away*, they'd be thinking. If they thought at all. Nobody seemed to think about what they were doing anymore. Including me. But it's different when you're trying to save a life.

My head was damp where it rested against the rock. They'd taken all my armor before dumping me in there, so I couldn't even make a pillow between me and the hard stone. The smell of moss and mushrooms had finally gone away as I got used to it. I thought I never would. Being between a rock and a hard place is even worse when it smells like—never mind.

All I could think of was singing. So I did.

"Oh, come, oh, come, Emmanuel...and ransom captive Israel...who mourns in lonely exile here..."

My voice cracked and I couldn't breathe. With my eyes shut against the hot tears, I didn't realize my head was dropping until my forehead touched my knees. I couldn't make a sound, but at least I could get a little air again, some nice, musky air in a nonexistent cave that I didn't belong in. There was nothing fair about this.

"...until the Son of God appears..." gently called a small voice.

I pulled my head up. Across the room in another cell were a pair of eyes, very small eyes, and a pair of hands on the bars. Then there were another pair of hands on the bars and another pair of eyes. They were twins, a boy and a girl. They watched me as I forced myself carefully onto my stiff feet and took a deep breath.

"Rejoice, rejoice..."

A rough but melodious voice of an elderly man rose from a distant corner: "Emmanuel..."

"Shall come to thee..." came a sweet sound from a few cells down. A thin, pink-winged lady with dirty blond hair materialized from the shadows.

"...oh, Israel..."

They stood at the edge of their cells, focusing on nothing but the song. Though barely capable of thinking from the immeasurable time they had spent in there, without sunlight or wind or river, they emerged from the darkness. Even in the deepest dungeons and the most reclusive recesses of the world, there was hope.

Then the door banged open. Intense white light poured in. A soldier stood at the top.

"Silence!" commanded Locknut. The singing stopped. A pair of Guards tromped down the stairs toward my cell.

"Rejoice, rejoice, Emmanuel," I sang in defiance as they unlocked the door. They grabbed me by the arms, and when I tried kicking them off, I earned myself a headache and a long scratch with a massive slap across the face. They cuffed me and shoved me up the stairs.

But before the door slammed behind me, I heard something billowing out in renewed strength.

"...shall come to thee, oh, Israel..."

CHAPTER THIRTEEN
STORM'S COMING

The boys picked their way through the northern edge of the forest. Wearing a camouflage of sticks, leaves, and muddy clothes, they hiked most of the afternoon and evening. They might've looked like very small trolls from a distance. Tracer guessed from the position of the moons that it must be around eleven or twelve, and as proof of the lateness of the hour, his face was overcome by an enormous yawn.

"Hey! Shush!" scolded Kael.

"Sorry," he whispered, glancing around the foliage for any ninja Guards. Tracer was glad to see there weren't any. "It's okay, there's nobody here but us," he whispered. "Or *are* there?" inquired Gator mysteriously. His face cracked into a very big, but very sleepy, grin. They worked their way further into the forest, stumbling and bumping into the dark things around their feet. Raven lost his balance and caught himself with Emma's staff. He couldn't quite think of it as his yet.

"Wait, so *where* are we going?" Gator asked.

"The mine, you numbskull!" Kael answered.

"Well, which part? I don't know where the entrance is. Heck, I don't even know where we are right now!" Gator grumbled, rubbing his hands together. He'd lost his gloves during their escapade.

"I know where we're going," assured Raven. Suddenly, there was more than moonlight hitting his face. A small, red glow emitted from the necklace, and they felt the cool, damp air move slowly around them.

"What's that sound?" Wayk breathed.

Falcon looked up the side of a tree. "It's moths. Beamers."

It was like a shower of stars coming out of the tree itself. The beamers flapped gracefully around the group of boys, a slow current of golden petals, and flew past Raven.

"It's a trail, isn't it? They're showing us how to get there," said Wayk. They stood looking between Wayk and the glittering path through the forest.

"Well? Let's go already!"

Kael took his turn leading, and they filed after him into the not-so-dense underbrush. The red necklace warmed Raven's chest.

They dragged me down a maze of halls, upstairs and then more stairs and more halls until I was practically sleepwalking. I could tell we were somewhere inside Skyglass from the grainy walls, but there were still no windows to tell me what time it was. The newer soldiers seemed tired enough to suggest a later shift in the evening. I had no idea where they were taking me, but I had a hunch, as usual, and I didn't like it. As usual.

Finally, we reached the top of a back staircase and went through a door. My jaw should've dropped, but it didn't. "This is the sanctuary!" I should have blurted in astonishment, but I didn't. They led me toward the back of the massive alter where the sparkling glass doors were, and I should've said, "But we can't go back there! It's the Hall of Silence," but I didn't.

The magnificent kaleidoscope-like doors swung outwards at our approach. A great shaft of light blasted us as we passed between them, and a great, cold wind bit into my bones. I could barely feel the wooden core of the tree under my boots. All natural smells vanished: no more damp leaves, no more river soil, no anything. Gone. Then I could see inside. Everything in my body told me to scream, but my throat closed tight.

It was more massive than the moons, than the mountains, than the great falls beyond the edge of the islet. It shone with a horrible hue of a nameless color, the color of death. The very lack of both scent and sound made it all the more dead. Living things are never silent, and they can never go unnoticed, for the very nature of existence implies that something is there. Seeing that *thing* there...it was like staring into the empty eye sockets of a skull, or looking straight through the ground into the thousands upon thousands of graves, all the ones that were filled with people and all the ones that were not. This thing was absent of everything. This thing was Death itself.

Then I saw her. The soldier. The lifeless one.

"Welcome to the Generator Room. Please take a seat."

Sameela O'Klurn strode out of the shadows, bow strung over her shoulder, and watched as they hauled me over to the torture chamber and locked me in.

I didn't need a room to be tortured.

"Quiet!" whispered Falcon. The boys froze in their tracks. Foggy breath, puffed in nervous clouds, was barely visible in the fading moonlight.

"What is it?" breathed Kael. The moths suddenly flew around them and vanished into the trees in every direction, leaving the boys practically blind. "Now what?" groaned Wayk.

A faint, red light emanated from Raven's tiny chest. The stone seemed to be calling their attention. Rays of light were gleaming out from its center, and a great wave of brightness engulfed their senses. With a jolt, they looked around and saw there was no more forest.

"What—" started Gator.

They were surrounded by green, glittering walls with a great rock ceiling above.

"The mines!" cried out Kael, as a platoon of Guards hustled...*through them?* A bizarre ripple fanned across the entire cave.

Raven stammered, "Wait...it's not—"

"—real." finished Tracer. "We're still in the woods."

"It's a projection," added Falcon, in awe of the illusion. He stuck his hand through it, touching the leaves on the other side. "Whoa!"

As if triggered by his motion, the picture whirled in a frenzy of colors and shapes. The boys jumped back from it, bumping into each other. Out of nothing came a door, a stone door hidden deep in a dank outcrop in the mountain. There were flashes of a Guard, a pass card, and the door opening, and a tunnel of many side rooms with mysterious lights seeping through the doors. Then a great room. Raven blanched at the sight. Children of all ages stood in an assembly line, hammering and heating metal things and welding them together.

"Hey, wait a second...those are Blasters. We haven't made those since the Great War," said Kael. Tracer and Gator nodded in their understanding of the ancient weapon. "Does fire powder even exist anymore?" wondered Wayk.

"No question. I saw what happens when you use too much by a forging station," replied Raven, a cold authority lining his voice. "It was really bad..."

The image switched again. There was set of stairs and a room with lots of lights and screens and a panel of switches. It paused on one labeled, "Emergency Floodgate Shutoff." Then it was gone, and there was a rush of tunnels, another great room, and a tunnel and a cave and a flood of water and a ball of fire, and then it was all gone.

They stood, breathless, as the light faded from the stone, and they were alone in the dark forest. A low rumble rolled in the distance, a threat of thunder and storms and wind.

"We have to find the entrance to the mountain. Like, right now," demanded Wayk.

"But how do we find it?" asked Tracer, flexing his hand on his sword hilt. His "borrowed" gun was gingerly fastened to his pack. He didn't plan to use it for a while, if at all. Stealth was their best option.

"We don't need to," quipped Raven. "It's right there." He pointed out into the darkness, and like a parting curtain, there was a door ahead of them in the side of the mountain. A ring of light surrounded it.

"Another projection?" wondered Kael.

"No," answered Raven. "A portal."

"All right, let's get this over with," Sam growled as she strode over to the room I was locked up in. They'd done all kinds of weird scans with different kinds of lights, and instinct told me that they were checking to make sure I wasn't some sort of decoy or diversion. There was no chair, no bed, no table, no anything for me to sit on, so I just crossed my arms and leaned into one of the corners to keep from falling over asleep. I wasn't sure I could remember what real sleep was; the plague of nightmares of death and destruction had consumed me for so long that I never felt truly rested, regardless of whether the visions remained in my mind's eye after I woke or not.

I pulled my eyelids back open as Sam grabbed a chair, flipped it around backwards, and sat on it, with her arms crossed on the back ridge. Her gentle, understanding smile was extinct, her peaceful, blue-gray eyes had turned cold and icy as the river in winter, and hatred for my soul pulsed from her as heatless rays from the hiding sun.

"Nice to see you, too, Sam," I muttered, unable to think of anything else to say in response.

She jerked her head to the guy at the control panel. The walls jolted me like fire, and I jumped away yelping. My wings and right arm prickled all over as if they'd fallen asleep.

"That was at 10 percent capacity. Don't push me to full-on electrocution, prisoner. My superior would be less than pleased," Sam said hollowly, unblinking.

Exhaustion and anger surged as one unit through me. "Your superior, huh? Since when is old man Locknut greater than God?"

Her response was another nod. The pain that crackled through me was far greater than I had expected, at least 30 percent. Somehow I laughed to myself inside my head: *At least my brain is still working to tell me how much this incredibly hurts.*

I hadn't realized I had shut my eyes until I opened them and found myself on my knees. Sam stared at me. There was no compassion, no history, no shared secrets. There was nothing of the Sam I knew left in the person sitting on the chair in front of me.

"So," she began as I pulled myself off the floor, "how shall we start? With your last rights that no longer exist or your explanation of everything you know about the High Order and all its affiliates?"

Sore and wobbly on my electrified legs, the disappointment and rage of being abandoned by the closest friend I had forced me to realize that I had nothing left. Nothing left to fight with. Nobody on my side. I was done listening, done obeying the rules, done trying to pretend that I could actually come out on top victoriously and be called a hero. Or even just a "good guy." In a game that you're meant to lose, there's only one chance at survival. Improvising.

I stood for a moment, keeping my balance, and stared straight at Sam. She looked back, unblinking, waiting for my answer.

"Oh, I dunno," I started nonchalantly, "I'd rather start with your surrender and *your* explanation of what the blazes you're all up to."

I knew she'd nod again, and in the concern of keeping my mind sharp, I drew strength out of some reserve deep in my cells and pulled my feet off the ground. The lightning popped and sizzled around me, frying the air. Heat built as it searched for me, for some living thing to course through and turn into a blob of cooked mush.

"Well?" I asked innocently. "Do you surrender or not?"

Sam nodded again. The energy tumbling, darting, zapping through the room was almost too much to bear, like being stuck in the middle of a thunderstorm covered in armor. A thought crossed my mind: *Bring it on.*

"Hoy, Sam! How's Raven doing? I haven't seen him for a while. Is he still tagging along after his sweet, big sister?"

The walls were turning white-hot from the pressure. The control panel man was yelling something at Sam. The shock wave burst out of my chest. I saw the walls crumble, the glass shatter, and Sam tumble away, shielding her face.

I stood triumphant in a pile of rubble, under the horrid Generator, in the room where every lie began.

Then there were red lights, and sirens, and a million soldiers in every direction, all with guns. I heard myself yell, "Come get me!" with heat surging to my hands. Then something hit my head, and it was very dark.

Raven ventured through the portal first, and the others trickled after him. There was a blur of color around them as they walked through, and then they were standing not a hundred feet from the door into the mountain. After Tracer walked through, the portal closed up behind him. No way back.

"Now remember," said Raven, turning to face them all, "We move quiet, and we move fast. We get the kids out, and we don't look back."

"Hang on," interrupted Kael, "since when are you the captain of this ship?"

"Since you guys didn't take it," replied Raven. He loaded his slingshot and peeked around the rock to see the door.

"Wait, what ship?" Wayk whispered.

"Shut up! Here comes somebody," retorted Falcon, drawing back his bowstring.

A soldier walked past their rock. In seconds, they'd jumped him, knocked him out, and hidden him. Their own efficiency startled them, given that they were a hodgepodge of barely trained boys with only one day of military experience. Raven grabbed the soldier's pass card and ran to open the door.

"Hey, Raven, watch it! You're not the toughest one here, you know!" called Kael as quietly as he could. Raven slid the card through the slot. There was a clicking sound, and the door slid open. He peeked in, slingshot ready, and looked back at them.

"Are you entirely sure of that?" he asked curiously. Then he turned and darted inside.

"Ouch," whispered Gator, a slight grin morphing his normally serious composure.

Falcon and Kael glanced at each other as they hustled after him. Tracer glanced around one more time, pausing just enough to look at the stars, the moons, and the clouds festering on the horizon. He knew he certainly didn't feel like the toughest one there, but even more so, something in his heart told him that they were in the wrong place to be rescuing anybody. In fact, he knew it. But he couldn't prove it. He just wanted to find Emma, and something told him she wouldn't be here.

Tracer got one last look at the silhouette of the Skyglass Temple, towering tall and black against the darkening, storm-clouded night before he shut the door.

A horrific, grinding, cackling noise woke me. A screeching laugh. A far-too-recognizable laugh. Somebody who had my hair in an iron grip pulled back so my head was tilted up to the ceiling.

"No-no-no, I bet...I bet it'll take less than *five* minutes! No, four and a *half!*"

From the sounds coming from outside the room, I guessed we were in some kind of dressing room near the stage I would die on. Without the help of my cuffed hands, I pulled my gummy eyes open again.

Black eyes and black hair and red-and-brown speckled wings flickered into view. Shadela cackled once again, dropping my head back down to my sweaty chest. I realized I was drenched. It was sweltering, wherever I was. Then a frigid blast came from nowhere and sent me shivering all over. I couldn't take this for long. I just wanted them to kill me and get it over with.

There was a light in front of me. When I was finally able to open my eyes again, I saw it was actually a mirror. My hair was sticking every which way in great auburn fluffs, held in place by honey spray. Shadela was frizzing it up to an appearance of chaos I thought unachievable, even to my own standards of static hair craziness. It made me feel like the crazy caterpillar lady a few floors down from our house. When I finally got to see what my own face had become, I understood why it was so hard to open my eyes: they were crusted over from the cut on my forehead. It was an ugly purple-yellow color, besides the black-red blood smears trickling down.

"Showtime, princess. Let's show them what you got." Shadela dug her claws into my scalp one more time, then turned and flounced away like a diva.

I looked at the outfit she'd stuck me in: a gaudy, neon-green evening gown, covered in sequins and exotic feathers and other cheesy stuff. It hurt my eyes just to look at it.

At least I'll look like a psychotic, gypsy, caterpillar lady.

I decided to buy time to get the kids out alive, if the boys had any chance at it in the first place. These High Order freaks seemed bulletproof until I came along. And I knew why. I laughed at the thought.

"What's so funny, Princess? You got something to tell us?" Shadela reappeared to grab my hair again and pulled my head back.

"You're scared of me. I think that's pretty silly, given that you act like you're indestructible," I said weakly. Her grip on my head started ripping out hair, but I didn't care.

"Everyone else you could just kill off or make disappear. But not me. I'm too dangerous." I smiled.

She smirked at me, just inches away from my face. "Oh, but you're wrong. We *can* kill you off because you're *not* so dangerous. And now everybody is going to get to see it, Princess Perfection. Isn't that right, Senator?"

"You got it, Agent! Would you enjoy the privilege of leading her out to the stage?" The Senator's footsteps sounded painfully loud by my left ear, and his sadistic, toothy grin flashed into my barely existent view.

"Yes, sir!" she cheered. As they led me, or dragged me, down the hall and onto the spiral stairs, I wondered how, at a time such as this, when my heart was pumping so hard, when my lungs were screaming at me for oxygen, when I was so close to dying, all I could think about was eating a bowl of nachos and watching Sky Trek episodes all weekend in my pajamas.

The clan of boys ran down the dark, craggy hall, past the rooms glowing with weird lights and filled with more mysterious concoctions, and down the steep steps of the forgotten mine. Raven led them on, guiding them with the glimmering red stone on his tiny, thin chest. They reached an overpass tunnel with windows on both sides and came to a screeching halt. Falcon stared down into the room below.

"What the heck?"

"Where is everybody?" asked Gator breathlessly. They looked out both sides of the tunnel. The massive assembly-line room that they'd fled through not a day before was completely vacant.

Kael turned to Raven. "Well, kid? Where are the slaves we're supposed to be rescuing?"

Raven's face drained of what little color it had. "Oh, no," he murmured, eyes darting through images in his mind. "Come on!" he yelled and bolted down the tunnel. They had no choice but to race after him.

No sooner had they rounded the corner at the end than they ran face-first into a patrol unit. Swords slashed, fists bashed, and a moment later, the six young men stood with their chests heaving over the knocked-out soldiers.

"Well, that was fun," grumbled Gator sarcastically. "Let's just leave a trail of dead guys for them to follow us with."

"Shut your face, man. They're only out of order," snapped Tracer. Before another brawl could break out, Raven sprinted down another passage, waving his staff–sling hybrid, calling them along. There were only a few encounters with some unlucky soldiers, each brief and to the point. By the time the six boys had trouble recalling where they were going in the first place, they tumbled over a pile of rocks, wood, and scrap metal in an abandoned room.

"This...this is the refining room," gasped Raven. "I know a...passage that takes you to...to this cave place. That's where they have everybody. I just know it."

"How?" moaned Wayk. "There are a million caves in this mine."

Raven stared at them with the cold, hard knowledge rarely seen in a child.

"There's only one chock-full of fire powder."

Ashleeka lay on her bed, staring at the ceiling. Mom and Dad were gone for the ceremony at Skyglass. They didn't say what about, but she knew. She just never said so, lest she end up in the same predicament as Emmaline.

Umala watched from her crib as Ashleeka tossed a toy ball up into the air. It was a game she did when she was bored or too preoccupied to sleep. The goal was to get as close as possible to the ceiling without touching it. She was quite skilled at it. There were many nights that were too filled with thoughts too important to sleep off. Up and down. Up and down. She could do it with her eyes shut.

Ashleeka tossed it again and held her hand up to catch it. The ball didn't come down. It didn't hit the floor, either. She opened her eyes.

It was floating by the ceiling, spinning gently. Ashleeka looked at Umala.

"Fine, what do you want? It's bad enough being trapped here, but if you can't even play by the rules—"

Umala cut her off. *It's time,* she said. *You know the drill.*

Ashleeka nodded, rolled off the bed, and pulled out her backpack from under her bed. The ball dropped softly onto her bed, and

Umala shut her eyes. Quiet snoring soon sounded from the corner of the room.

Figures, thought Ashleeka. *The world's getting blown apart, and I'm the one who has to pack everything.*

CHAPTER FOURTEEN

JUSTICE

The cheer of the crowd behind the curtain pounded against my ears as the Guards yanked my wrists and cuffed them to the bars, stretching my arms apart to the point I couldn't move them without breaking something. They cuffed my ankles to the floor of the platform, shaping me into a cross. All I could think about was my family's reaction to seeing their "little diamond of joy" strung up on the stocks in that stupid, hypnotic dress—if they recognized me at all. They tore the edges, to make the brainwashed people think there was a struggle before they brought me to the Courtroom. Nice name for a place where the defendant couldn't defend herself.

My spastic hair drifted in front of my eyes. Sweat continued to trickle down my back and drip off my hair. I stared with one eye at the ground, dizzy from lack of food and almost nauseous with a terrible feeling about what my fate was going to be in a matter of minutes. My heart pounded steadily—not what I would have expected, given the circumstances of certain death and having made the city's number one wanted poster. 9:57. I had three minutes to do something before the curtain drew open and everyone saw Emmaline O'Meern tied up like a mantis on a spider's web. *God, why is this happening?* I begged, I prayed, I pleaded for His help.

9:58.

A Guard strode up to me with the air of an executioner. So I was going to die. I stared at his boots, dark green and luminescent as the dying light from the window far to my right glinted off the tanned and treated forest leaves. Oh, how I'd love to walk the forest, the rivers, the mountains, the world, just once more before I died. He said, "Traitor." That was my new name, and my cue to obey if I didn't want another smack across the cheek like the one I got in the cell hole. The first cut had finally gummed up all the way, so it wasn't bleeding, but it itched like crazy.

I pulled my head up, struggling to keep looking straight at him as my head swam. It felt like I was falling to one side, but there was no way to fall. *You're all hung up like a wet, smelly towel, remember?*

His eyes glinted with a maniac's pleasure. "Traitor," he smirked, "you still have a way out of this. It's really quite simple, Traitor. Admit you were wrong to disobey the High Order and all its affiliates, and we'll let you off with a simple expulsion. Beyond the Wall."

Nobody could survive beyond the Wall. That's what they said, not that I believed anything they'd said anymore. But if it was true, I was dead either way. It was hard to keep my good eye open. Exhaustion crawled up from the floor. My knees started failing. I started crumpling up like a wet paper sack, but the cuffs on my wrists kept me from falling all the way to the ground. So this is what the Crucifixion must have felt like, minus the crown of thorns and metal stakes and the perfection of being God.

9:59.

"So, Traitor, what do you say? Confess? Or die?" The executioner stared intently at my scrunched-up eyes and bloody face. That was their game: they threatened to kill your self-respect, and even if you said yes, they'd just plain kill you anyway. Some game. I refused to play.

I rose from my half kneel in front of him, pulling my feet back under me, straightened up, and stared squarely back into his face.

"You're going to kill me one way or another. If I'm dying, I'll die as myself."

"Oh, but we're not going to kill you," sneered Shadela as she strode in front of me, wearing an elegant, dining party dress, shimmering red. "They are."

I heard the roar of the crowd rise again from ebb to tidal wave as the speaker called them out to face their enemy. He didn't seem to be aware that the Traitor was a female or at least didn't specify otherwise. *Maybe that's to make the shock universal. At least none of the younger kids I know will see me die. Thank God for the age restriction.*

Shadela snickered sadistically, grabbed the ceremonial mask from the approaching Senator and shoved it over my pulsating head. She disappeared into her natural habitat of darkness behind me, and the Senator put a chain around my neck for an extra dose of theatrics and terror, grinning all the while. He gave my shoulder a friendly smack. "Knock 'em dead, kiddo." He winked and walked away with a hop in his step.

The group of soldiers lined up on either side of the stocks. Any blood left in my face drained away as two of them pushed the platform forward to within three feet of the curtain, and the mob of angry and bloodthirsty citizens beyond it. Sparks jumped amongst the soldiers from the very twitchy, very sharp weapons they carried.

It was 10:00.

Falcon drew an arrow from his quiver as Raven waved him towards a tunnel at the far end of the room, a tunnel he recognized from their first mission. It had the mining tracks running in and out of it, but the carts were motionless and, for the most part, missing. A whooshing noise came from behind.

"Dang it, Tracer! Quit tryin' to chop off my head!"

"Sorry," he replied and stopped swinging his sword. "So what exactly is our plan?"

Falcon opened his mouth, but the voice came from behind.

"We flood the tunnels and ride it out through the escape-ways down the river," Gator announced. They all turned to stare and saw a large plaque on the wall behind him. He waved them over. "According to these charts," Gator began, "we're above the water table. I wouldn't be surprised if the tunnels lead out to the base of the falls. They're really not that deep at the bottom, right, Raven?"

Raven nodded. "Right."

"And if they designed the system like I think they did, we just might manage to flush out all the prisoners with us," added Kael. He pointed back down the room. "Did you guys ever see the control panel for this place?"

Wayk's hand shot into the air. "I'll get it! I'll get it!" Energy seemed to radiate from him, despite all they'd been through. His enthusiastic grin let them all smile briefly.

"No, Wayk, I need you here. You're the best at stealth," ordered Raven. "I'll go," offered Gator. "My father helps regulate the water-ways. I'll probably understand things that none of you would. No offense," he added.

"Good. Tracer, go with him. There'll be company waiting," said Kael. They nodded and disappeared around a corner, the echoes of their thudding steps chasing after them. Raven put Falcon and Wayk on the left side and himself and Kael on the right side of the tunnel. He took a deep breath and looked at his older comrades.

"Alright, then. Let's bust this haystack!"

The cheers following the call to war were amplified by the massive chamber. To Gator and Tracer, it sounded like a raging army.

"Are you ready to see your enemy?" the announcer boomed, just feet in front of me. I could tell now that the raucous mob saw the shape of somebody tied up just behind the red, silk curtain. A wave of despair and horror hit me as I put the pieces together. The curtain was white at the top. The bottom half was stained with blood.

Whatever the announcer said next, I missed because I was overcome with a coughing fit, but he got the roar to an almost deafening level. Even the soldiers flinched.

Then he boomed, "Behold the Traitor!"

The tainted curtain pulled back from each end, sliding towards the center. In a few seconds, it would reach the middle and rise up and away. My heart jumped to my throat with terror. Choking with despair, I prayed with what composure I had left.

The Lord is my Shepherd; I shall not be in want...

The voices crescendoed as the curtain pulled back. A light like the sun blinded my already sore eyes, and I blinked away from it. The intensity of my senses at that moment was astounding: I smelled the pine from the newly polished floor, tasted the cool dampness of the air that wafted in from the open windows, sensed the heat of bright lights on my skin. When I finally got my eyes open again, my heart broke.

I saw the hatred and betrayal of my city on the face of every man and woman. I saw the poise of an attack in every one of them, ready to strike their Traitor. My teachers, my neighbors, my classmates. My parents' friends from work, the little old ladies I'd helped step into the carriage, the recluse who sold tiny flowers in the marketplace. The janitor guy who always tipped his hat politely when I walked by, the hummer trainer, and the couple whose little girl I'd played with years ago. Everybody I knew and everyone I didn't. I spotted my friends' families, staring at me, unaware that their kids were part of this "plot" as well.

And then I saw my parents. In the third row. With flickering spears and arrows. Unaware of who was before them. I screamed for them, but the chain around my neck cut off my voice.

On the screens flicked up a list of options for my demise: Beating, Beheading, Hanging, Drowning, Burning, Poisoning, Stoning, Crucifying, Devouring, and the worst of all sat accursed at the very bottom of the list: Confiscating.

"Behold your Traitor, ladies and gentlemen. Do as you may." The announcer ended ominously and walked offstage. His boots clapped like thunder against the stifling silence. And to think this was the same guy I heard on the news almost every night. Even the breeze had halted its soothing movement in the curtains around the Courtroom.

I waited for my mom to scream, to convulse in agony at seeing her child's kill options. For Dad to hold her thrashing figure back and yell out, "That's my daughter! You filthy liars, that's my daughter!" For Mom to sob in his arms as she reached out to me, crying, "We're going to get you out of this, Honey!" For Dad to scream, "Where's your evidence?" while raising his spear. For tears to slip down his face, contorted with a violent mix of anger and disbelief.

I saw nothing but blank faces staring into nothing at all. Nobody asked who I was. Nobody ever asked. You found out after they were dead.

The Senator stood square to the crowd. "Ladies and gentlemen," he began with an air of displeasure and impatience, "The Traitor is convicted of High Treason. Rest assured that the evidence is clear and convicting. Now, let's get this over with, so we can bunk down and ride out the storm, shall we?"

As he forged the lies of my lawbreaking endeavors, I screamed that this was tyranny. As he elaborated on my evil conniving of destruction, I told them everything, about the caves and the slaves and the manipulation of our minds. But there was nothing I could do to make them hear me. They were dead to me, just as I would be dead to them.

Tears sprung anew and mixed with the dirt and blood, racing down and away like the time left on my clock. My parents, blind and heartless, were just another wave in the sea of menacing faces. Sam stood further down the row of soldiers in the arena. She ignored my gaze. Her stone-faced parents, having completely forgotten they even had a son, a son I helped rescue with the cost of my own life, didn't move.

My soul folded up in despair, and I sagged to the floor, hanging on my wrists. I cried without a sound, for even my voice was stolen. I was alone in the city I had loved my whole life that had raised me and cared for me, and only now, in my moment of need, there was nobody to stand by me.

I prayed for a miracle.

The Senator had the crowd chanting, "Death for the Traitor! Death! Death!" In unison, he orchestrated them in rows to choose how to kill me. "Death for the Traitor! Death! Death!" They beat the ends of their spears on the wood floor. I felt the rumbling waves churn beneath me in the chant. "Death for the Traitor! Death! Death!" Thousands of qualified adults and adolescents voted for how I would die. My bones shook. "Death for the Traitor! Death! Death!"

The Senator halted the chant in an instant. The void created by it was overwhelming. My heart thumped about so hard I thought it was thunder, and my chest drummed as the results flashed up on the screens surrounding the magnificent auditorium.

Beating—93.

Beheading—47.

Burning—85.

Devouring—176.

I flinched at the thought of a swarm of spiders ripping me apart. But it wasn't done.

Drowning—17.
Hanging—131.
Poisoning—28.
Crucifying—394.
Bats. Well, I've been strung up this long, so I'd die quick. Maybe.
Stoning—502.
Great. Either they knock me out and it goes easy, or they break everything first. I stared at the marvelously polished floor only a foot below me and saw how bloody my face already was. But a rumble of both alarm and exhilaration told me to lift my soggy head.
Confiscating—518.

The instant I saw that on the screen, a dormant animal instinct reared its head. I lost the controls as it bucked and thrashed me about, rattling the chains and making me convulse harder than I thought physically possible.

518.

I shrieked, banging my throat inside the giant metal clasp trying to choke me, and shook my head violently in a futile attempt to rip it off and tell them the truth about their precious Elders and High Order, how it was all a lie. They watched me with the nervous delight of seeing a beast locked in a cage: one overwhelmed by their presence yet ready to tear them to pieces, but also with the thrill of a hunter, with the savage anticipation of scarlet pools filling the arena.

518. That was my number. That was my name on the list. It was the next name to be crossed out. Me. Crossed out. I was next to die. 518. That's the number of people who chose Confiscation. It was my fate.

518. Confiscation.

The metal doors to the far left opened, and six brick-like soldiers rolled in the machine. The slanted blade glinted at me menacingly from its throne up high, stained deep red from its last victim. 518. Confiscation. The Guards surrounding the room turned simultaneously to shut the windows and pull the curtains tight. Airtight. No escape.

My people, my executioners, cheered for the death of the silent Traitor, for her Confiscation. Death for the Traitor, they demanded. Shadela cackled from behind me. "Oh, my, oh, my. How wonderful this will all be!"

The machine was rolled to the middle of the arena before me, stopping long enough for me to get a good look at how it worked. Then soldiers grabbed the stock they'd cuffed me to and began the descent to the machine. My feet burned as I fought it.

518. Confiscation. A guillotine.

They were taking my wings.

Tracer and Gator raced down one passage then another, finally stumbling up the steps leading to the Control Room. They overthrew the few Guards still present with some well-timed combat moves and burst into the room.

Three sides of the room were lined with massive boards, covered with light indicators, switches, dials, and sliders. It would take hours to figure out what they were all for, let alone find the right one.

"There are no labels on any of them!" panicked Tracer, pacing the length of the panel on the far wall. "How are we supposed to know what it is?" He glanced up to see that there was live broadcast footage being played on one of the security monitors overhead. A strange, blue light flicked on. Tracer whipped around to find Gator by a light-switch panel by the door, grinning at his discovery. "Not bad, huh?" Letters and words glowed everywhere.

"Well, which button is it, smarty-pants? We don't exactly have all day!" Tracer growled.

"Uh, how about this big red one that says 'Emergency Floodgate Shutoff'?" answered Gator, pointing at the most prominent button on the board.

Without the grace of a retort, Tracer headed back down the long panel. Sure enough, the displays surrounding the area indicated pressure, temperature, and output of all the water entering the main waterways, as well as the floodgates keeping the water out of the mines. "Makes sense," Tracer granted. "Just make sure you're not trapping or exploding anything."

"Right," said Gator, checking the readings and adjusting the dials to flood the tunnels. Tracer turned back to the screen. The news broadcast had finally gotten to the event, whatever it was, and the host had the audience out of their seats cheering. One camera faced out into a huge arena with a tiny figure chained up in the middle.

"Did you hear about any ceremonies this week, Gator?" he asked, still staring at the screen. Without waiting for a reply, he sent the image to the massive screen at the other end of the security room. The lens seemed to have dust on it. Or maybe it was out of focus. Either way, they couldn't see the prisoner clearly. But Tracer had a bad feeling.

"Wait a minute...is that?" asked Gator. The person looked straight at them.

"No! I knew we were in the wrong place!" seethed Tracer, shaking with rage. He cursed profusely, wings pulsing deep red, blue, and yellow, and threw a chair over the balcony into the security room below with a raw, guttural yell. Several computers crashed to the floor, sizzling from the impact.

Gator fell back into the remaining chair and dropped his head. He covered his eyes, shaking. Neither of them moved for about ten seconds. Eyes watering, Gator stood up and flipped up the glass cover on the big red button and whispered, voice cracking, "Tracer, we have to help the others."

"We can't just leave her there! You know what this is. It's an execution! They'll kill her!" Tracer thundered.

"Dang it, Tracer, I know that! But there's no way we can get to her, much less in time!" retorted Gator. "You really think that we don't care about Emma? Huh? She's our friend, too, you know!" he shouted. Tracer stood smoldering, his knuckles whitening. "But there's nothing we can do about it," Gator persisted. "Right now, our job is to help the ones we can. Emmaline gave us this mission. Falcon, Raven, Kael, and Wayk need us here to help get that done. Now, are you with me or not?" he demanded.

Face flushed with unbridled fury, Tracer drew his sword and smashed the button with the broad side. Alarms triggered, red lights flashed everywhere, and a countdown system began: "Three minutes to self-destruct. Evacuate using the emergency exits."

"Like we'd want to stick around," muttered Gator.

They bolted over the soldiers' bodies, down the steps, and back through the tunnel, water already splashing under their feet, with two-and-a-half minutes to save every slave and none to save Emma.

I couldn't think of anything else to get their attention. If they couldn't see me, they could hear me.

Stop! You don't know what you're doing!

Everything halted. Women screamed in fear, and men took up their weapons again. They moved their sightless eyes, searching for the source of the disembodied voice, and finally locked on me.

Listen to me! Everything you know is a lie. There are no Elders. The High Order controls everything, including your decisions. We live in fear as our children vanish and destruction claims lives, and yet nothing happens because they won't let us think for ourselves. That is not freedom! Is that not what we claim to be our greatest treasure, even over life itself?

Somebody yelled, "Witch! Witch! She's reading our minds! Witch!"

Jeering and calls for so-called justice echoed once more in the massive chamber. Somebody started up a new chant: "Death for the Sorceress! Death! Death!"

Would you all shut up for half a second and think for once?

"Death for the Sorceress! Death! Death!"

Is there nobody listening to me?

"Death for the Sorceress! Death! Death!"

I couldn't even hear my own thoughts anymore and sagged like a worn-out, hand-me-down doll, not caring about the pain stabbing into my wrists. Why wouldn't they just leave me alone?

Fine! You can kill me! Go ahead! Kill me!

The chant faded away.

You can kill me. Just listen. There's going to be a fire, a terrible fire. Tonight. It's going to burn down this whole tree. Everyone has to leave now. It starts soon, tonight. You have to leave! Please, I begged, *please go. Nobody else should have to die tonight.*

There was silence. And then there wasn't.

"It's a trick! She's going to kill us all! Kill her first! Kill her now! She's a Sorceress! Kill her! She wants us to leave, so she can escape!"

All voices merged into one. The chant started again, and for all I knew, it was the last time I would hear it.

"Death for the Sorceress! Death! Death!"

I thought of Tracer, and Gator, and Falcon, and Kael, and Raven, and even Sam, the best friend they'd stolen from me. How I would never see them again and couldn't apologize for all the things I'd said and done that I wished I hadn't.

"Death for the Sorceress! Death! Death!"

The Senator raised his hand into the air to show my time was up. My wings would be Confiscated, and nobody could stop it. I blinked away hot tears, remembering the tortured expression on Tracer's face. *I'm sorry*, I thought, looking at one of the several hundred cameras hidden around the arena. I felt his mind disappear from the monitor at the other end of it as a new camera went live. Over the screaming death chant, Shadela screeched from behind me, "Can't wait to see the look on their faces when you're dead!"

The Lord is my Shepherd; I shall not want...

Soldiers dragged me back against the guillotine and scraped my now blood-covered wings through the holes, clamping them flat against the backboard. With nothing to do but see my fate, I turned my watery eyes upward, only then realizing how narrow the crack was between my wings and my back. "Death for the Sorceress! Death! Death!"

He makes me lie down in green pastures; He leads me beside still waters...

A soldier checked that the pulley for the blade was well oiled. A drop grazed my blood-caked forehead as I watched. "Death for the Sorceress! Death! Death!"

He restores my soul.

Weapons and tools sharpened for only one purpose danced up and down to the beat of the chant. If the shock didn't kill me, they'd hack and shoot and stab and slice until there was nothing recognizable about me anymore. Unless I ran fast enough. While bleeding out my back. That'd work really well. "Death for the Sor-cer-ess! Death! Death!"

He leads me in paths of righteousness for His name's sake...

The Senator flicked his finger. The dark-skinned soldier who'd last spoken to me was back. So he was the executioner. As he pulled the blade up to its full height of twelve feet above my wings, I noticed a large obsidian saber knife on his belt.

Even though I walk through the valley of the shadow of death...

"Alright everybody, here we go! Countdown! Five!"

I will fear no evil...

"Four!"

For You are with me.

"Three!"

I knew what I had to do.

"Two!"

Ashleeka stood with Umala by the window, looking at the grumbling clouds. They watched together through their minds' eyes at their older sister, chained up against the guillotine, and saw the people of NeverSeen calling her Traitor and Sorceress. Including their parents.

They held each other closer as they heard the crowd reach two.

I closed my eyes, shutting out the hatred.

"ONE!"

I forced myself to be motionless.

"ZERO!"

The blade screeched down as thunder clapped for joy.

CHAPTER FIFTEEN
THE ARSONIST

"Guys!" Falcon screamed over the chaos, "We have to get them out of here!"

Kael yelled in return, "Well, how are we gonna do that when every Watcher of NeverSeen is trying to slit our throats?" He hook-kicked his attacker and shot another arrow across the room. A shock wave pushed everyone to their knees with perfect timing, as another series of arrows and bullets pummeled the wall behind their fort of boulders and pockmarked pillars. "Emma's Army" was lucky enough to have the low ground in this cavern.

A sudden pause in battle to reload left both sides staring at the ceiling. There were red lights everywhere and loud noises. "There's your answer," panted Wayk as he held his shoulder. He'd been badly hit, and his breaths came in hisses between his teeth.

All the kids and prisoners, several dozen of them, were huddled in a small trench between stalagmites to avoid being shot. They started screaming, not in horror, but delight as fresh, cold water began racing under them. A second shock wave blasted them, and part of the roof caved in, sending rocks tumbling past the boys' meager shelters. The soldiers raised their weapons again to fire, but several suddenly dropped with a great splash.

"Die, you filthy cowards!" bellowed Tracer as he stomped his soaking way into the middle of the room and took shelter behind a stalagmite. "Where's the exit?" he growled at Raven, reloading. He fired his rounds at the soldiers on the other side of the trench and turned around, eyes blazing. "Well?" he demanded.

"There isn't one," said Wayk, shooting a few soldiers with a handgun as he stumbled over to Tracer. "There's no way out."

"We're hosed," added Raven casually, as he fired a volley of well-placed shots at the Guards.

"Ninety seconds to self-destruct," said the alarm system. A loud boom sounded down the tunnel, and the children shrieked as the water rose. The soldiers looked around and backed away into a hidden tunnel, fired at them one last time, and shut the door. Gator sloshed over and pounded on it, but it was sealed shut. The water lapped at their knees, and the kids started crying and climbing onto rocks as it reached their sensitive wings. Tracer frantically looked for a way out. "There's gotta be a way!"

Kael stood staring up. "Found it," he said. "There's just one problem. It's up there, and there are no more stairs." He pointed to a small crevice at the edge of the ceiling, glowing red under the emergency exit light. Fragments of stone steps jutted out from the wall, but ended about ten feet short of the top.

"Well, that's just great," sighed Gator.

"Seventy seconds."

Raven helped a tiny girl onto a rock face jutting out from the wall. "We can make it."

"And just how are we going to do that, Raven, when none of us can fly?" Wayk snapped, struggling to tread water. Whenever it hit his shoulder, he grimaced, and the water turned red.

"With this." Raven splashed the water swirling around him. It was gushing in faster than Wayk had realized, and shortly they were dodging the undamaged stalactites nearing their heads.

"Sixty seconds to self-destruct."

Falcon swam to the crevice's edge and hauled himself out. "Come on, let's go!" shouted Raven, pushing a group of smaller kids to the edge. Tracer grabbed the collars of two distressed boys and towed them over as well. As space at the cliff's edge filled up, Falcon led a group of teens further back. Something hard bumped his knee. "Ouch! What was that?" he shouted to nobody in particular. Water was now sloshing around their ankles. Someone replied, "It's a giant boat! Get in!" Orange light erupted from the staff as Raven guided the remaining groups towards Falcon and the vessel. Working in pairs, they packed the youngest kids together like sardines in one seat, then another. Some tried unsuccessfully to keep it from lurching. Yelps that the boat had started moving downstream arose. Progress stalled.

"There's too many." Gator surged through waist-deep water to Falcon. "We can't get them all in." He grabbed the boat edge to stabilize it, dragging his feet. Tracer held the other side as he tried to anchor it.

"Five seconds to self-destruct."

"Wanna bet?" asked Raven. He raised the staff like a baton, and everyone not in the boat was floating above it.

"Four."

They fell in, between seats and on each other. Falcon felt the boat pick up speed.

"Three."

Raven shouted from the bow, "Hold on!"

"Two."

The boat tipped forward and shot down the trench into darkness.

Falcon couldn't hear the countdown end, but he felt it. In the midst of the splashing and screaming, there was a shuddering jolt through the tunnel. A whooshing, rushing noise of a bomb exploded behind them. The heat of dragon fire chased them down, down, down the turns of the tunnel, luring them away in a sweaty, breathless sleep in the jolting twists of darkness. All they could do was obey.

Right when Gator thought they'd all fry to death, the space in front of them opened into a magnificent cavern. The fireball flew over their heads, acting as a short flare for their surroundings. In the few moments Gator had to take it in, the stone formations seemed to be subterranean castle ruins, like none he'd ever seen in the history books. The pillars they rushed by had mysterious carvings on them, and what remained of the archways had strange symbols on each one. Seven symbols.

The fire vanished. The trench dropped out from under them. They tumbled through the deep darkness, screaming in terror. They plummeted for what felt like hours with no end in sight. Then they hit water again. Children flew into each other, bumping heads. Some passed out.

Tracer opened his eyes for the first time since jumping in the boat and looked around. They were still in the boat in the freezing, smoldering tunnel. At least, it seemed like the same tunnel. But it couldn't be. They'd floated away from where they'd landed, and another tunnel had swallowed them up. He looked back upstream. *What did you expect to see?* he thought, *Something other than darkness?* But there *was* light where they had come from and the orange glow of the fire. It appeared that there was more than one explosion caused by their escape, and it was following them. Fast.

Tracer turned to face downstream. Splinters of light broke through ahead, illuminating the scores of rescued children, some still unconscious. The rumble of fire grew behind them, and the tunnel felt like an oven. Moonlight refracted through streams of water ahead of the boat. The horrible shriek of the fire howled around them. All at once they were soaked from above and fell into the open air, and the fireball that nearly consumed them crashed head-on into the waterfall.

The plume of steam stole his sense of direction, but he knew which way was down when they hit the water. He tumbled back, landing in a pool of twiggy arms and legs. All that was heard was the panting of children and the thunder of the storm swirling over them like an inverted whirlpool. Their teeth chattered and, like him, they shivered madly in the frigid hours of the night.

Shortly after, they ran aground in the soft soil of the cave. Over the course of several long minutes, the tangled mass of kids discombobulated themselves and set to tending to their injuries, satisfying their immense hunger by way of edible mosses and flowers, and seeking shelter from the rain coming from the few cracks in the cavern's roof. Raven heated small rocks for warmth with Emma's staff.

Catching his breath and waiting for Raven to come to his end of the group, Tracer took in his surroundings. *So we haven't gone through one of the main waterfalls at all,* he thought, *just a minor outlet into this giant place. That's fine and dandy not to be drowned, but it's still absurdly cold.*

It was a surprisingly large quarry, and a deep one at that. The entrance to it was almost straight up a steep slope, a lot like the one they'd tumbled down. He wondered if it led somewhere, maybe to a tributary of the river. If it did, it would plummet down the sharp twists and turns of the cliffs, run between the growing fields, and flow under the great Wall into the lifeless land beyond. That's what they'd been told. But there was nothing he'd been told anymore that he could trust, except the knowledge that he had fiercely loyal friends, and they were in the same cave as he was. And Emma, wherever they'd locked her up, and if she was still...

Exhausted and shaken and unsure what to do next, if he could do anything, Tracer stared up through the entrance. Between the sweeping curtains of rain, he saw no stars, and horribly red moons, and...a strange, flickering glow on the clouds.

His heart jumped into his throat. "Nn-no-OO!"

Tracer stumbled to his feet and sprinted up the slope at the edge of the quarry, phased neither by the weight from his waterlogged wings nor the sheerness of the ground. He didn't hear the other boys running after him, hopping between arms and legs and coughing bodies. They clambered up the slope after him, afraid to find out what he had discovered. Raven crested the ridge and gasped.

Tracer was standing in the damp grass below the knoll, his hands hanging limp at his sides. His face was lit a pale orange, and his eyes and cheeks glistened as his tears fell. Raven drew himself reluctantly out of the shelter of the cave's mouth and into the dark rain—and shrieked.

Far in the distance, parting the river into its falls and rising like a beacon from the far end of the lush islet, burned Skyglass Temple.

I didn't have a Plan B. All I had was this crazy idea, the kind you only get when you're about to be executed in the middle of the only place you know by all the influential people you've ever respected and obeyed. It was stupid and insane and had a 99.999 percent chance of failing, but it was all I had.

I had to melt the blade.

My blood surged with fiery pressure, my soul-fire erupting inside my chest. I was focused so hard on turning into a super-heated torch-person that when the piercing, biting pain in my wings vanished, I didn't notice.

Then it hit me.

It was very cold and very dark.

There was no rescue in this rain: there was no way for anybody to fly there safely to perform an air rescue. There was no hope for the people in Skyglass. Raven wailed with grief, at how long the list of victims would be, and how many funerals there would be, for entire families, maybe even generations...

"I killed her, I killed her!" screamed Tracer. He fell to his knees on the soaking grass and sat cross-legged, blindly staring into the bonfire of broken trust. He brought his broad, gentle hands to his glistening face and sobbed.

The other boys reached the summit and came out into the unyielding rain. Falcon thought back to their last conversation with Emmaline, right before she was captured. Emma had been so unyielding about taking the fall on her own. She wouldn't let a single one of them come with her. A fury so powerful he couldn't decide what to do with exploded inside of him. He threw off his pack and proceeded to break the branches scattered across the ground, screaming at the tree so far away. Kael cursed profusely, kicking rocks down the slope. Gator and Wayk fell down beside their distraught comrade in the wet grass; Gator just barely engaged enough to continue bandaging Wayk's shoulder.

Tracer blubbered behind his hands. To Gator, it sounded vaguely like, "She's dead, and it's all my fault. Why did I let her go?" The rain had slowed to a trickle where they were, but far off over Skyglass, they could see the sheets of rain, pale and silky in the light of the twin moons. Cautious about startling him, Wayk gently put his hand on Tracer's shuddering back.

Tracer sat up quickly, wiping his tears and drying his hands on his pants. He side-glanced at both Wayk and Gator repeatedly, mortified to be caught. But it didn't stop him from sobbing.

Gator sat back from his work and turned his weary eyes to the burning Temple. It was fully engulfed now; not even the torrential rain could hinder its destruction. The avenging actions of Falcon and the foul words spilling from Kael's mouth were mournful whispers over the tree's requiem.

Tracer put his hands to his face again and blubbered something again.

"What?" Gator whispered gently.

Tracer took his hands away, letting them lay limply over his crossed legs. He sniffled away another heaving sob and sighed. "I...I never got to tell her."

"Emmaline?"

Tracer nodded his head, watching the tree beginning to tilt to one side. More tears raced down his cheek.

"What did you want to tell her?" Gator whispered, barely capable of containing his own chaotic emotions. With a breaking voice, Tracer wept, "I never got to tell her...how...how much I loved her." He wiped his face with his hands, unable to speak anymore.

"She already knew, Tracer."

Falcon, Kael, and Raven stood behind them further up the slope. Kael repeated, "She already knew," then took his glasses off in a hurry. The other boys were wiping tears away and sniffling, struggling to remain strong in spite of everything. Falcon added with a shaky voice, "We all knew." Tracer stayed quiet, hiding his face, but Gator felt him still trembling. Behind them in the mouth of the cave came a trickle of rescuees. A little boy who stepped into the open and saw the burning tree collapsed to the ground, wailing. Those who followed him joined his chorus of despair with howls, screams, and moans, crying for the home they'd prayed to be delivered back to for all the years they'd been locked away and were now banished from once again.

The overflowing catharsis broke the final barriers of the teen titans. Losing control as the tears streamed down their faces, they collapsed by their friends, arms around each other's backs, and mourned the loss of all the goodness they knew.

"Umala, let's go!" yelled Ashleeka, as the smoke filtered up through the windows. It was getting harder to see. The smoke stung her eyes and choked her. She coughed violently as another plume enveloped her.

The floor suddenly jerked under her feet. She fought for her balance as Umala zoomed back around the corner with the pack. It held their lives in it: food, clothes, and a few precious artifacts. Ashleeka grabbed Umala in her arms and raced for the master bedroom. For a moment she forgot where it was. The girls were staying in a guest room in Skyglass for storm protection and for an important assembly in which their parents were required to "decide on something very important," as they had said. *Yes, I would say that voting to have your eldest child's wings confiscated is rather important,* thought Ashleeka darkly.

Another change in the angle of the tree sent her flying through the air, and she smacked her head on the edge of a door. She would've fallen if Umala hadn't kept them up and pulled them the rest of the way. Ashleeka peered through the stream of red coming down her face to see Umala lift a chair with the flick of her finger and shoot it at the window. With everything she had left, Ashleeka pulled Umala to her chest and fell out the window.

Heat blinded them and they choked on the smoke invading their lungs. The flames reached like greedy hands and fingers out of the windows and passages, perforating the immense side of the tree. Ashleeka struggled to stay conscious as she angled right and left, but the fire seemed to follow her, reaching out further and further. *Umala,* she thought, *what's going on? I can't get away!*

The tree is going to fall into the river. Turn left!

But the right bank is closer!

Just do it! Umala screamed. The tree groaned, leaning, exhausted, out over the river's dark waves.

Ashleeka angled her wings as hard as she could, but it wasn't enough. They were diving too steep and too fast, and she didn't have the strength to make it to the other side of the river. She lost consciousness and they continued to plummet from the smoke-filled sky.

Stumbling up the stairs to the exit at the back of the arena, I knew I was supposed to be dead. I hadn't melted the blade. My wings were gone. I'd awoken in a scarlet pool of my own blood, abandoned in the arena, screaming from the most malicious pain imaginable, with the executioner's saber knife in my red and white hand. I didn't know if I'd taken it or if it was given to me. I ran. The ground rumbled under my feet, and the blistering heat told me that despite every last desperate prayer I'd made, my nightmare was reality. I threw the door open. Columns of smoke rolled up through the great spiral staircase, in through the windows, and encased people in dark poison. Men grabbed buckets of water from the spouting fountains, but it made little difference. The fire was outside, coming in. Flames already crept up the stairs, sending people screaming in every direction.

A Guard crashed into the wall next to me and grabbed the emergency phone, shouting, "Fire on level five! Fire on level five! Evacuate immediately! No, sir, we can't stop it! Something is working against us here!" He paused as he realized whom he was looking at. As I sprinted up the clearest passage, I heard his yells follow me, telling the soldiers to stop the Sorceress.

"Stop right there! You're under arrest!"

I'd reached the top levels of Skyglass with almost no memory of how I'd gotten there. Snippets of screams echoing in burning hallways were all I could recall. Balancing precariously on one of the branches protruding from the side of one of the greater branches, I glanced back to see the face of someone I'd once loved like a sister, hiding behind a pointed arrow, glistening with poison.

"Sameela O'Klurn, you are my friend. You always will be."

She opened her mouth for the next order but hesitated. "Drop the weapon! Hands in the air!"

Remembering the knife, I looked down in my hand to realize it was streaming with blood from my back. Blood was everywhere, on the singed green dress, on my skin, in my hair. "Or what?" I laughed despondently. "You gonna shoot me? Throw me back in a cell?" I held my hands out around me. "Look around you, Sam! The people needed protection from the High Order, not from me. Why else do you think I'm leaving? Nobody can stay here and live to see tomorrow!" My vision blurred but stayed enough to see Sam flex her hand on the bow hilt.

"Who are you?" she asked, more in bewilderment than anger.

I shook my head, just able to whisper. "I don't know anymore."

My hand tossed the knife. It arced gracefully through the air and clattered at Sam's feet. She stared at it, longer than a Guard should. Her bow twitched downward as she looked back at me, her rusty hair waving in the scorching breeze. "You're my best friend, Sam," I breathed. "Don't die on my account." The tree shifted. My legs folded under me, and I fell off the branch into the endless inferno.

Umala watched the river's surface approaching ever faster. Ashleeka would never wake in time. She brought her tiny hands by Ashleeka's ears. An enormous shaft of light appeared, shining out from between her fingers. She squeezed her eyes shut in concentration, and a pulsing light grew out of her chest. When the light became blinding, Umala opened her eyes.

The radiant beam shot from her chest into Ashleeka's. Ashleeka's arms and wings flew out rigid, and her eyes flew open, pupils shining white. She caught Umala tight again in her arms and guided them safely over the swirling depths of the river and spraying breaks on the rocks. They were halfway to the far bank, away from the Temple and the tragedy, when they crashed off the shore of a small island. The rocks stung as she waddled up the slope on her knees, but Ashleeka wasn't thinking about the pain. She'd just been Regenerated from her baby sister turning into a star. Her heart still raced. She crawled into the grove of trees, dropped her pack on the ground, and fell onto her back, Umala lying on her heaving chest.

How in Heaven's name did you do that?

There was no answer. Instead Ashleeka found Umala sound asleep, drained, and she had nothing left to do but to stare at the waters glistening orange with the firelight.

Still sniffing, the friends of Emmaline O'Meern lay against each other, too tired and too full of grief to speak. Gator absentmindedly rested his head against Tracer's shoulder, gazing gloomily into the dying glow of the remains of Skyglass, now leaning precariously over the river racing below it. Nothing stood in the way of falling asleep to shut out the grief, but he couldn't. None of them could. Something deep in their hearts told them that Emma couldn't be gone. But there was no proof she would come back, and as the terrible night wore on, hope was painfully draining out of them.

Tracer broke the aching silence first.

"What do we do now?" was all he asked.

Gator breathed heavily. "I don't know."

"Can we go home?" moaned Raven, half asleep, from Wayk's lap.

"Are you kidding?" exclaimed Kael, looking down the row. "Those Guards saw us! And there are, like, a million cameras in every tree. You really think they wouldn't put two and two together?"

"Yeah, he's right," Falcon groaned solemnly, running his fingers through his short, dirty hair. "They'll have records of our attack. The second any of us step inside the boundary again, we're all hashed." He made eye contact with everyone, searching their faces for understanding. "We can't go back."

A sudden noise from across the darkness made them snap their heads around. A critical support root of the tree had finally collapsed with a vicious crack, and the still-burning tree moaned its last. They watched as the Temple slowly tilted, then gained momentum and plunged into the dark river, hissing like a thousand evil serpents as fire met water. Its death was a final piercing into the hearts of everyone: their Temple was lost, their friends and family were lost, and Emmaline, dear, brave Emmaline, was lost. There was nothing left for them here.

Raven hid his face from the sight and began whimpering into Wayk's leg. Gator, Falcon, and Tracer wiped newly sprung tears from their eyes, and Kael shielded his face behind his tendrils of blond-turned-brown hair. Wayk stared at the shadowless landscape in front of him and wondered aloud, "Where are we supposed to go?"

"We go home, we die. We stay here, we die. There's no way to escape this madhouse," ruminated Tracer. "Dang it, I'm so tired of fighting this place, its rules, its secrets. Why does everything have to be so screwed up?"

As the immense, stubborn fire continued blazing from the river, enough that ash began to fall, Gator inquired, "Couldn't...couldn't we change our names? Make disguises? You know, like on spy movies? Or—"

Falcon laughed frantically. "I don't know, Gator, I just don't know. I'm too tired to even think about thinking about it, and frankly I'm not sure I care anymore!" He stood up abruptly, fumbled his way a few feet down the slope and turned around. "Don't you guys get it?" he demanded incredulously. "There is no way out of this! We're trapped! We always have been." He waved his arms about, trying to convey the hopelessness of their situation. "We can't pass the Wall, and we can't stay here either! Even if we did manage to keep low, whoever's left of the Guard will search every corner of NeverSeen until they find us! See? There's no place that we can hide, no place that we can rest! They're going to hunt us down and make us Traitors! They'll kill us just like Emmaline!"

Tracer jumped up, yelling, "Shut up! SHUT! UP!" Gator and Kael were dragged several feet down the slope as they seized him, struggling to hold him back. The fury churning in his eyes startled them all, but it smoldered back into grief. "I knew we were in the wrong place. Why didn't she tell us..." he murmured as ash settled on his head. Wayk, Kael, Gator, and Falcon returned to their seats around him, unable to speak.

It was several hours of waves of grief, anger, and hopelessness laced by semiconsciousness. The fire had faded greatly by then, and its light was replaced gradually with the glow of dawn: burnt blacks, raging reds, and poisonous pinks with smoke blanketing the forest. Ash fell steadily now, making a quilt of its own amongst the trees and across the lush green fields. It settled on the rescuees and the rescuers, all consumed by universal misery. There was nothing to do or go back to. So everybody did nothing at all. If and when they slept, they found no rest.

Startled from a dream, Raven lifted his head up out of the now-gray grass and squinted across the clearing. His eyes opened in disbelief, then belief. He bolted upright and screamed a name.

"Emmaline!"

Heat and toxic air washed over me as I plummeted. Blood pulsed freely now, and I could see it falling up away from me like little scarlet beads from a broken bracelet. I kept seeing the same flames in the window and on the trunk and on the branches. It blurred to streaks of orange and white and yellow, until I couldn't keep my eyes open. The lights swirled to a pearly whiteness as I blacked out.

Then, after either a second or a lifetime, my feet hit wet dirt. Gagging on the fragments of poisonous air, I stumbled back and forth between trees, searching for a clearing. Scarlet rays shone between the branches of the dark trees, and I found myself unable to take my eyes off them.

Lights swirled in front of me, brighter this time. Wait, please wait. *Just a little longer*, I pleaded. Nobody wants to be alone when they die.

My legs continued to blunder through the trees. I thought it was snowing, but it didn't melt when it touched me. Everything was gray with ash, but it shone like ice. It was so cold now, so cold. The swirling lights returned, and everything shone like gold and silver. I found a small hill and somehow crested it upright, swaying on my lifeless feet.

It was so very bright, and so cold...

Somebody yelled my name from far away.

Heads jerked simultaneously to see Raven scramble to his feet and tear down the hill, shouting repeatedly, "Emmaline! Emmaline!" A small figure in a dark dress stood on a hill across the ashen, smoky field. Gator, Kael, and Falcon stumbled onto their numb feet and bolted down the hill. So did Tracer.

"Emma!" he bellowed and outran them all. He outran Raven's flying feet, he sped past Falcon, and he would have outrun even Emma, had she been part of the race. All the while Emma stood there, blankly gazing into the space in front of her. As Gator grew closer, his gut told him something was terribly wrong. *It's not just her dress that's red*, he realized, seeing the dark streaks on her bleached skin. "Emma!" he shouted, trying to catch her eye.

Emmaline didn't respond. She kept looking out above their heads at nothingness, and soon it became obvious something was terribly wrong. Before any of the sprinting crowd reached her, Emmaline's knees gave, swaying gently to her right. She collapsed silently onto the hillside, ash fluttering around her.

"No!" cried Tracer, seconds before reaching her. He leapt up the hill, but when he got to the top and looked down at her, he stopped. His face turned the same color as Emmaline's.

"What? What is it?" Gator demanded a few feet from reaching him.

"Dear God...her wings...oh, Lord," he faltered. He turned away shuddering and started coughing violently. "Stay back! All of you! Kael, Falcon! Don't come up here!" he commanded through his coughs.

Against Tracer's orders, they scrambled like mad fools to the top. Gator fell to his knees, and Wayk cursed vehemently, sitting abruptly on a rock. Kael bumped into him on the way up, but what he saw made him run into a nearby hedge of bushes. Falcon stood motionless, breathing heavily. He stopped Raven from reaching Emma. Wisely, Raven sat where he was, eyes brimming with tears. He could still see what was missing.

Emmaline's wings were gone. There was nothing but dark red where they had connected to her backbone. The abomination was beyond any of the grotesque violence they'd ever seen, imagined or not.

Falcon knelt and checked for a pulse. It was hardly there, unbelievably weak. Emma wouldn't survive to see the dawn, which was just minutes away. Falcon bent down, took off his coat, and calmly pressed it into Emmaline's back. "Guys, I'll need your help," he worded carefully. "We have to stop the bleeding."

Kael emerged from the thicket, wiping his mouth with his sleeve. "Stop torturing us, Falcon, we know she's already—"

Before he could finish, a faint moan came from the ground. They stared, unmoving, as Emma's white fingers moved slightly.

Tracer pulled himself up. At Falcon's instruction, Tracer carefully lifted Emma's head and shoulders into his lap. She was a frail rag doll, trembling from blood loss. Her eyes were glassy, but she still recognized his face.

"Tracer," she whispered, unaware Falcon was bracing his coat to her back with his own leg. Tracer sniffled and whispered back, "Hi, Emma." Tears ran down his face as he gave a trembling smile.

"It's bad, isn't it?" she asked needlessly, tears running across her nose.

Tracer straightened his face out as best as he could. "Nah," he answered, voice cracking, "it's just a scratch. You'll be...you'll be fine. Right, Falcon?"

Falcon lowered his eyes. Wayk looked on from his rock without speaking.

"See, Emmaline? You'll be fine. Falcon says so." His smile trembled through his lie and slowly disappeared. "You have to get better. You...you have to..." he told her. Emma didn't seem to hear him. Her eyes half opened. "Will you do me a favor?" she asked quietly. "Anything," Tracer answered immediately.

"Don't let me come back as a zombie."

Despite the tragic night, Tracer found himself laughing. Emmaline smiled faintly at the sight. More seriously, she added, "Don't stop being...yourself, either...or I'll come back...and kick your butt."

"Hey, come on, you can kick my butt any time you want, Emma." She blinked slowly. "Promise?" she whispered.

Tracer looked away then turned back. "I promise, Emma."

It seemed like he was a stained glass window, and she could see through to the other side. She whispered, "Thanks," and stared at the ominous glow of the horizon. Tracer didn't take his eyes off her ghostly face as he gently stroked her golden hair, turned red from the morning light and black with the dried blood gathered from her back.

"You are my Sunshine...my...only Sunshine..."

Tracer sang softly to Emmaline as he rocked her gently in his lap. The simplicity of the lullaby broke them. Falcon squinted his eyes, and a single sob gasped from his lips. Kael crawled up the knoll on all fours and collapsed on his side, breathing through his tears. Wayk and Gator dug their nails into their hair, rocking side to side. Raven sat with his legs splayed on the hill, blatantly staring into the gray meadow broken by the rescues, engulfed by their already shattered hopes.

"...please...don't take...my Sunshine...away..." he whispered. Tracer watched as Falcon took Emma's pulse again, both of their faces contorted in anguish. He'd felt her stop breathing during his song, and he knew there was no escape from it this time. As the sun breached the edge of the mountaintops and flooded the valley with its cool, pale, red light, Emmaline O'Meern died.

⟶⟶ ⟵⟵

Umala woke from a deep sleep. She knew it had happened. So did Ashleeka.

"You didn't tell me she would die," accused Ashleeka, trembling. The ash fluttered off of her gently.

It was merely a possibility. You know that the future shifts with every given second.

"I don't care!" she cried. "You lied! You said...you said everything would be okay! You said we'd all make it!"

The baby clinging to her chest sighed.

That is yet to be seen.

Before Ashleeka could decipher this new revelation, Umala shut her eyes and entered a deeper realm of her mind. Time was fleeting, and there was still a chance.

A one-in-a-million chance—but still a chance.

Raven, surprising himself, had no reaction. Somehow, it didn't feel definite. None of them wanted it to be. But Tracer knew it was real.

Raven stood up from his seat on the damp, ashen hillside and walked up slowly until he could see Emma lying in Tracer's lap.

Tracer saw Raven and held his hand out. "No! Don't touch her! Stay away!" he stammered. "She...she needs to...to rest now. Leave her alone."

"Fine. But if you want even a remote chance of getting her back, put this on her." Raven thrust out the necklace. At once, all their heads snapped in its direction. Tracer calmed enough to think again. "Please," he whispered. "Please, let me." Raven gave it to Tracer.

He wrapped it around Emma's neck with blurred vision and trembling fingers. "Please work, c'mon, please," he whispered, finally clasping it. He pulled his hands away, shaking in anxiety, and waited.

Emmaline's eyes didn't open. He couldn't feel the rise and fall of her chest. She just lay in his lap with a ruby necklace on her white skin. Ash fell lightly on her cheek, undisturbed, and hid in the camouflage of her lifeless skin. Disbelieving, Tracer put his left hand under her head and carefully turned it upwards, brushing away the ash. He stared at her face, searching for a sign. "Emma, wake up. Please. Wake up, Emma!"

"Tracer, she's not coming back," Falcon said, dried tears on his cheeks. Tracer shook his head, eyes watering. "No, no, she will! She has to! Emmaline! Come back!" He shook her gently. "She's got to come back! Emma!"

"Tracer," started Kael, with a dejected expression, "Emma's gone. She's—"

"No!" he protested, rocking back and forth with Emma's still form in his arms. "No! Please, no!" Tracer turned his head skyward, shouting, "God! Please! If you're here, don't take her now! Not now! She's not ready! She's...she's gonna be an engineer...she's got her whole life ahead of her..." he trailed off, sobbing. "Oh, Emma," he cried, "why didn't you let me go with you?"

Everyone watched despondently at Tracer, rocking back and forth, with Emmaline's face shining a pale red in the light of the rising sun.

Wayk gasped. "What's that?"

The crystal hanging around Emma's neck had started glowing. Everyone's eyes lasered in on it as it pulsed, looking around hurriedly as they wondered what it meant. Red light radiated brightly from it, making strange shadows opposing the rising, orange sun.

"Over here!"

"Surround them!"

"Watch your backs, they have weapons!"

Gator snapped his head up in dismay to see a force of several dozen soldiers racing towards them from across the river, with eyes glinting and ready to kill.

"Circle up!" screamed Kael, grabbing his sword. "Wayk, Raven! Get the kids back into the cave! Nobody touches them!" He glanced back to see Tracer still holding Emma's ashen form, watching the light grow and pulse faster. "Gator! Falcon! Guard them!" Kael backed up in their direction, flourishing his sword before plunging it in the dirt to exchange it for his bow. Gator and Falcon followed his lead.

The Guards circled them, at least thirty, with super-bows that looked built for battle. *This isn't an arrest,* Kael thought. *This is a massacre!* His eye caught on one small figure dressed in a brighter green. The smaller Guard had her bow trained on them, but stared vacantly at the funeral on the hilltop. The leader shouted at her, but she didn't respond. She stared at the form amongst the ashes.

"Sam! Stop! You don't know what you're doing!" shouted Raven from the mouth of the cave. Wayk yanked him down as three soldiers broke off from the group and flew towards them.

"O'Klurn!" the Chief yelled again. "At the ready, soldier!"

Sam paused, still looking at Emma, and Falcon saw her whisper something: "You killed her." She finally turned to the Chief Guard and something snapped.

"Go myrhh yourself, Locknut."

Sam fired at him. He dropped to the ground with a thud. No sooner had he done so than the whirring of arrows filled the air, and Sam fell, six sticking out from her gear. A seventh for good measure struck as she pulled herself up the hill, gritting her teeth, with her bow still in her hand. The next soldier in line stepped up and ordered the troops to draw. "Get ready!" Falcon yelled, aiming his bow, knowing very well that they'd never survive. They braced for impact.

A blast wave blew around them, sending the Guards flipping through the air and spiraling to the ground. Massive rings of ash particles exploded from the ground, swirling in a tornado of red light around them. Bright white blinded them from the sky, and they were all being lifted off the ground. *I must be dead already if I think I'm being abducted by aliens,* Kael contemplated, floating sideways in the air. There was no way of tracking how high they were tumbling: they couldn't see past the ash column, and nobody could have escaped if they'd tried.

Tracer was still holding Emmaline's limp, ash-blanketed figure in his arms as they approached the source of the light. And for a brief, peculiar second, Gator imagined he saw Emma's eyes flicker in the brightness.

All at once the ash vanished, and Raven found himself splayed on a smooth, white floor in a huge chamber, surrounded by all the kids they'd rescued, and Wayk, and Kael, and Gator, and Falcon, all completely silent. Several adults in white suits came rushing through a door with a stretcher. He tracked them to Tracer, who sat with pale Emmaline lying in his arms like a child. The people in white suits tried to take her from him, but he protested, clinging to her. They spoke softly to him, and a moment later, Tracer's head fell back to the floor as he passed out from exhaustion.

Raven caught a glimpse of more adults, *Doctors*, he thought, coming in from other doors, but everything got dark and swirly. He called Emma's name gently, setting his head down and sleeping for a long time afterwards.

Gator was astounded, in his bleary, semiconscious state, at how kind and gentle the healers were to him. He didn't feel any of the cleansing of his wounds, or the wrappings, or anything. But he couldn't help asking repeatedly about Emmaline and what they were doing with her. Everyone simply told him "Everything will be alright."

Yeah. Everything. Our Temple incinerated, us almost killed half a dozen times, and our leader Confiscated. Nothing is going to be okay!

He wanted to tell them. But they said, "You'll see her soon enough. Now, it's time for you to sleep."

They helped him into the softest pajamas he'd ever felt, and he sat on the bed. He couldn't think of even dreaming as he fell onto the pillow.

Gator wasn't conscious when they pulled the covers over him.

Cool, fresh air washed across my face and weaved its way through the soft sheets. My head rested comfortably on a downy pillow, and a clean set of pajamas sat lightly on my skin. I felt a strange texture of wrappings on the right side my face, where it pressed into the pillow, but mostly I felt it covering the whole top section of my back.

Why do my wings hurt so much?

I don't have wings anymore.

I opened my eyes gradually. They stung, at first, from the white light shining through the open window, as silk curtains waved gently in the breeze. In fact, just about everything was white. Not a blinding white, but a soft, cream white that makes you feel warm and fuzzy: the bedsheets, the ceiling, the hall beyond the door and the inner window. Everything I saw was a lovely shade of cream, with dancing shadows caused by light coming through the windows.

Except...

I smiled. Slumped over in a row of chairs arranged in front of me were Wayk, Kael, Gator, Raven, and Falcon, all dozing off. Raven's face was smushed into Wayk's lap, and Wayk's head leaned against Falcon's shoulder. Kael sat at the other end, turned sideways with his glasses askew, and Gator sat next to him, arms and legs crossed and head tipped to one side.

I already knew where Tracer was.

He sat in a chair to the right of the bed where I would see him first, with his hand holding on to mine, and his head resting on his left arm on top of the table. His face was peaceful and fast asleep, as it should've been.

I remembered a lullaby and slipped off again, but he was still there when I woke.

And so was I.

EPILOGUE

"How long have we been here?"

"Dunno, Emma. We've been sleepin' half the time. None of us can keep track of days and nights." Falcon yawned. It was a day or two after I'd first awakened, and we all had questions. Especially them: first I was a prisoner, then I was dead, then I wasn't, then I was, and then we were all alive in wherever this place was. I asked about that, too.

Tracer said, "We don't know that, either. They've kept us mostly in our rooms, except for a few tests." He looked at me carefully, watching my reactions. I blinked slowly. The excruciating pain pulsing through my back at the moment made me want to frantically rip the bandages off and claw it to death. But I couldn't even move my shoulders. So instead, I asked, "What kind of tests?"

Nobody answered right away. I glanced at each of them. Kael finally spoke up from the corner. "We dunno. Weird tests, like how much stuff we know from school, and training exercises, and questions about everything that happened to us, and all sorts of random stuff like that." He phased out for a minute. Gator jumped in for him. "I think they're testing us to see if we can still function properly after...um...you know. What happened." He scratched the back of his head.

The words took a while to sink in. "Yeah, what did happen?" They all stared at me. "See, I remember the fire...and running up stairs...to the top...and falling...and, and..." I struggled to recall. "There was a hilltop, and everything was really bright...and somebody called my name..." I squeezed my eyes shut, and I saw the glimpses clearer.

"And I was really cold...somebody was talking to me...and singing...and that's all I remember from there."

"From there?" asked Wayk.

"Well, after that I was...um...somewhere else, I guess. It was really nice," I sighed peacefully. "And nothing hurt, either. I liked it. But I couldn't stay."

The hand in mine started shaking. Tracer had tears in his eyes. Since I couldn't give him a shoulder hug because of the bandages, I squeezed his hand. He relaxed, but only a little.

Raven broke the silence. "So you don't remember Sam?"

Sam? "What about her?"

He bounced up from his chair and started waving his hands around fanatically. "She came with the soldiers an' they were gonna kill us an' then...an' then she shot one of them, and she got shot back! But she's here now. She came up the tornado with us!"

"Tornado? Guards? She...she came with us? What? Wait, she's here?" My brain hurt. Raven nodded so hard I thought his head would pop off. Everyone shifted nervously. I wasn't sure if I was glad or not about Sam's presence.

"She's in the detention ward way down the hall. She got a couple of chest wounds, but not as bad as...um...I mean..." Falcon dropped his head in embarrassment at the slipup. The room was thick with silence. I blinked away tears.

"It's okay. It's fine...it's not...it's not your fault..."

Exhaustion took its bite. I closed my eyes, mostly so I wouldn't cry, and the others retreated into themselves and eventually slipped off to sleep as well. Tracer and I were the last ones awake. I moved my hand to show I was still awake.

"It was you, wasn't it?" was all I asked. He turned his head to me then understood. He looked away quickly. I smiled faintly.

"Thank you. That was one of the nicest lullabies ever."

He cleared his throat. "Thanks. I'm glad you're back," he whispered.

We fell asleep, hand in hand.

Thirteen days later, I held gently onto Tracer's right arm and onto Raven's left as I took my first steps out of my room. I could stand on my own relatively fine. The bandages had come off, and I knew my wings were gone, but I hadn't seen yet what my back looked like without them. Now I had a better understanding of what war amputees felt like.

The nurses had helped me get dressed. It was hard to move my arms without regretting it. They tried putting me in a dress like the one I'd arrived in, but I said I'd rather jump off a cliff before I wore that color again.

I felt like a baby as they tied my hair back like I asked them to. There was no way to get my arms that high, not for a long while. *One day at a time, Emmaline, one day at a time.*

I hate one day at a time.

I felt myself teetering between Raven and Tracer as they led me patiently down the hall. Wings were like cat's tails for faeries, and having them gone was forcing me to relearn, well, everything. I had to balance differently, walk differently, get up and down differently. It was a long, hard road I had to take, but like they say, nothing worth having is ever easy.

It wasn't.

They guided me to an open area, where I found all my friends waiting for me. They stood up from their seats, cheering me on. I couldn't help but smile. Dividing, they made a path for me to walk with Tracer and Raven to where the room of mirrors was. As we drew close, I told my two friends I could walk the rest of the way by myself.

"But...um...stay close, okay?" I added.

They nodded in understanding. Breathing deeply, I put one foot in front of the other, arms out slightly for balance, and moved forward. Numerous reflections of my blue-shoed feet, indigo like the rest of me, surrounded me. Blinking furiously in preparation, I pulled my head up and looked at the mirrors.

From the front I looked normal, but from the other angles...

I hyperventilated. Every cell in my body told me my wings were still there, glistening with red and gold and indigo and magenta and green. My eyes showed me they weren't. Two four-inch and two three-inch bumps spaced out in my upper back were all that was left. There was no sign that something gut-wrenching had happened: no setups, no accusations, no disownment from all the adults I cared about, no torrential Confiscation or fire or blood or anything—*oh, GOD, why did this happen to me?*

I put my weight against the wall to stop from falling over. Tracer and Raven heard my cries and came running to me, keeping me from falling. They walked me, trembling, to a pale-blue couch, and sat with me as I cried uncontrollably, hiding my face from the world. Nothing could bring my wings back. Nothing. Everyone understood. Nobody stopped me from crying.

But Raven still sat at my feet, like all the times he had when the world was still in one piece. He set his chin on my knee, and I saw behind him a pair of familiar feet with brown sandals below a turquoise dress. Sam looked at me vacantly as she walked by, her jingling cuffs holding her between the pairs of guards leading and following her. We were in the same space without codes, orders, or secrets. For a few moments. Then she disappeared down the hall. It had been a long, torturous, week leading to what happened, and then the three-and-a-half weeks after that to where we were. Time made no sense.

In time, my tears subsided. My mind was blank, and for the first time, when I felt Tracer set his hand lightly on my shoulder like all those times back at school, I set mine on top of his. We looked at each other with a new appreciation for each other's existence.

That brought me back to a question.

"Wasn't I dead?"

Tracer's eyes watered as he nodded his head wordlessly. He put his hand over them, trying to block out the memories of holding my dead body in his arms. I squeezed his hand gently to remind him: I was still here. *Still?*

"How...how did I come back?"

Raven shrugged wordlessly. I looked around for an answer from the crowd of rescuers, my friends. "We haven't...um...really been told," answered Falcon. Kael, Gator, and Raven nodded in agreement. It was weird to think that they each had a distinct memory of me, a dead me, and that I didn't. Backwards logic of course, but still weird. Because I had my own set of memories.

"That's because we weren't cleared to give you that information."

A man in a silver cloak strode in from around the corner. His sharp blue eyes held the air of command in them. The evidence was presented as the boys moved well out of his way. He nodded his head to them.

"Until after the tests, mind you. I am Professor Ticort, and I can tell you now that 'Emmaline,' as she's known by..."

Tracer and I glanced at each other with confusion. Raven's forehead scrunched up, and he glanced at me like I might change into somebody else.

"...is a Flamerider."

A collective, "Huh?" burst from us all at once. "Say what?" I asked. "And what do you mean 'as I'm known by'?"

Professor Ticort turned. "I beg your pardon, Miss," he apologized, bowing, "but 'Emmaline' is not necessarily your true name."

"Why wouldn't it be?" I countered.

"You are a Flamerider," he replied cryptically, like that solved everything. He stood by a window, contemplatively looking at whatever was out there. We didn't know yet.

Flamerider. Why do I feel like I've heard that before?

"Wh-what's a Flamerider?" asked Raven, from the floor.

The professor spun away from the curtain. "You mean to say—can it be—that you've never heard of the Council of Seven?"

We all shook our heads.

"Oh, dear, oh, dear...you will need debriefing on all of this...oh, my. But first, come with me!" he ordered. "Yes, all of you!" Gator, Kael, and Wayk almost bumped into him when he abruptly stopped. "Don't worry, Miss, we're only going for a short walk outside."

Yeah. Outside. More like way-up-high-side.

"Outside" was on an enormous walkway wrapped around a magnificent domed building in the center of the most gigantic city I'd ever seen, bigger than the medieval ones or the ruins of the Great War we saw on TV. It wasn't spread around in different trees like NeverSeen was. It was all broken up into building after building, structures made of stone and wood and metal and who knows what else, on a massive stone platform. Sections were separated by colored flags and bizarre symbols, all surrounded with a high-rising solid marble wall and turrets posted around the circumference.

Like they needed it.

"Welcome to Pellabor, capital of Skyline Country," said the professor.

We were on a city in the clouds.

If you enjoyed this book, please leave a review here! The author (and other readers) will appreciate it!

PLEASE LEAVE A REVIEW

ABOUT TAYLOR

Taylor Hunter lives in Southwest Idaho. She shares her home with her elderly cats, who tolerate her. After several "wonderful years" of challenging college coursework, Taylor is now a full-time mechanical engineer.

ALSO BY TAYLOR

If you want to read more works by Taylor Hunter, click here or scan the QR code below: